●●●●●●●●●●●●●●●●●●●●●●●●●●

You tried not to think of dying because it wasn't a natural thing for young men to brood about, and besides it could undermine your fighting ability like nothing else. We knew that some of us were going to die, but there wasn't very much we could do about it. We had all volunteered for the air force, so we couldn't say anybody had pushed us into it. Perhaps the risks had never been fully explained, but we'd seen enough British and American war movies to know that death was one of the principal ingredients of war in the air. It was only that I'd never seen a war movie where they showed a close-up of a hero with one side of his face blown off....

That's Bill Sutcliffe talking, bombardier of the Halifax bomber "Nan", losing his combat innocence night after night over Germany, and in England making love as if every woman were his last....

ON TARGET

Bestsellers From NAL of CANADA

This book is for Art, without whose kind help many of these pages could not have been written; for Harry, who believed in it and so kept me going; and for my wife, whose patience at times outmatched even my own stubborn persistence.

It's a Sunday morning like many, many others. Last night it was my turn to have the boys in for the regular Saturday poker game, and as usual I ate too many potato chips and peanuts and drank too much beer. Add to that the fact that the game didn't break up until two, and you can easily appreciate why I've slept in late and went right away for the Bromo Seltzer when I finally hit the bathroom half an hour ago.

Now I've washed and shaved, and with half a cup of my wife's good perked coffee inside me, I'm slowly beginning to feel human again. The lead weight has almost gone from my stomach. I sit at the breakfast table and wait for my toast and marmalade.

Due to all the confusion last night I didn't have a chance to look at Saturday's Star. It sits now beside my plate, still smelling slightly of printer's ink. Well, I follow my usual routine. I pick out the sport's section and begin to read it thoroughly, starting with a front page column on the Maple Leaf hockey club. If there's any time left I may look at the financial section, glance at the editorial page. The rest I may safely ignore.

Midge sits down with me now and joins me in a second cup of coffee. She's telling me something which doesn't sink in right away. But she's used to this and merely repeats herself the first time I look up from the paper. Apparently there's an article in the magazine supplement I might be interested in. The Air Force in wartime Yorkshire. I think it's even about your old base, she adds.

But it isn't until a good half hour later when I'm comfortably settled in my favorite easy chair in the livingroom that I pick up the glossy section of the paper she's mentioned. On the front cover, underneath a very self-consciously posed picture of seven ground-crew clustered around a thousand pound bomb on a trolley, the caption reads: "Come with us on a nostalgic visit to the weedy runways in England that were home to Canada's flyers. Page 34." Behind the airmen is the familiar outline of a Handley Page Halifax, probably a B.III. I turn to Page 34 and what hits me right away is old Air Vice-Marshal McCowan looking out at me, very much more stern-faced now in his old age than I remember him from the several times he visited our station. There are other coloured pictures of an abandoned Nissen hut at West Moor, part of the mirror in Betty's Bar with its myriad scrawled signatures, the entrances to Ye Olde Starre Inne, both in York, and the Golden Fleece in Thirsk. But the best one of all is the black-and-white picture headed "Off-duty aircrews headed for Betty's Bar—with periodic stops for repairs." This shows four or five jokers struggling to get their old car going again after it's stopped along a muddy road, with a sign in the background reading "Two mi. to Betty's Bar." This one really makes me smile and with good reason.

I start in to read the article, noting that the date of the magazine is February 18th, 1967. On February 14th, 1945, the night after the infamous Dresden raid, I flew my first op to Chemnitz, fifty miles to the south-east. That's twenty-two years ago now. It seems more like a hundred.

I learn as I read on that Croft is now an auto track, Linton and Leeming are R.A.F. training stations, while

Middleton St. George is a busy commercial airport. But the runways at Skipton, Tholthorpe and West Moor are surrounded by waist-high fields of grain, and West Moor itself is to have its old buildings used as a piggery. It shakes me a little, but I'm not really surprised. Nothing is more obsolete after a war than its artifacts, its participants. And I've read where there isn't a Handley Page Halifax intact anywhere, they all very quickly found their way to the scrap dealers.

I've had enough nostalgia for one day and lay the paper aside. For a change of pace I put a favorite jazz record on my stereo turntable. But even when Buck Clayton lays down a beautiful opening muted solo, then Ruby Braff follows behind with an even more impressive one, and old Buck sneaks back and steals it all away again, I find my attention wandering. I picture myself back in England. The years are first 1944 and then 1945. I recall London of the V-1's and V-2's, the old walls around the city of York, standing in the Fleece in Darlington and fighting through the Friday night crowd to get to the counter and cool pints of beer, the long cold hours sweating it out in the navigator's and bombardier's compartments, always chilled through even with heavy boots, extra socks, thick gloves and flying suit. The Yorkshire countryside seen from the air, vast, green-stretching, lonely. But most of all I see the faces again, the faces of my old comrades, some dead, some still alive. And suddenly I want to relive all those impetuous, foolish, brave and tender months right from the beginning just one final time. . . .

1

I'd met up with a lot of pilots during my training days in Canada with the R.C.A.F. But from the time I began to fly with Slim Cochrane in the early fall of '44 at O.T.U. in Nottinghamshire, I rated him strictly number one as far as I was concerned. Slim was from Vancouver, at twenty-one a whole year younger than me, and self-appointed God's gift to English women. The way he could walk into a roomful of females and have them falling all over him within minutes had to be seen to be believed. The rest of our bomber crew were naturally more than a little jealous of his magnetic personality at first. Quite logically, though, they decided that they could afford to let him have this advantage as long as he continued to make flying our two-engine Wellingtons seem like an elementary training exercise.

As it turned out, his flying ability was very quickly put to its supreme test at a certain moment of a bright September afternoon. We were leaving on a combination bombing air/sea firing practice run off the Yorkshire coast. There were only two more tiresome weeks to go before our graduation from Gamston Operational Training Unit run by the R.A.F. In my role as bombardier, and partly because of my brief, previous pilot training, I was understudying Slim as emergency pilot. I had to handle the throttles and generally perform the engineer's job on take-offs and landings. We'd hardly begun to lift off from the runway when I happened to notice the starboard R.P.M. gauge strangely unwinding like a clock in reverse. This meant only one thing—the starboard engine had conked out.

"Slim," I yelled at him, my left hand gripping the shoulder of his flying-suit in utter panic.

His reflexes had been perfect. He'd taken one quick look where my hand was pointing on the instrument panel, then

1

spoken crisply, only slightly louder than his usual voice over
the intercom, "Hang on, gang, we're greasing it. Wish me
luck." At the same time he frantically began reversing petrol
cocks, pulling up the undercarriage, all the time firmly holding the wheel. Frozen instantly by a sudden rush of fear, I
watched first with detached amazement, then with complete
horror, as first we touched down with a tremendous jolt, then
ran out of runway and began to slide, slip and grind terribly
over bare, rough farmland. And suddenly ended up with a
neck-shaking, body-flinging jerk as Slim fought the wheel and
finally won out. The Wimpey ground to a dead, dusty halt.

I was more than ready to give in to a powerful urge that
seemed to rush through my body, commanding it to collapse
completely, to remain limp while I tried to recover from the
shock of those last thirty seconds. But there was Slim half-
prodding, half-pushing me out of my seat. He was pointing
urgently to the hatch-way above, at the same time yelling
over the intercom, "Run for it, guys, she could blow any
time." That was when I realized that in addition to the risk of
a gasoline explosion we were carrying live practice bombs in
the bomb-bay of the now-smoking fuselage of the aircraft.
Fear gripped me again, this time propelling me like a mad
man up through the hatch, which thank God opened instantly. I clambered down the wing and jumped clear of our
Wellington half over on its side. I didn't even turn over to see
if Slim or any of the others were getting out. I panicked and
ran to get clear of the crash.

Out-of-breath, still shaking all over, I stopped running
twenty-five yards or so from the aircraft where the runway
began again. I looked back. I counted five other figures all
clear of the Wimpey and dashing toward me now. So we'd all
made it. Thanks to good old Slim.

I dropped half-panting, half-shaking now to the runway.
The others followed my example as they came up to me. No
one said a word at first or hardly looked at anyone else. We
were still getting over the shock. I could feel myself swimming in sweat inside my flying suit. In the distance now I
heard the sirens of the fire-truck and then the ambulance
hell-bending it down the runway. This time we'd need only
the fire-truck. Thank God for that. I watched a thin trail of
smoke still rising from the Wimpey. She was really smashed,
probably a write-off. She'd come close to taking us with her.

Slim had his helmet off now. His usually calm, slightly pale face under the fair hair was flushed, his eyes had an animated look I'd seldom seen before.

He half-grinned at me as he spoke. "I never saw you move your ass that fast before, Sutcliffe. Too bad it was all a wasted effort. Doesn't look like she's going to pop after all."

"That's a bloody shame, isn't it?" I answered, feeling slightly more relaxed now. "Just imagine how much surplus b.s. would have hit the fan if you'd gone with her."

The rest of the crew—my buddy Dave, Fred, Pete and Joe—didn't crack a single smile at our feeble exchange. They sat there on the runway in their flying suits still looking pretty grim-faced. I couldn't say I blamed them in the least. It had been all too damn close for comfort.

"Rough luck, you bums," Slim said to the others, "I guess we won't get to the gunnery range after all. You crack shots sure could have done with some practice. By the way, anyone get badly shaken up in there? If you did, better not play the hero but hop a ride in the meat-wagon and get looked at in hospital. No? Well, looks like I got a small souvenir out of it. Must have banged myself against something in there."

He had a sizeable bump by now on his forehead over one eye. It was cut very slightly. It didn't look like much.

"Hope this lousy crash doesn't bugger me up any for graduating," he told me quietly on the drive back to our flight hut in a station lorry.

"Why the hell should it? It's not your fault if some Limey maintenance crew doesn't do its job," I told him.

"You know as well as I do they'll not blame them one damn little bit. We're the ones who'll take the roasting."

"For Christ's sake, quit worrying. You're the best pilot on the station. You're the last one they'd give the axe to."

Still he sounded worried. "You don't know these R.A.F. bastards. I know a couple here at least who'd really like to nail me good."

But he seemed to brighten up as we went in for interrogation. Two desk jockeys asked the crew a hundred and one stupid questions about the crash. I think we managed to tie them up very well and they knew it.

"This head of mine's starting to ache like a son-of-a-bitch," Slim complained as we came out of the flight hut together. "I think I'll just trot up to the hospital and get me some aspirin. See you up at the mess for a cool one in half an hour."

"And I'm buying, chum. No shit, you were really great out there today. Especially with me freezing up like a creep. Bloody good thing I wasn't flying that crate."

"Bill," Slim said, "I'll let you in on a little secret. I came so close to crapping my pants out there I can still smell it."

And with that he walked away with that easy stride of his, headed for the station hospital. I watched him go around the corner of the Nissen hut and out of sight. At that moment I was more convinced than ever that Slim Cochrane was the greatest pilot I'd ever met. I had a lot to make up to him for the way I'd acted out there in the Wimpey today. I knew it would take much more than simply buying him a couple of lousy beers at the mess.

2

Slim never did show up for his beer. I learned at supper that he was being kept in hospital overnight. It seemed they wanted to check up on that bang on the head he'd received earlier in the afternoon.

The next day when our crew reported to the dispersal hut we were told that Slim would be in hospital for a day or two. That was all right with us. It was nice to have some time off for a change. They'd been training us too hard anyway. It was starting to come out our ears.

That evening we went to see Slim at the hospital. He was sitting up in bed very much in command of the situation.

"Sorry to hold you guys back," he wise-cracked, "I know how much you were counting on flying today."

Good old Slim. Always the joker. It wasn't until four days later that they moved him up to the hospital at Northallerton. It was only then that we learned he was having serious trouble with his eyes. It had hard to believe at first. We'd always thought of Slim as having some kind of charmed life. We figured the doctors must be crazy.

That's when they told our crew that we would graduate from O.T.U. in the usual way but then we'd go on to a holding unit at Dalton, a Six Group station near Ripon in Yorkshire, one county away. There we'd pick up another pilot from pilot's pool. So it was goodbye Slim Cochrane.

At the end of that week we made the short journey from our O.T.U. in Nottinghamshire to what we hoped was an even shorter stay at the holding unit. Dalton, we found out, was a satellite of neighbouring R.C.A.F. Station, Topcliffe. It was used as a training base along with several other stations in this part of Yorkshire. We found it nice being with Canadians again. We also approved of the considerable number of

5

very attractive English WAAFs in the various ground trades.

Our third night there, more by accident than anything else, we met up with our future pilot. Dave and I were in the officer's bar having a night cap and generally crying in our beer at being held up at this critical stage in our Air Force careers. A short, stubby Flying Officer pilot walked up to the bar. Right away I recognized him. Walt Gibson. I'd last seen him in transit camp at Quebec City a good year ago. He'd been badly overweight then and the stiff P.T. handed out to us there had been sheer agony for him. Now he looked heavier, if anything, than before.

After introductions I asked him what in hell he was doing at Dalton.

"You won't believe this," he said, "but I'll tell you anyway. I was at Wombleton H.C.U. with the course nearly over when suddenly for no good reason two of my crew went A.W.O.L. to London. They caught the stupid buggers right away, but they battled the S.P.'s so they drew four weeks' detention. That busted up our crew. So to end the sad story I'm back here looking for another bunch. Now tell me what in hell you're doing here yourself?"

I told him, and after a half hour and two more beers he said we were definitely the guys he was looking for.

"After that last screwing I took you can't blame me for being choosy, can you?" he asked us very seriously.

We certainly didn't, we assured him. We'd felt much the same way ourselves. We hadn't been in any great flap to line up another pilot. It was still damn hard to think of flying without Slim at the controls. But we knew we had to make a move sooner or later, and this certainly looked like the right one to me. Dave didn't seem to have any objections, I decided. So the two of us ended up taking Walt over to the Sergeant's Mess, where we had Fred, Pete, Joe, and our newly-acquired flight-engineer, Max Babinczuk, dragged out by the ears and introduced all round. It didn't take them too long to give Walt the nod. And that was that.

Life at Dalton was a lot more pleasant from then on. We had a pilot and were ready for Heavy Conversion Unit whenever the brass got its finger out. It didn't hurt to know either that Walt had logged twenty-five hours already on Hallys, four night hops included. We should be a breeze at Con Unit.

The next Saturday afternoon our old bunch went up to Northallerton to see Slim. We wanted Walt and Max to come along but they both said we'd better make it without them. I suppose they were right in a way. Slim was probably feeling bad enough as it was without having to talk to a couple of strangers.

"Christ, it's great to see you boys, but you sure went to a lot of trouble," he told us after we trouped into his room at the hospital.

We assured him it wasn't any trouble at all. Then a little later we learned that he'd been invited to a party some of the nurses were giving in town that night. Trust old Slim to make the best use of his time.

"How the hell do you swing that?" Dave asked him. "We thought you couldn't leave the hospital."

"Officially, I can't, son," Slim said, "but regulations were only made to be bent a little, I always say. By the way, how'd you boys like to tag along? I'm sure you'd all be very welcome and it would be whizzo for me."

"Our train doesn't leave until eleven," Pete conceded. "I'm game if you guys are."

That settled it. We really didn't need to be persuaded. On the way to the dance in a taxi Slim produced an unlabelled bottle from a plain paper bag he was nursing very carefully.

"Pass this around, you sad sacks. Pure grain alcohol. Beautifully smooth on the stomach. Just save a drop or two for me, please."

"Where'd you get this stuff?" someone asked him.

"Sorry. It's a military secret."

"You're going to get some nurse court-martialed up there before you're through," I said.

"Easy, Bill, easy. Those are hard words. Actually it was a thank you gift for services rendered."

"Above and beyond the call of duty, of course."

"You can say that again."

"You've really got it taped," was all I could find to say.

We were made to feel very much at home at the dance. So much so that we barely dragged ourselves away in time to catch our train. Earlier, during an intermission, Slim had gotten me alone in a corner.

"How about this new pilot? Does he know his stuff?"

"Walt's already had Hally time. He knows what the score is. He's a hell of a lot better than I ever expected we'd get."

"Great. I'm glad for you guys." Slim's carefree manner was mostly gone now. I'd rarely seen him this serious. "You know, it's been a bloody bind to find myself grounded. After all that goddamn training. I was really itching to go onto the big jobs."

"I know you were. I think I know exactly how you feel," I said.

"No, you don't. How could you? It's hell. And all because of a shitty little accident. Tell me, why did it have to happen to me? No kidding, Bill, sometimes I could shoot myself."

"How are your eyes now?"

"I still see things a little blurred. The doc says I'm probably going to have to wear glasses. Me with glasses! And most of my depth perception's gone. You know what that means. I'll never fly again."

"It's rotten luck. What else can I say? And just when we were shaping up into a shit-hot crew."

"You guys were the greatest. You still are, and that's no b.s. By the way, what's this about getting a mad Cossack for an engineer? What's he like?"

"Max Babinczuk? Mad like you say. Drinks like a fish, too. Looks like he and Walt are going to become great boozing pals. But a wizard mechanic, so we're told. If there's anything left to fly those two boys will bring it home between them."

"Maybe so, but I'm still depending on you to look after these guys, Bill. They look up to you and respect you. I'm really serious about this. If anything happens to them I'm going to blame you. After this bloody war's over I want to get together again with you bums. So you mustn't do anything to spoil it."

"I'll do the best I can, Slim," I promised solemnly. I was very touched by his concern for all of us. He was one great guy. We were really going to miss him in the days ahead.

"Enough of this crap," he said suddenly, "I'm making this dance into a private wake. Take care, Sutcliffe."

That was the last thing he said to me. I never saw him again after that night. A couple of months later I had an airmail letter from him postmarked Vancouver. It was sure good to be back in the old home town, he said. But he missed flying and especially the crew. He didn't mind being out of the Air Force except for that. He signed off saying he had to rush to keep a date with a blonde. I didn't doubt that in the least. Good old Slim. There were no more letters after that.

3

It was almost three months and a new training station later. 1659 H.C.U., Topcliffe, Yorkshire, to be exact. My roommate, Dave Malone, and I were lying on our beds catching up on the news after a late Sunday morning breakfast. I was somewhere in the middle of a slightly crumpled six weeks' old copy of the *Toronto Daily Star* while Dave was skimming through the latest *Sunday Times* fresh in from London.

Suddenly, without any warning, Walt Gibson swept into the room, banging the door back against the wall. I didn't know about Dave, but I jumped an inch off my bed.

"Didn't you ever learn to knock on gentlemen's doors, you clod?" I asked him cheerfully.

"Go piss up a rope," he countered, leaning over and punching the newspaper out of my hands. There was a big wide grin spreading from one end to the other of his reddish, slightly pudgy face. "All right, you two, let's get the rag out. We're kissing this dump goodbye."

That made me sit up straight. But I still didn't really believe it. Something like that was just too good to be true.

"Of course you're kidding, aren't you, fat boy?"

"You know me better than that, buster," he said to me. "No, it's absolute official gen. Tomorrow at nine we're off for West Moor. Looks like we're going to end up bloody Algonquins."

I glanced across the room at Dave. His mouth was still hanging half-open, and he was one of the coolest, most unexcitable characters you could imagine.

"That's great, Walt," he finally managed. "I understand West Moor's only five miles out from York so it couldn't be handier. And I hear the Algonquins are a damn fine squadron. Matter of fact, I have a buddy in the Muskrats there. They've even got some new Mark Sevens this year."

10

"How about our flying today?" I asked Walt. We were down for a 1200 hour cross-country.

"Scrubbed. Like I told you, we're finished here. So you'd both better move your asses. We're going to log some real pub time tonight. O.K? Now I've got to press on with the good news. Can't you imagine Max's face when I tell him?"

As soon as Walt had gone I jumped up off my bed. He was right. We'd have to shake our asses. There were a lot of loose ends for both of us to tie up around the base before the end of the day.

"I figured this wasn't going to happen for at least another week or two," I told Dave. "I still can't get over it. Getting a squadron at last! It's really the greatest, isn't it?"

"You can say that again," he agreed, "but it's what we've been sweating blood for all this time, isn't it? You know, I was beginning to wonder if we'd ever make ops. Now it's happened it's still hard to believe."

I knew better than most what he meant by that. For almost my first year and a half in the R.C.A.F. now I'd been training as aircrew, first as pilot, then as navigator, finally as bombardier. I'd been stationed back in Canada all the way west to Winnipeg and down east as far as Chatham, New Brunswick. Late in 1943 I'd come overseas to England. But that really didn't mean a thing, because I'd started my training all over again from scratch. They were going to teach us Canadians how to do things the right way, the R.A.F. way. Of course there were some new things to learn as a bombardier such as H2S, but basically it was the same old stuff. And for a bonus we had R.A.F. instructors, each one of them bent on making us feel that as "colonials" we had no real business even being associated with the Royal Air Force in the first place.

But in spite of a few drawbacks things had gone rather well until Slim's crash-landing at Gamston. His washing-out meant that our crew was removed from the regular flow of things, and would have to stand by and wait its chance to get back in regular training again. For us it was the holding unit at Dalton and endless hours sitting around on our butts. Even after we'd met up with Walt there were more weeks of idleness to endure with no end in sight. Then, in early November of the previous year, our new crew had been posted from Dalton to 1659 H.C.U. at nearby Topcliffe.

Topcliffe was another station in the Canadian Six Group of Bomber Command. There we'd take our final training before going on ops.

Now the old year was well behind us. It was early February, 1945. The war continued to grind on. The newspapers which had talked about the fighting being over by Christmas now talked about it ending by the fall. I supposed it was a good thing for the war to end as soon as possible. Still, I knew now I'd feel cheated if it finished without me flying at least a few token ops against the enemy. . . .

"Well, sport, I'd better get mobile," I said to Dave. He had resumed reading his newspaper, very much the unperturbed young airman again. "I gave Betty my dress blues to press for tomorrow. Now I'd better have them this afternoon."

"My pants are a mess," Dave decided. "I'll give them a quick run-over with the iron. We want to look sharp when we hit West Moor."

"That's us, sharp, sharp, sharp," I mocked him. I headed down the hallway to the tiny room where Betty, our barrack floor WAAF who handled all batman duties so cheerfully and efficiently, could usually be found between eight and five. As I'd expected she was hard at work with iron and pressing-cloth. She promised to have my uniform ready by four-thirty.

"Mind you look after yourself, love," she cautioned after I'd told her the big news. "Don't go playing the bloody hero whatever you do. Keep alive so you can enjoy yourself after this rotten business is over."

"Don't worry, sweet, I'll do just that little thing," I promised, more than slightly touched by her sudden protective feelings toward me. She was a good girl and I hoped she'd find herself a decent man after she got out of the Service. From the little I'd heard it sounded like she hadn't had too much luck with the boys at Topcliffe.

The rest of the morning and afternoon were gone before I knew it. It was a busy few hours. I had to find someone to take my bike, turn in my flying clothing and other gear, make arrangements to have my laundry and mail forwarded—all those dozen or so things that make up being cleared from a station. By five, when I finally returned to our hut, I had a copy of a clearance paper in my pocket. I was finished with Topcliffe and training stations, more than ready to move on to the real thing.

Dave showed up not too much later, and we walked over to the mess for supper. We had to pass by some of the hangars and flight rooms we'd come to know so well checking out on the Handley Page Halifax. The Halifax was the aircraft we all admired. Far heavier, more complicated in every way than the Wimpey, it was the ship we'd voted as a crew to fly instead of the newer Lancasters at the time of our transfer to Topcliffe. For us the clinching argument had been the fact that the Hally could climb like an elevator on take-off. With an extra-heavy bomb-load aboard we'd decided that could be one hell of an advantage.

"One thing's for sure," I said to Dave as we made our way along a slightly muddy foot-path, "I'm not going to miss this drome one little bit. I couldn't tell you exactly why but I've hated almost every day of it here."

"Wait until you get back into a smoky, grimy Nissen hut again and have to take your turn keeping the blasted fire going all night. Then maybe you won't think it was all that bad. Don't forget, too, we had a damn good leave from here."

Perhaps in time I would regret leaving the hotel-like rooms of our Permanent Force barrack block. But I didn't really think so. He was right about the leave, though. That Christmas week, first in Edinburgh and then up to Glasgow, had been terrific. Our whole crew of seven had gone and we'd stuck together most of the time. Our waking hours had been divided equally between the pubs and the girls in the dance-halls. Those rosy-cheeked, quick-tongued, bare-legged Scottish girls! They'd been unbeatable. And the rest of the Scots had been fine, too. Still, I was glad to be moving on now. To finally belong to an operational Canadian squadron in Six Group. To take crap from no one. To fly at last against the enemy.

As we turned off the path to go into the officer's mess a Hally came over, readying its approach into the circuit. It hung up there, dark, gracefully awkward, engines roaring out solidly. It could have been us coming back from our cross-country flight. But we were through with instructional flying. Our busher days were over. Tomorrow we were moving up into the big leagues.

4

<hr/>

Next morning by some minor miracle we all managed to catch the nine-twenty local for York out of Thirsk station. The whole crew seemed in high spirits as we pushed our way into an empty compartment with only seconds to spare.

I had a lousy headache from too much beer-drinking the night before and only half noticed the bleak Yorkshire countryside flashing by outside the train windows. Almost before I realized it we were pulling into York. I hadn't been in the old place since coming back off leave. It felt somehow good to walk again through the loud-echoing vault of the station. The voice of a woman train announcer could be heard, her very proper English accent rising over the noise of shunting engines and assorted baggage sounds.

I was in the mood for a good cup of coffee at Betty's Bar, but sensed the rest of the crew wanted to move on out to West Moor at once. Well, we might be keen as hell at the moment but I had a feeling it wouldn't take very long for the novelty of a new base to wear off.

Walt left us to go into the R.T.O. office to arrange transport to the base. The rest of us stood around with our suitcases and kit-bags, indulging in a little horseplay. You'd have thought by our mood we were waiting for the London Express to pull in for the start of a seven day leave in the big town.

Within fifteen minutes a panel truck arrived. There was a bench in the back along both sides. Walt and I sat up front with the driver. The others piled in behind.

We didn't find out very much about West Moor from our L.A.C. driver except that it had been a bad summer and fall for aircrew casualties and the new year hadn't started out too much better. His pal drove the station ambulance on the

14

night shift so he knew all about that. We asked him how York was for women. He shrugged his shoulders. You boys should do all right, he said. It's a whole lot tougher for us. But it's a very friendly place. When he heard we were from Topcliffe he told us he'd spent a good year and a half there. His principal achievement seemed to have been knocking up a WAAF. Came pretty close to having to marry her, too, he told us with a grin. But I managed to wriggle out of it somehow.

Driving in from the main gate West Moor looked very unimpressive. Set down in very flat countryside, it lacked the solid look that Topcliffe had with its neat stone buildings of a former R.A.F. Permanent Force station. The Admin. Building was fairly substantial, but everything else except the hangars seemed to be Nissen huts of several varying sizes. The whole thing gave you the impression of having been thrown together in a hurry with no thought at all for the future. It was there to do a job and that was that.

We soon found out, however, that what West Moor lacked in appearance it made up for in quiet efficiency. Within roughly an hour Dave and I had been assigned an empty room in a hut occupied by Algonquin air bombers and navigators, had sampled our first meal in the officer's mess, and hoisted a beer with a bunch of fellow aircrew in the bar off the dining-room.

We were finishing up our second when Walt came in. I introduced him to the boys standing around.

"Your room O.K.?" he asked me after the bartender had drawn him a pint.

"Fine, Walt," I said. "It's not as fancy as Topcliffe but it feels more like a flying station."

"An Algonquin crew went for a Burton two days ago, so maybe that explains your empty room. I've got the pilot's bed myself. The guy I share it with was pretty close to him and hasn't got over it yet by the looks of things."

"Any idea when we start in?" Dave asked.

"We're all due down at 'B' Flight dispersal hut at 1400. Incidentally, we've been attached to 'B' Flight. We'll probably meet the Squadron C.O. and our Flight Commander. Looks like we might be flying fairly soon. I'm going on a familiarization flight tonight, which should give you guys tomorrow off anyway. Better make the most of it. After that we could be busy as hell. I'm told they really sweat your balls off around here."

"I guess they want to give you the feel of going right in to the target and back," I said. "I sure wish we could tag along with you."

"You'll all get your chance soon enough. Now, did I hear either of you guys say you were buying this next round?"

"You must be hearing things, Walt," I told him, "but anything to help quiet your nerves."

"That's about what it is, too, nerve food. You couldn't have put it better. Up your kilt, Sutcliffe."

Good old Uncle Walt. He hadn't changed one bit in the four months I'd known him now. An awful man for his beer, at least thirty pounds overweight, but a damn fine pilot, at the ripe age of twenty captain of a seven-man bomber crew. In a few days now he'd be leading us over the Channel, across Holland or Belgium, and into Germany. There we'd steer our evasive courses, maybe get shot at, try our damnedest to get back all in one piece. One thing we could count on, we'd either live through it or die. Perhaps in the process we might learn how to be men.

"Come on," I finally said to Dave, "let's get out of here before this joker hits us up for another round. Besides, I could use an hour's sack time right about now. Then tonight while our noble captain fights his way through the flak and the searchlights, I'll be fresh as a daisy dancing real close to a cute little blonde in York."

"You'd better get it all tonight," Walt warned us, his face beaming now. "Starting tomorrow Max and I are going to close in on the whole damn place. You won't even get as much as a smell then."

"Dream on, fat boy," I retorted as Dave and I walked away from the bar. If Walt came back with an answer we didn't catch it, but it wasn't too hard to imagine how it would go.

"Walt's a great loveable guy, isn't he?" Dave said as we walked back in what we'd decided was the general direction of our hut.

"Just about the greatest," I admitted, knowing that I still had Slim Cochrane at the top of my list.

"Wouldn't it be weird if he got knocked off on this lousy familiarization flight tonight?"

It would be weird, all right. That was one thing I liked about my roommate. He was a real solid optimist.

5

Later that same afternoon, while picking up my flying clothing at Q.M. Stores along with the rest of the crew, I made what was for me a very quick decision. If I was going to make the most of my precious off-duty hours at West Moor I'd need a car. I was fed up waiting for station rides, taking buses and trams, and generally spending a small fortune on taxis. A bank draft for ninety odd pounds had arrived only the week before, the balance of my savings account back in Toronto. While I still had the money I'd better make myself independently mobile.

As Walt had predicted, the rest of our crew had the next day off. I slept in late, then headed into York right after lunch.

The third garage I tried had exactly what I was looking for, a thirty-seven Standard nine that didn't sound as if it had all the guts knocked out of it. The garage owner let me take the car for a trial run. I managed to keep it on the left side of the road for several miles. By the time I got back I felt like a veteran English driver. There was considerable rust and wear around the body but the inside was clean, the upholstery in good condition. Eighty pounds didn't seem too bad a price. I then paid a visit to the nearest branch of the London bank which handled our pay account. After signing innumerable papers I was allowed to deposit my bank draft and withdraw eighty pounds. It took me another hour to get an automobile license, with my three year-old Ontario driving permit appearing to impress the clerk at the vehicle office. At three o'clock I became the official owner and driver of what my crew was shortly to christen "The Relic".

Three gallons of gas came with the purchase. After that I'd have to scrounge my fuel back at the base, my use of the car not being considered essential enough to the war effort. I'd al-

18

ready checked around the hangars and found petrol wasn't too difficult to obtain. The present going price for a tankful of one hundred octane gasoline mixed with oil was a carton of Canadian cigarettes. I was reliably informed that with this concoction in the tank your car did everything but take off on the highway.

I spent the next couple of hours strolling around the old city. I passed through the Shambles where the upper storeys of the houses bulged out over the roadway, along streets like Stonegate with its fine old book and curio shops. And visible from almost anywhere you happened to be, brooding above this very ancient city, the Minster. It still looked very grand, very impressive, even though when you got up close you saw how it was boarded up all around to protect the windows and the interior in case of an air raid. I ended up window-shopping and then gift-buying along Piccadilly. It was the first real chance I'd had in a long time to pick up a few souvenirs to send to my folks back home.

It was almost five o'clock when I remembered I'd promised Dave to cash in our candy ration coupons at the big NAAFI in town. He was a real nut for milk chocolate in any way, shape or form. By the time I'd located it my feet were actually sore. Like most aircrew any blisters I developed usually were on my backside.

I remembered now I'd been in the place once before. It was a large, modern building. My impression was confirmed from the time before that it was filled mainly with R.A.F. personnel all with hair carefully combed and slicked down with Brylcreme.

The candy counter was right off the main lobby and carried an impressive variety of chocolate bars. The girl behind the counter had the largest pair of breasts I'd seen on any woman in England. I had a hard time keeping my mind on filled and plain candy bars with something like that hovering above the merchandise. Imagine dating a girl like that. You'd be conscious of people staring at her every minute of the time you were out with her.

As if that wasn't enough to please me, I heard faintly from somewhere Les Brown and His Band of Renown go into *Dancing in the Dark*.

The girl behind the counter must have been a mind reader.

"That's the tea dance music you hear. It has another hour to go if you're interested. Right down there to your left."

I thanked her and walked along in the direction of the music. I couldn't have told you why. Right now I felt like doing almost anything but dance. I wanted nothing better than to sit down in a comfortable chair and give my feet a well-earned rest. But that music was almost irresistable, and besides, I had over an hour to kill before meeting the gang for a pub crawl.

There were about thirty couples dancing in the large, rather bare room, with an equal number of airmen, a few Army, and civilian girls in bright dresses either sitting or standing around the edge of the dance area. It was something right out of my Bournemouth Reception Centre days, the daily tea dance at the Hermitage. I'd never enjoyed the few I'd attended then, and this one would probably be no exception. I certainly was a sucker for punishment.

A woman with striking blue eyes and that soft delicate skin so many English women seem to have as standard equipment moved across the room. She was obviously the hostess, the official greeter.

"So nice you could come along this afternoon," she crooned sweetly. She was perhaps forty or forty-five. "Would you like a dancing partner or would you prefer a cup of tea first?"

"Thank you," I said. "The tea sounds fine to me."

"Very well. Right this way."

She led me around the edge of the floor to a large table on which was laid a fine white tablecloth. Tea cups, sugar bowls and small cream jugs were littered over it.

"Go right ahead and help yourself," the hostess invited. "By the way, my name is Beatrice Halliday."

"I'm Bill Sutcliffe," I said, "now stationed at West Moor."

Before I'd even had time to reach for a tea cup my hostess turned and called to a girl who'd just emerged from behind the scenes, "Prue, do you mind stepping over here?"

As the girl approached the table I sucked in a deep breath of air. She was wearing a light blue dress that set off perfectly her shoulder-length brown hair. It was, however, the combination of her head held proudly yet a little shyly, the look of perfect calm in the dark hazel eyes, and the easy yet deliberate flow of her fairly tall body as she walked, that made me forget everything else in the room at that moment.

"Bill, this is Miss Prudence Warwick. We all call her Prue, as you may have gathered. Prue, this is Bill Sutcliffe."

"How do you do?" I said.

"Hello, Bill," she replied, trying to sound relaxed but hardly making it. Her voice went perfectly with my first impression of her, friendly yet slightly inaccessible.

"Well, I'll leave you two on your own," our hostess said, beginning to move away. "Mr. Sutcliffe was just going to have a cup of tea."

"Thanks," I said, and then asked the girl, "would you like a cup? Or is it pretty horrible?"

"At least it's wet. Yes, I'll join you. And let me pour it. Women are supposed to be much better at these things, you know."

She could be twenty-four or five, but then it was hard to tell girls' ages. She wasn't wearing a ring, which was a good first sign. I watched her hands, one holding the cup, the other pouring the tea from a large tea-pot. Even they looked unusual, very thinly-tapered, soft-looking. When she turned to give me my cup of tea the quiet smile on her face and the way her eyes lit up made me want to breathe in even more deeply than I had a minute before.

"Thanks." I took a couple of sips of tea to gain a little time. It suddenly seemed very important to say the right thing to this girl. Prudence, that was an unusual name. Very English, of course.

"Good tea," I said finally, which was a safe enough opener.

"It could be just a shade warmer," the girl said, "but tea is tea, isn't it?"

That was safe enough, too. We were both playing it very cosy, weren't we?

"Do you live in York?" I asked.

"No. Close nearby, you could call it. But I work in town. I suppose you're stationed somewhere around here? Most of the Canadians I've met seem to be."

"West Moor. Do you know where that is?"

"I've never actually been out there, but I know it very well. I rather think it's your planes that fly over our house late at night."

"Probably. They'd be coming back from a raid."

"I suppose that's quite an experience, being on a raid, I mean."

"To tell you the truth, I wouldn't know. I only arrived at West Moor yesterday, so I'm still wet behind the ears. But I hope to go on ops any day now. Incidentally, before I came here I was at Topcliffe, outside Thirsk. Do you know that part of the country?"

"Thirsk is a cute little town," the girl called Prue said. "Or didn't you think so?"

"I have to confess I didn't see very much of it. Most of my time there I seemed to be in one pub or another."

At that point whoever was running the gramaphone must have decided that it was time for more dancing. Glen Miller's *Chattanooga Choo-Choo* woke up the room with wonderful sound. Nearly all the people in the room seemed to pair off quite naturally this time and begin dancing.

"Do you want to dance?" I asked the girl sipping tea beside me.

"Let's wait till the next one, shall we? Otherwise the tea won't be worth coming back to."

We continued sipping at our tea in silence, watching the dancers navigate around the floor until the Glen Miller ended and the next record came on. It was Vera Lynn singing *The Nightingales Sang in Berkeley Square*. It was a song I'd heard a few too many times to enjoy any more. But now on the floor, dancing in the crowded room with this girl I hardly knew, it seemed to take on an unexpected freshness.

"Do you come here often?" I asked. It didn't look as though she'd do much talking on her own, so if any ice was to be broken I'd have to break it.

"Actually it's only my third time. I'm taking the place of a regular girl who's sick. I fill in like that occasionally."

She was only an average dancer, I found out, which was fine by me, as I wasn't any Fred Astaire. But she moved very gracefully and easily; my hand held very loosely around her waist told me that.

Before I could think of another opening to get the conversation going, all the nightingales had fled from Berkeley Square. Then there was a tap on my shoulder and a rosy-cheeked R.A.F. sergeant-pilot was standing there waiting for me to hand over my partner for the next dance. I nodded to her, she smiled sweetly, then was whirled away as Tommy Dorsey's *On the Sunny Side of the Street* came on.

I moved slowly through the throng of dancers to the sidelines. My interest in the tea dance had disappeared almost as quickly as it had begun. I had met a girl who attracted me greatly, but who didn't appear to have the slightest interest in me. That of course was hard to understand. But it was a fact. I could hang around this place until the dance ended trying to make some more time with Miss Warwick. But I had the certain feeling now that I wouldn't get anywhere, that I'd only be wasting my time. It seemed much smarter to make a strategic retreat and live to fight another day. Next time I meant to do a lot better.

Or so I told myself as I left the NAAFI and headed over to Betty's Bar in the Standard. I hoped some of the crew would be there already. I badly needed a mild and bitter to get that NAAFI tea taste out of my mouth.

6

On our last night at Topcliffe all the crew had attended a bash at a pub in Thirsk. Uncle Walt had rented us a back room of our own and it proved to be one of our better evenings together. Later in the proceedings when things had developed into toasts and speech-making the following approximate dialogue had taken place. Walt had risen to his feet and started it off.

"You know, you guys, I hate to say this, but looking back on it all now I realize that I should have shook my ass a little harder back there at Pilot's Pool. Instead of sitting around running up a big bar bill I should have been seriously handpicking a crew. Then I'd have ended up with a real bunch of fly boys instead of you dead beats."

I was almost as sloshed as Walt at this stage and found myself rising up to defend both myself and my buddies.

"If my good captain will allow me," I'd said in reply, "I don't think he quite realizes what a dinkum crew he's got—probably one of the finest in the whole of Bomber Command."

After the cheers and the clapping had died down I'd continued: "Take Dave here, for instance. He was among the top ten in his graduating class—a class of ten, I'll admit, but still no mean achievement. Max we all know was one of the very few at T.T.S. to flunk both his airframe and aero-engine courses—so he ends up a flight engineer, what else? I'm told Fred's last C.O. in Canada tried to keep him there as a hockey player—he figured he could shoot a puck a hell of a lot better than he ever would a Browning .303. And I'm a washed-out pilot myself—they decided I couldn't hurt anybody but the enemy if they let me drop bombs."

That had been several days ago. Tonight as I entered Betty's Bar I saw them all gathered again at a table in a corner—six Canadians aged nineteen to twenty-one impatiently waiting to try their luck against an enemy they'd read about only in the papers or seen in movie newsreels. Six Canadians whose hometowns were almost right across Canada—Walt Gibson from Calgary, Dave Malone from Niagara Falls, Fred Waters, St. John, N.B., Pete Yarish from Montreal, Joe Petosky out of Windsor, Ontario, Max Babinczuk, Winnipeg. I was the lone Hogtown representative.

"Where the hell have you been, Sutcliffe?" Max wanted to know, pulling up a chair for me. "We've been waiting to get this meeting officially called to order."

"None of your business, sport," I told him cheerfully, dropping my greatcoat on top of a pile on a nearby chair and sitting down. Max sounded as though he'd started his own party a couple of hours ago. "Anyway, you told me six," I reminded him.

"Just to show you there's no hard feelings, Bill, you can buy the next round," Walt said. He looked a lot better tonight than he usually did. It might even be that having a taste of operations agreed with him.

"Thanks a lot," I said. But I signalled one of the girls serving behind the bar and she came and took the order. I'd decided that I'd be stuck for a round sooner or later, so I might as well spring for it now.

"Well, how did the op go, Walt?" someone at the table asked.

"Did you come out of it with clean drawers is what I want to know," Max grinned.

"Cleaner than yours'll be after your first one, wise guy," Walt advised him. Then he went on.

"No kidding, boys, it was almost like a routine training flight. We were trying to clobber the synthetic oil plant at a place called Wanne-Eickel. It was a piece of cake. We went right through to the target without any flak to speak of. When we got there the cloud cover was solid all the way up. At first we lost the sky markers. Then we could see them glowing faintly, and we got our bombs away. We heard a couple of bloody loud explosions down below right after. Then on the way home we could see a big red glow in the sky behind us."

"Any kites lost?"

"One from the squadron. Some crew took it on their first op, the poor bastards."

"Wasn't much of a piece of cake for them," I said.

"I guess not," Walt admitted.

"Did you do any flying yourself?" someone asked him.

"Most of the way back. Jerry had fighters up apparently, but we didn't see any. Sometimes they follow you part of the way back, then jump you when they think you've lowered your guard."

"That isn't jolly old cricket, is it, what?" Fred mimicked.

"But it's damn good football," Pete countered. "And the way I look at it, Fred, we should be damn glad we're sitting here drinking good beer instead of being out there getting an assful of flak."

"I'll drink to that," Walt said. "Any time we spend in the air is that much less drinking and wenching time. Don't worry, though, eager beavers, we'll probably get airborne tomorrow if this weather holds."

"Bugger the flying," Max said. "You guys should all have been born with wings attached, then you could float around up there all the time. Give me good solid ground any time. Say, anybody feel like some fish and chips yet? Right now I could eat the asshole out of a skunk."

"That's the first thing you've said today that's made any sense," Walt told his engineer.

"Up yours."

"Up yours with a hunk of glass."

"Hey, you guys," I said, trying to be as serious as possible, "what are all the nice people at the other tables going to think hearing such language used? You trying to give Canada a bad name?"

"You mean it's still good?" Joe Petosky wanted to know.

"Pure as gold, chum. A shining example of young Christian manhood and unselfish devotion to duty."

"You know what that smells like, Bill," Pete said.

I knew, we all knew, so we had a long pull on our beer to celebrate such secret knowledge.

"Seriously, though, I think Max has a point," Walt said "I could use a few chips myself."

"A few truck-loads, you mean," someone quipped as we drained our glasses and got up from the table. After a much-needed emptying of bladders we emerged very happily onto the now darkened streets of York.

"Hang onto your hats," I announced, "you're in for the surprise of the month. Right this way, gentlemen." And I led the group around the corner to where I had my car parked.

"I don't see any broads, Sutcliffe," Joe Petosky said, taking an exaggerated look up and down the street.

"Maybe that's his big surprise," Max said. "This boy is full of fun and games."

I stopped dramatically in front of the car.

"Honestly, chaps, what do you think of her? Isn't she perfectly whizzo?" I asked.

"What is it?"

"Does it need only four wheels?"

"Did you haul it out of the garage yourself or did they help you push it?"

"No kidding, Bill, how much did they pay you to take it off their hands?"

"Thanks, gentlemen, I knew you'd all like it," I said. "Now hop in and let's get to those chips."

After stuffing our hunger-crying stomachs with two orders each of well-greased, heavenly-smelling fish and chips, we moved on to Ye Olde Starre Inne, which we'd been told was one of the better pubs in York and a favourite Six Group haunt. It was so comfortable there and the beer so good that by nine o'clock we hardly felt like leaving it for the local Palaise de Dance. But tonight we were all together, and what we did or where we did it didn't matter too much; it was bound to end up a ball whatever happened.

At the dancehall there was the brief question of the management letting us in or not, due to our somewhat jolly condition. But we put on a collective show of being hostile and that was that. It was a large, pleasant ballroom with a fair dance-band on the stand. Most of the girls present seemed to be sixteen-year olds trying to act like twenty. I danced with a couple and couldn't work up the slightest interest in either of them. I suppose I still had a picture in my mind of moving around the floor at the NAAFI tea-dance with my hand behind Prue's trim waist and her eyes not too distant from mine going right through me, the mere touch of her making my head swim. I was feeling no such vibrations now.

I looked at my watch. Nine-thirty. If we moved out of here

smartly enough we'd still have enough time to hoist a couple of quick ones somewhere.

And we managed it, barely. When the first shout of "Time, gentlemen, please," echoed through the smoky cavern of a pub close by the Palaise, I was well into my second glass of mild and bitter, and the evening had been saved after all. With that good feeling of warmth all over my body the whole business seemed less and less important—the Air Force, going on operations, women, even Prue's face grew indistinct, blurred in my mind. My whole world was reduced to the smoke-filled, noisy-warm, brightly-lit room I was in, the shouted talk across the tables, the animated faces reddened with beer, the steady clink of glasses. But even that little world had all the hard unpleasant edges taken away. I felt very happy and a little sad all at once. It was time to go home.

Driving back to camp through the darkness, driving with both eyes glued magnetically to that white line which showed like a wavy ribbon in the weak glare of my headlights, I didn't feel like joining in the singing at first. But the crew's carefree voices bellowing out the familiar words finally won me over. I was still very young, wasn't I, and nothing else mattered very much as long as you had that. That and your health. The rest would all fit somehow into place. They couldn't take all of that away from you no matter how much they wanted to, no matter how hard they tried.

"There was flak, flak, bags of bloody flak.
  In the Ruhr, in the Ruhr,
There was flak, flak, bags of bloody flak,
  In the Valley of the Ruhr."

Once I'd started singing I felt better. I wanted to shout out louder than all the rest those stupid, precious words:

"My eyes are dim, I cannot see,
The searchlights they are blinding me,
The searchlights they are blinding me."

7

After I and the rest of the crew had stowed our flying gear in our lockers we left the flight hut in a group. We straggled along a foot-patch in the half-dark to the much larger Nissen hut called the dispersal hut. One half of it was used as a flight office, the other half was the Station briefing room, now doubling as a de-briefing room with the attack on Chemnitz over.

As we pushed open the door a welcome mixture of noise, warmth and coffee struck us all at once. The long narrow room was packed with sweaty, tired-faced aircrew, most of them talking very animatedly in pairs or in small groups. We slowly made our way through the crowd to the far end of the hut, where we could make out two WAAFs busily at work serving coffee. I spotted an air commodore with bristling moustaches and a chestful of ribbons, probably the base C.O. down from Linton. He was talking very happily with our squadron O.C. Perhaps this was a sign that our raid on Chemnitz had been a good one. But it was probably too early to tell yet. It would take the Photo Section some time to develop all the flash pictures taken by our aircraft cameras during the attack.

It felt very good to have a mug of fresh hot coffee in my hand again. Drinking it out of a lukewarm thermos in the aircraft wasn't somehow the same. Now it was even better when I'd managed the first couple of scalding sips, tasting the strong navy rum it was liberally laced with. The rum at first singed my gullet, then caught fire deliciously throughout my stomach region.

"That urn must hold at least five gallons," Walt pointed out as he joined Dave and me in the centre of the room. "I hope the I.O. calls me soon so I can keep at this coffee. Some Chase and Sanborn's. Must be at least one hundred proof."

Right about then a fellow bombardier in our squadron, whom I'd met before in the mess and who had only a couple of trips left to complete his tour, joined us. You could tell the rum had got to him quickly by the way he talked, very loud and a mile a minute. He was the old battle-scarred veteran giving the new recruits the benefit of his experience. He told us very solemnly that we were lucky as hell to be starting our tour now the ops were strictly milk runs. Like his first two which were leaflet raids on France. But from then on it had been a real son-of-a-bitch. The Ruhr had a bloody good defence network last fall. Jerry's night fighters had swarmed like bees, the flak was unbelieveably heavy and well-directed. Even the searchlights could sometimes be a real menace. Tonight he'd been bombing at the bottom of the stack and there'd been little or no flak. He'd heard that Jerry had fighter flares marking their course from the Leipzig area to the target and back, but he hadn't seen either the flares or the fighters, so it could be a lot of crap. They claimed the fighters were twin-engine jobs, but who had tangled with any? Don't get him wrong, he wasn't complaining. He didn't mind going back to Canada all in one piece.

Before he could tell us how lucky we were all over again Walt and I excused ourselves, leaving Dave to have his ear bent off. I couldn't stand that bombardier any longer. Right now the last thing in the world I wanted to talk to anyone about was the attack. I wanted to forget for a few minutes that there were bombers and fighters, targets to be bombed, burning cities lighting up the night sky. But I knew there wasn't much chance of that while I stayed in this room.

"Looks like a few guys are really enjoying this war," Walt said as we watched a cute little blonde WAAF serve us up another cup of pain killer.

"He's not too hard to figure out. He's probably been through that same routine so many times he almost believes it himself by now. Well, all I can say is, I hope he makes it."

"You know," Walt went on, "I'd stay in the Air Force the rest of my life if all I had to do was sleep all day, drink in the mess and chase quail all night. The only catch is they expect you to fly part of the time. Even now every time I release the brakes and we beetle down the runway I'm wondering if we're going to make it. I guess I've seen too many guys go for the chop in the last two years."

"Ever since that engine failure with old Slim at Topcliffe I feel exactly the same way," I said. "I'm nervous as a cat every time I step into a crate. Once we're airborne it's all right. But getting up and down has me in a solid sweat every time. I only hope I've got enough nerves to last me."

Our conversation ended there. My name had been called out by one of the Intelligence Officers behind the big table half-way down the room.

When I was seated across from him he asked me if we'd encountered any strong anti-aircraft fire or spotted any enemy aircraft. No. Anything at all I'd consider unusual? Again I had to answer no. Then he showed me my target pictures fresh from the photo lab, each one looking more like one huge cloud than anything else.

"Looks like you were bang on the aiming point when you released, Sutcliffe. Good work. That's all, then. Get yourself some more coffee if you feel like it. This batch tasted a little more potent than usual to me."

By now I was full of coffee right up to here. I'd leave my third cup for Walt or some other thirstier type. All of a sudden I felt very warm and very hungry both at once. I moved over toward the door and ran into Fred Waters standing there at the edge of things looking a little like a lost soul, that blissful Number-One-Op-behind-him-look written all over his face.

"Had enough of this nonsense?" I asked him.

He nodded and we left the de-briefing room together. We went out into the cold dark night again. Back at the flight hut we removed our battle dress and sweaty underwear and luxuriated in the warm showers. The hot water seemed to soak into every tired inch of my body. Beautiful, simply beautiful, I didn't want to leave the shower room. But I forced myself finally to turn on the cold water to finish it off, then worked my towel frantically to get my body warm and dry again. Gradually I felt myself coming back to life.

Then, a little later up in the mess, with bacon and eggs on the plate in front of me, luxuries reserved for returning heroes, I imagined myself seated once more in that hushed briefing-room as the Chief Briefing Officer mounted the platform, moved directly over to the huge map, and with the wooden pointer in his hand indicated a city in south-east Germany.

"We've got a long haul tonight, lads," he announced with just the right amount of relaxed seriousness in his voice. "The target is Chemnitz in Saxony, a large manufacturing centre with an important rail junction and numerous railway repair shops. Jerry has to bring his troops and supplies through here; we're going to smash it and him at the same time. Last night we hit nearby Dresden hard, tonight we want to do even better."

Then I was hunched over beside Dave in the navigator's compartment much, much later, totally concentrated on the pale green fluorescent picture tube we called H2S, watching Frankfurt appear as a bright patch of light to right of centre, then Leipzig come up on the left. I was still in my crowded bombardier's compartment in the nose, sweating above the Mark XIV bombsight with the aiming-point approaching far too rapidly to suit me. I was still awed and more than a little shaken by my first sight of a target area, all that mass of hell come alive down below, glowing like one huge seething diamond. A blood-red sea of flames underneath which streets, factories, houses were disintegrating block after block. . . .

One phrase kept surging through my mind now as I got busy on my bacon and eggs, you've made it, you've made it. That first op I'd been dreaming about and working toward for two years and more. That big first entry in my log book: Date: 14/2/45; Hour: 1655; Aircraft type and number: Haly VII "V"; Pilot: F/O Gibson; Duty: Operations; Remarks: *Chemnitz*, ground markers; Flying Times, Night: 8:55." The first one, the one that would always be the big one. The one that would remain clear and unclouded in your memory long after all the others that followed had somehow all blurred together. Like your first time with sex—more than a little awkward, more than a little tight across the chest, wanting it to happen perfectly and easily, and worrying a little that it wouldn't go right. But it did, and suddenly you were relaxing and very sure all at once and enjoying it like no other sensation on earth. Flying that first one today had been a little like that; the same rocket-like elation and just as sudden let-down of feeling. The knowledge now that you'd proved yourself and were fit to walk in the man's world of this squadron and this Air Force. A knowledge which made you proud and gave you an inner bond nothing that happened later could destroy totally though it could be badly scarred and shaken; some of that would always remain from this moment. Remain as long as you did, and nothing they could do would spoil it or cheapen its memory. . . .

Around about the end of the meal huge waves of tiredness began to spill over me that I knew I couldn't fight off for long. It became a tremendous effort simply to keep my eyes open. I began to yawn and couldn't stop. Dave said it was time he got me into bed, before he had to carry me.

Next morning I could remember nothing about walking back to the billet, nothing about somehow undressing and flaking out in bed. But neither did I remember any bad dreams; for me it had been solid, dead-tired sleep. Without even meeting once those dark penetrating eyes of Prudence Warwick.

8

"You don't know it but you scared hell out of me about four o'clock this morning," Dave informed me as we tackled our sausages, leeks and mashed potatoes up at the mess at noon the next day.

"How do you mean?"

"Oh, you suddenly gave out with a loud scream which made me jump a mile in my bed. Then you threshed around for about half a minute, throwing your blanket right off. All the time you were muttering out loud to yourself. That was a real beauty of a nightmare you had, chum."

"Sorry if I buggered up your beauty sleep. So that's what I do in bed at night, is it? You know, my mother used to tell me my old man had a bad habit of every now and then reliving his World War One adventures in bed. A couple of times he kicked her in his sleep and once his arm caught her on the head. She was always joking about getting single beds, but come to think of it maybe it wasn't that much of a joke if he kept getting those dreams fairly often."

"Maybe I do the same thing myself, Bill. Be sure and tell me if you notice anything. But what the hell, we were all keyed up after that op."

"No doubt about it. That was a bastard to draw on the first one. A nine hour haul right across Germany."

"Like Walt said about his first flight last week, it seemed like just another training run at first. But after we hit the Dutch coast it began to feel very different to me. Maybe because we had radio silence, while on those cross-countrys over England we always had the R/T going and somebody babbling over the intercom most of the time. Then I was plotting the headings taking us closer and closer to Saxony. I kept expecting someone to call out a fighter attack or at least have some flak booming up at us. Tension like that can really

34

build up in you, and when there's no release it wears you down after a while. How did things look on the bombing run?"

"All I could really see was a mess of glowing circles, like red-hot embers on a fire. They were spread out, so I'd have to say our bombing was fairly scattered. But there were hundreds of those glowing embers, so that adds up to one hell of a blaze. I guess the cloud cover had moved in by the time our bunch got there. We must have been on the tail-end of the attack."

"Did it feel any different dropping real bombs this time?"

"Not really. I guess I was so damned busy making good and sure I had the bombsight bang on the aiming-point that I didn't have much time to think about it. I'll tell you one thing, though, you feel mighty exposed up there in the nose."

"I suppose you would. What do you think yourself, though, has Jerry given up defending a place like Chemnitz?"

"Maybe it's just that he doesn't figure it has enough strategic importance at this stage of the game. It could be, though, that we had him fooled all the way. You know how they always mount about three phoney attacks on these big shows. So maybe their night-fighter controllers got sucked in. They sure had plenty of chance to attack us along that route. But I can't figure out why we didn't get any flak unless they've moved their guns to more important cities. We can't expect to get it as easy the next time. But it was a nice bonus on our first run."

Dave and I gas-bagged our way through the rest of the meal. It was good to have a long talk with him again, nice to know we could still open up to each other. We'd been very close at the start of our O.T.U. training, then gradually had drifted apart to some extent. While still roommates we didn't spend much time together. Dave was shy as hell with girls and after several disastrous attempts had pretty well given up serious skirt-chasing. That and the fact that he wasn't much of a drinker made it easy to understand why I'd looked around for more adventurous company. But we still shot pool, played a little bridge, and took in station movies together. I was glad we could stay as close as we did.

"Coming down to dispersal?" he asked as we left the dining-room and wandered out into the lounge.

"You go ahead. I have to make a phone call first. You

don't think those bastards up at the Castle will have us down for something tonight, do you?"

The castle I referred to was Allerton Park Castle, east of Knaresborough, our Group Headquarters. From here "Black Jack" McCowan, our Group A.O.C. kept his fourteen heavy-bomber squadrons scrambling night and day.

"I wouldn't put it past them, though by rights we should have the night off. See you down at the hut, then."

I was in luck. Neither of the two public telephones in the lobby was in use. I thumbed through the letter "W" in the thin York and District telephone directory. Lucky again. Only one Warwick was listed. But the listing read "Herbert Warwick, Dispensing Chemists". Well, that could be her father. It was the only lead I had at the moment.

I dropped in my money and waited for the operator. It was like using a phone in the country.

A female voice answered.

"Warwick's."

"Is that you, Prue?"

"Yes. Who's that? Do I know you?"

"I hope you remember me at least. We met at the NAAFI dance last week. I'm Bill Sutcliffe. One of those Canadians, you know."

"Yes, I remember you. You're a bombardier, aren't you? I remember that 'B' on your wing."

"I meant to call you sooner," I went on rather lamely, "but I've been flying all the time. I was wondering if we could go out together somewhere. A dance or the cinema. I have a car so I can pick you up any time."

"You know, I'd love to, Bill, but I'm frightfully busy all this week. And I work at the shop here in the evenings until eight. Would you care to call me next week like a good boy?"

"Fine." What else could I say? "But I'd hoped I wouldn't have to wait that long," I added.

"I'm sorry. Fortunes of war, you know. Goodbye for now, then."

She was gone and I was left holding a buzzing receiver in my hand. She had been quick, polite, and yet unmistakeably clear. It was a model brush-off.

Yet she'd left the door open. She had invited me to call her next week. It still wasn't hopeless. Impossible, perhaps, but not hopeless.

I walked out of the mess and across several branching footpaths between desolate-looking Nissen huts until I reached the dispersal hut. The rest of the crew were there, along with most of the boys in the squadron, looking over some of the photos of the raid. Chemnitz looked like it had taken quite a pounding in spite of the cloud cover. One Algonquin crew was posted as missing, but they'd been seen bailing out as their Hally went down in flames. It had been hit by a Ju.88 an hour after leaving the target, which went to prove you were never really home free until you touched down on your own field.

Around three o'clock I felt the compelling need of a little shut-eye. I checked out of the bridge game I was in with Dave and a couple of WAGs and wandered back to our billet. I was still tired from those nine hours in the air last night. No sooner had my head hit the pillow than I was away. When Dave came into the room at four-thirty it seemed as though I'd only lain down minutes before. Relax, he said, stand-down until 0800. Thank God for that.

I had every intention of making it a quiet evening on the base. I had late supper with Dave, drank a beer and shot some pool with him afterwards. Then it turned out I'd seen the movie they were showing at the NAAFI, and it was such a lousy picture I couldn't face sitting through it a second time. I told Dave to go ahead himself and then I went back to the hut. I was going to catch up on a couple of letters home I was a week late now in getting off. But I was too restless to write letters. I started one and then tore it up. To hell with it. I shaved, put on a clean shirt, and drove into York.

I knew damn well what was eating me. That telephone conversation with Prudence Warwick. The more I thought about it the more unhappy I became. It all boiled down to the fact that I couldn't wait until next week to know where I stood with her. I had to know now. Tonight if at all possible. Until I did I knew I'd be on edge. Maybe I'd only feel worse after I found out, but at least the thing would be decided one way or the other.

I had the address of the chemist's shop. It was on Piccadilly, near Copper Gate as it turned out. By the time I got there it was well after eight and the shop looked like it was closed. But there was a light at the back so perhaps someone

was still working there. I parked my car and waited. It was a
very slim chance but I had nothing else going for me at the
moment.

About fifteen minutes later the single light went out. Then
I saw a female figure step out into the street and lock the
door carefully behind her. The woman began walking down
Piccadilly toward the Copper Gate corner. With any kind of
luck it had to be Prue.

I started the engine and moved slowly away from the curb.
If it was Prue it looked as though she was heading for the
bus stop on the corner. Would she take a lift from me? There
was only one way to find out.

I drove past her slowly and pulled into the curb again. As
long as a bus didn't come along in the next minute I stood a
chance.

I rolled down the window as she came abreast of the car.
It was Prue all right. My heart began to beat very fast and I
felt myself tightening up all over. Very silly but it was happening.

"Hello, Miss Warwick, may I offer you a lift?"

I tried to make it sound very casual, but I didn't know
whether I succeeded or not.

She stopped and looked at me. I couldn't tell what was going on behind that pleasant face with the wonderful eyes.

"Don't tell me it's you," was all she said.

"Quite a coincidence, isn't it? I was coming down Piccadilly when I looked over and thought I recognized you. Can I
drive you anywhere? I'm probably going in your direction
anyway."

"Oh, I'm sure you will be. All right," she said, "you can
drop me off at the station if you like. I have a train to
catch."

"And where does the train take you, if I may ask?"

"You are an inquisitive man, aren't you?" Prue said as she
sat down on the seat beside me and gave the car door a little
slam. "Well, if you must know, I go to Tadcaster. It's about
five miles from town. That's where I live."

"Why don't I simply drive you there? Wouldn't that be
easiest?" I asked her. "It's not much fun standing around stations at this time of night waiting for trains."

"It's really no hardship. I do it almost every night."

"Five miles is nothing. I can have you home while we're still arguing about it."

"Do you always get your own way, Mr. Sutcliffe?"

"Most of the time when it really counts," I admitted. "So it's on to Tadcaster then. You'll have to be navigator on this run."

I started up the car and we headed through the old streets. Prue directed me across the Ouse Bridge and along Micklegate. We crossed Queen Street, heading out along The Mount.

I offered her a cigarette and she said, "No thank you." Now that there weren't any more directions to give she was sitting very quietly beside me.

"You're working late tonight," I ventured.

"We close every night at eight. Then I usually have a few things to finish up. Tonight there were several last minute prescriptions."

"Does that mean you fill prescriptions?"

"Why, yes. That's my job, really. I'm a dispensing chemist."

I must have looked surprised, for she laughed slightly. That was a good sign. Get them smiling or laughing and half the battle was won.

"My father didn't have a son so I had to be the other chemist in the family," she explained. "Actually, I've only been doing it less than a year. Say, perhaps I will have one of your cigarettes. I like the aroma of the one you're smoking."

"Sweet Caps. Best cigarette in Canada."

Now things were starting to roll. The iceberg slowly beginning to melt at last.

She leaned over slightly to accept the light I gave her, and in the split second of the lighter's glow I saw how fresh-looking her skin was, how firmly-red her lips, how perfectly groomed her brown hair. Then the flame of the lighter died and her features became only a vague outline once more beside me.

"I'm afraid the car's bloody cold," I apologized. "There's something wrong with the heater."

"It's fine. We English get along on a minimum of heat, as you've probably discovered by now."

"Yes, I've noticed that you're only beginning to become

aware of central heating. You wouldn't last too long through a good Canadian winter without it, let me tell you."

"I suppose not. Do you find it very cold here?"

"Cold enough. This last couple of weeks I could imagine I was back in Ontario without too much trouble."

"Is that where you come from?"

"Yes. A city called Toronto in the southern part. It's on one of the Great Lakes, Lake Ontario, to be exact."

"We probably studied it in geography at school, but I'm afraid I've forgotten all about things like that."

"It's a big small town," I told her. "Everywhere else in Canada they call it Hogtown." How did the conversation stray off onto this tangent? I was wasting valuable time now.

"That certainly is a quaint name."

No doubt about it, I was rapidly running out of small talk. Before I could think of a way to change the conversation around, Prue said, "Tadcaster's just around the next bend, Bill. Slow down a little or you may miss it completely."

A minute later I was turning off the High Street and pulling up in front of a large old-fashioned house with an iron railing around the front of it. Only one light was shining inside, probably in the hall.

"Thanks awfully for the ride," Prue said, opening her door and beginning to get out of the car before I had a chance to say anything.

I clambered out on my side as quickly as I could and caught up to her at the gate. She certainly wasn't waiting around for me, and she was making that very plain indeed.

"I hope you didn't mind me barging in on you like this tonight," I said. "Faint heart never won fair lady and all that rot."

"Rot is right. Actually I didn't mind that much, you know."

"When can I see you again?"

"You were going to call me the beginning of next week, remember?"

"Yes, I know, but couldn't we settle something right now? I never know when I'm flying these days."

Prue went through the iron gate and closed it behind her. Then she turned around. A slight smile was playing around the corners of her lips.

"All right. Tuesday night. You can pick me up at the shop if you like. I'll be there until eight at least."

"Thanks, Prue. See you then."

"Goodnight, Bill, and take care."

Now she was fitting the key from her purse into the front door lock and before I knew it the door had closed behind her. I was standing there alone in the quiet, dark street.

But I had a date with her Tuesday. I'd made the first breakthrough. I could see I still had a long way to go. But I was over the first hurdle.

I got back in my Standard, started her up and drove back into York. The five miles seemed like nothing at all. With any luck I had a full hour's beer time left. But that was really unimportant. None of it was important beside this girl I'd just said goodnight to. That's the way it is when you fall suddenly, completely in love.

9

"Skipper." It was Joe Petosky on the intercom. "Just got a message from base. It's socked in solid. We're ordered to East Fortune, wherever that is."

"How's that for good news, gang?" Walt's voice lacked its usual light-heartedness. "Looks like spam and spuds for us tonight. Bill and Dave, see if you can spot this lousy drome on the map and give us a heading."

"Balls," I said as Dave spread a map out on his navigator's desk. "This has been one bitch of a day, hasn't it? And now we get this to top it off."

"You're absolutely right, mate," Dave agreed, as I came around and looked over his shoulder.

It had all started much too early that Tuesday morning. At eight-thirty Dave had shaken me awake for an early briefing. By 1139 we were airborne on our first daylight attack. The target was Wesel in the Rhine Valley. Bomber Command had pasted it the night before and expected a repeat performance from us today.

After circling around above the countryside we followed our lead aircraft on a heading which joined us up before too long with other Hally squadrons until there must have been a hundred aircraft in one huge gaggle. As we left the coast of England behind we picked up a large fighter escort of R.A.F. Mustangs. They stayed with us right across Holland and part way into Germany. The trouble was the visibility grew steadily worse. By the time we reached the target area the cloud blanket was all the way up to the top aircraft at 18,000 feet. Finally the Master Bomber called out over the R/T "Mission abandoned, all aircraft return to base". It had been one hell of a frustrating day all round and when Walt bumped "L" for "Love" down on the slightly fogged-up runway at East Fortune we'd been six and a half hours airborne. Good old

Air Force. My date with Prue was buggered just when I was starting to make a little progress. She'd be cheesed when I didn't show up and I couldn't blame her in the least. I was bitching louder than the rest of the crew as we climbed onto a waiting lorry and were driven off to Flights.

After storing our gear in a special visitor's room, we showered, dressed up, then went looking for beer and supper in that order. As officers Walt, Dave and I headed for the Officer's Mess Bar, the rest of the crew had to settle for the Sergeant's Mess.

The beer proved to be good, the meal ordinary. The R.A.F. officers were very polite, but gave you the impression that they were trying a little too hard to be friendly. We were allies and all that sort of thing, don't you know. I always had the feeling they were sitting a little on the edge of their chairs waiting for those crazy Canadians to put their foot in it in some completely, unexpected, nerve-shattering way. To be completely fair, most of the time we tried our best not to disappoint them.

"I sure hope the weather clears up at base tomorrow," Walt moaned as we consoled ourselves after supper with more beer in the officer's bar. "Imagine having to spend another day in a hole like this."

Beyond the fact that I'd missed my date with Prue I wasn't feeling too badly myself about our aircraft being diverted. I rather fancied Walt didn't mind it that much either, but of course he wouldn't admit it. As long as we stayed here we couldn't be flying over Happy Valley. It seemed like a pretty good deal to me. Our first two ops had taken most of the frosting off the cake as far as I was concerned. The glamour of being part of the R.C.A.F.'s highly-trained heavy bomber crews fighting the good fight with the Luftwaffe had worn thin very quickly. Now it was more a case of doing a dirty job that had to be done with the one thought uppermost of somehow coming through it alive. Even that, we knew now, was strictly a matter of luck, and could run out on us the very next time up.

"Why don't we collect all the bums, scrape up a taxi and head for the nearest pub?" I suggested. "Better than climbing the wall around here."

"Great idea," Walt said. "Let's find the sergeant's mess and get mobile. Are you with us, Davey boy?"

Dave didn't have to be coaxed tonight. Less than an hour later we were all drinking together at a pub a couple of miles from the drome. It turned out to be one of the crew's better times together, as well as one of the liveliest.

Half way through the evening I found myself talking very seriously with Fred Waters, our mid-upper gunner. I'd begun by inquiring about Doris, his little Scottish lass up in Edinburgh, and we were off to a flying start.

"Wonderful," he said. "I had a letter from her yesterday. She's a little worried about me being on ops now but that's normal, I guess."

"You're pretty well stuck on her, aren't you?"

"I have been from the first time I saw her, Bill. I suppose it's that old chestnut about love at first sight. Something seemed to go all warm and funny inside me and I knew this was my girl for keeps. Has it ever happened to you?"

I was tempted to tell him a little about Prue, but decided against it. After all, we hadn't really gotten off the ground yet. It was too early to say how it would go with the two of us.

"A couple of times," I said, "but it never lasted. Still, it was great while it did. A little like being on a merry-go-round where the horses seem to go faster and faster and you think they'll never stop."

"I guess Doris and I are still going round and round. Say, you haven't heard anything more about a leave, have you? Doris is always after me about when I'm coming up again."

"As far as I know we still got one week out of every ten. But right now it could depend on how many hot targets the brass have left for us to blast away at. I certainly wouldn't count on any time off until we've done at least ten trips."

"The big reason we're so interested, Bill, is that Doris and I want to get married as soon as possible. You'll keep this under your hat, won't you? I haven't told any of the others."

"You can count on me," I told him. "But aren't you rushing it a bit? You hardly know the girl yet, do you? You were only up in Edinburgh for a week and even then you didn't meet her right away."

"That's true enough," Fred said, "but just the same I feel as if I've known her for a whole lot longer. Right now I'm as sure of what I'm doing as I'll ever be."

"Well, I wish you all the luck in the world, Fred. Seriously, though, I don't know how anybody goes ahead with something like marriage at a time like this. I know I'm living strictly one day at a time. I can't believe in looking ahead any further than that. That's why I don't even think about leave. Maybe it's only a few weeks away, but it could be a couple of years as far as I'm concerned."

About then Max wandered over with glass in hand and my conversation with Fred was over. As I'd told him, I wished him all the luck in the world if he was really serious about marriage.

Dave joined us a couple of minutes later. When he went to say anything he did it so deliberately, so solemnly, that I knew he must be fairly high. Which wasn't surprising if he was trying to keep up to real professional beer drinkers like Walt and Max. For a guy who never drank more than a pint during an evening he was managing very well.

It seemed hardly any time after that when the owner of the pub called out from behind the bar, "Time, gentlemen, please."

"Well, old sport," I said to Dave sitting next to me at the long table covered with beer bottles, "drink up. You've still got another bottle to kill."

"Don't bloody well worry about me, chum," Dave said, looking at me a little glassy-eyed, the words even more slurred now than before. "I can keep up with any of you dead-beats."

I knew right away he was drunk, really smashed. It was the only way you could explain that swear word he'd used. I'd never heard him say anything more colourful than damn all the time I'd known him, and even that was used very sparingly.

The pub owner finally half-jollied, half-pushed us out of his establishment into the cold night air. Twenty minutes later we were jumping out of a taxi at the East Fortune base, a very happy bunch indeed. We went through the guardhouse and up the main road toward our quarters.

We were almost there when Dave, who was walking beside me, gave a little cry. He stopped, staggered once, and started to fall over. Luckily it was toward me, so I was able to half-catch him.

He was out cold. Pete Yarish got his other arm and Fred held his feet. We carried him into our hut and down to the room assigned to Dave and I. He was a dead weight, and by the time we'd dumped him on the bed we were puffing heavily.

"How is he?" Walt asked. He'd followed along behind us.

"I think he's coming around now," I said, bending over and looking at his face. Just then he half-opened his eyes and looked up at all of us.

"Bloody bastard Limeys," he shouted out so loud it made us all jump a little. Then before we knew it he was off the bed, coming at us with his arms swinging wildly, a glazed look in his eyes.

One of his fists hit me in the chest but didn't do any immedate damage. He corked Pete right in the face, however, and Walt backed away just in time.

"Limey buggers," he shouted again, getting ready for another series of swings. By now I'd realized what must be going through his beer-fogged mind. He imagined he was back at O.T.U. surrounded by a hostile bunch of R.A.F. instructors. Why I didn't really know, but it had to be something like that. The problem right now was to quiet him down before he woke up the whole hut. We simply had to act fast. I signalled Walt and dived for his legs.

He may have been drunk and didn't know where he was or who we were, but he still had a few of his reflexes working. I received a good part of his shoe on my head as I hit him above the ankles and he fell over.

The others got the idea about then and went for his arms. We pinned him down and held him there, even though he continued to struggle like a madman. It was all I could do to hold his legs down. Finally I simply sat on them.

We must have kept him pinned down for almost half an hour. He was struggling as hard then as at the start of things. You wondered where he got all the extra strength from. Walt was kneeling across his chest now, holding one arm and trying to talk to him.

"Hey, Dave. It's me, Walt. Walt Gibson. Remember me?"

Dave's only answer was to suddenly spit in his face.

I had to give Walt a lot of credit. He took it without saying a word. I leaned over with a handkerchief and wiped his face off for him.

"Thanks, Bill. This friend of yours is sure a tough customer," he panted. "Sorry, Dave, but I have to do this." He pushed the handkerchief over Dave's mouth. "Now what the hell do we do?"

That was a good question. Nobody could expect Walt to take any more of that. At the same time we didn't want to hurt Dave if we could possibly avoid it. This was something he himself had no control over.

It was Walt who supplied the answer.

"I don't think we've got too much choice," he said. "Let him up when I say the word. I'm going to have to hit him but I'll try not to leave a mark."

He got his handkerchief out and wrapped it around his fist. We made ready to release Dave. There didn't seem to be anything else to do. He was still lying there, that crazy, glassed look in his eyes. We could be a bunch of Jerries for all he knew.

We got off him one by one. Walt was the last up. We stood there, waiting for Dave to get to his feet. He swore a couple of times. Then all at once he closed his eyes, his breathing became easier, his arms and legs loosened. He was suddenly sleeping as relaxed as a baby on the floor.

That's how we left him a few minutes later, after partly undressing him and putting him under a blanket. We were all dead on our feet, but relieved, almost happy.

"The silly bastard," Walt said, as the rest of the boys made ready to leave our room. "From now on he stays on soda pop, Bill. Happy dreams."

For most of that night my head felt the same way it had years ago after I'd been kicked in a high school football game. The last thing I remembered before turning out the light in the room was taking a last look over at Dave. His face on the rumpled pillow had an easy, almost smiling look.

10

The voice at the other end of the telephone could only be Prue's. I knew it well enough now not to mistake it for anyone else's.

"It's Bill, Prue. Sorry about last night. We couldn't land at West Moor and I only got back here an hour ago. Any chance of seeing you this evening?"

"I suppose so. I can't blame you if our Yorkshire weather isn't right, can I? There's no chance you'll fly at the last minute, is there?"

"No. I'm all on my own until 0800. When shall I pick you up?"

"I'm at the shop until eight. So you might as well come here. If the door's shut, just bang on it. I'll probably be out in the back."

"Fine. Goodbye for now."

"Goodbye, Bill."

I felt very lighthearted as I put the phone up. I hadn't expected things to go quite so smoothly. I'd been almost sure Prue would keep me waiting a day or two at least for another date. I was even prepared to have her tell me to forget it. Instead she'd sounded almost friendly. It was a nice break after a miserable twenty-four hours. I walked back to the hut to catch a little sack time feeling very light-hearted indeed.

I woke up at five, ate a leisurely supper with Dave, then had a couple of beers in the mess bar. By mutual agreement the crew had decided to say nothing to Dave about his rampage of the night before. We couldn't see how it would serve any useful purpose. And as he didn't bring the subject up himself all next day, we concluded that he hadn't remembered anything of it. It looked as though a large blank had been mercifully drawn across his mind. Knowing Dave as

48

well as I did, I knew he'd feel miserable as hell if he was aware how he'd put us all through the wringer.

I was in a very good mood as I drove toward York through the early darkness. The weather was windy and cold, but there hadn't been any more snow and the highway was completely dry. If I could only get my heater fixed it would be a pleasure driving in the car. I'd been by the M.T. Section and one of the mechanics had promised to take a look at it. If he could get it going it would be well worth a couple of cartons of cigarettes.

It was almost eight when I parked the car and walked around onto Piccadilly where the chemist's shop was. Prue was serving a customer when I walked in. She looked very neat and efficient wearing her white smock; it seemed to high-light her soft, medium-length hair. She greeted me with a look, then went back to wait on her customer, a middle-aged woman apparently confused about the directions on a prescription.

"These doctors," she muttered finally, when her customer had gone, and she had drawn the shade down over the front window and bolted the door, "they give their patients little or no idea of what their medicine is or how to take it; everything's left up to us."

"Problems, problems," I said, "everybody has their problems. I always thought the biggest trouble with doctors was nobody could read their handwriting."

"That's true enough, believe me," Prue had moved back behind the counter. "I've one prescription to make up for first thing tomorrow, then I'll be with you."

"You go right ahead. I'll take a look around."

I noticed two framed graduation diplomas hung up on the wall, directly outside the little dispensary in which Prue was standing now. One was to certify that Prudence Elizabeth Warwick, having passed all the necessary requirements, was entitled to all the privileges of the Degree of Bachelor of Pharmacy. It was from the University of York. The other was in much the same language, and made out to John Foster Warwick, and was from the University of London. No doubt her father's.

"I take it your father only works the day shift."

"That's right," Prue answered. "He has to watch his heart ever since his attack last year. He opens up and works until two. I come on at noon and work right through. That way both of us are here during one of the busiest times of the day. It suits me fine because I have the hardest job getting up in the morning."

I nosed around the various counters until Prue had finished work. I'd always been intrigued by drug stores. This one didn't have the wide-ranging sidelines of a Canadian store, but there was a fascinating selection of cough lozenges and throat pastilles, for example, which gave you the idea everyone in England must have some kind of throat problem. With the crazy weather they had I didn't doubt it in the least.

Finally Prue closed up the dispensary, took off her smock, and stood there looking at me, a little smile playing around the corner of her mouth, a mood quite familiar to me by now.

"I hope you didn't have anything planned," she said. "I didn't realize how tired I am until a few minutes ago. I suppose I'm getting old and don't know it."

"I was simply playing it by ear. I thought we might catch a drink or two somewhere and get better acquainted. Outside of that I didn't have anything definite in mind."

"Good. You know, I'd like a cup of tea right now in the worst way. Would you care for one? I have a small stove out back."

"Fine." It didn't matter to me in the least what we did or where we did it. Being with her seemed the only important thing. I noted with approval the black, almost tightly-fitting sweater which showed off her sharp-pointed breasts to good advantage. And as I followed her out into the back room I noted again that easy swing of her hips, the purposeful walk. This was certainly some woman any way you looked at it. Which led directly to some puzzling questions still on my mind, some of which I might have answers to before the evening was over.

I'd never been a tea drinker and still didn't drink it if anything else was available. But tonight for some reason I enjoyed sipping away at the cup which Prue put before me at the tiny table crowded in beside the miniature stove.

"How are you finding West Moor?" she asked me before I could think of something to get the conversation going.

"The quarters aren't much—smoky, crowded Nissen huts.

But I'm with a fine squadron and I've got two ops in, so I can't complain."

"Do you like flying?"

"Not really. I suppose if I was piloting the aircraft I might have a different feeling about it. It all boils down to the fact that I didn't join the Air Force with the idea of ending up dropping bombs. Of course I do a lot more than that when I'm in the air but that's the most important part of it."

"They made you an officer, didn't they? That must mean they consider you're doing an important job."

"I happened by a big fluke to graduate first in my bombardier's class, so a commission was almost automatic. That leads me on to one of my pet gripes about the whole flying business. We're a crew of seven, but only three of us are officers, although seeing we're a team one job in the air is as important as any other. But if we should happen to get shot down and taken prisoner, some of us would go to officer's prison camp and the others to an N.C.O.'s camp. Which means that the N.C.O.'s can be forced to do heavy manual labour while we as officers can't be made to work under the Geneva Convention. I say we should be together on the ground as we are in the air. I suppose that would cost the taxpayers back home too much money. But let's get off this flying kick. I must be boring you to tears. I want to hear more about you. I still don't know hardly anything."

"What is it you want to know?"

"The usual things. I can't remember whether you've ever told me your age, for instance."

"That's one thing women usually don't like to mention. I'm not sure I do myself. But I'm twenty-five, if you really must know. And I'm five foot seven, one hundred and twenty pounds. That's all the vital statistics you're going to get out of me, sir."

"You've mentioned your father, but you didn't say anything about your mother."

"Oh, she's very much alive and kicking. A regular dynamo, that woman. She runs both of us ragged."

"How about brothers and sisters?"

"Didn't I tell you I was an only child? One of those horribly spoilt brats, I should hasten to add."

"If you are it doesn't show."

"That's only because I keep it very carefully hidden. But you'd better watch out."

"Thanks for the warning," I said.

Prue sipped away at her tea for several minutes without saying anything more. I could see the lightheartedness slowly going out of her face, and a more serious mood taking its place. Finally she finished her cup and looked across the table at me with those wonderfully disturbing eyes of hers.

"Pardon me for being such a wet blanket," she said, "but I think you and I should come to some kind of understanding. As you've probably noticed I've tried to discourage you from seeing me but you don't seem to give up easily. It's not that I don't like you or don't want your company, it's simply that I don't want you to get serious over me. Because it can't lead to anything, Bill. To sex or anything else. So that's the way it is. If we can just be friends and have some good times together, I'd like nothing better. But if it's going to be anything else then we'd better end it here and now. I thought you should know this before I wasted any more of your time. Now that's my little speech. I suppose you'll think I'm a stupid old maid for saying all this. Don't worry, it doesn't bother me in the least."

"Nothing of the kind," I said. "If that's the way you feel about things the sooner I know it the better. Perhaps sometime you'll tell me the reasons behind it. But I should tell you that I'm fairly sure I love you. And if it has to be this way then that's the way it has to be. I don't really have much choice in the matter, do I?"

"You're sweet," Prue said, and some of her serious mood had left her face already. "You're a dear sweet boy. Let's not stay here any longer, shall we? Didn't you promise me a drink a while ago? I think I need something stronger than tea after all."

"We both do," I said, and left it at that.

11

Dave and I were walking back from the mess to our hut following an after-lunch game of poker in which I'd lost two quid and he'd won almost the same amount when the now all too familiar voice of Tannoy echoed in our ears across the drome:

"Attention. This is the Adjutant speaking. All personnel are confined to the station until further notice, effective immediately."

It was now a quarter past two. That meant it was too late for a daylight. But still meant another op was coming up. Our number eight to be exact.

"Christ, just when I was beginning to enjoy this war," I grumbled. "I knew it was too good to last."

"We've had almost a week," Dave pointed out. "I think we've been damn lucky. Some joker from Operations was telling me at breakfast that some squadrons in the Group have been out twice this month already. One was a daylight to Cologne. So at least we missed that much."

"I was only kidding," I said. "Of course we've been lucky. Any day you don't fly in this rat race you're damn lucky."

It was March fifth. We hadn't flown since the twenty-seventh of February. Right after lunch on that particular day we'd gone to Mainz on a daylight attack. Cloud had hidden our target indicators so the Pathfinders released sky markers. We had a fighter escort all the way out and back, so we weren't too surprised not to see any Jerry fighters. But the flak still came up pretty thick and hot. My log book carried this entry: "Four flak holes fin and wing."

A couple of days before that it had been Kamen and Essen, where there was also a fair amount of light flak. They were both daylights, amounting almost to milk runs. But Monheim on the twenty-first, where we went after an oil re-

finery, had been a night attack with moderately heavy flak
and fighter flares showing on our homeward run. But the next
night at Worms, a target every bit as miserable as the name,
Group lost three crews as opposed to one over Monheim. I
wrote in my log: "Intense flak and searchlights, good attack,"
and that covered it pretty well. By the time we'd gone in on
our bomb run large fires were burning down below. The
Jerry ack-ack seemed to be well concentrated here. Plenty of
powerful searchlights began to sweep the sky, and for the first
time we heard the loud rattling of flak fragments against
wings and fuselage. Our aircraft bucked and shuddered under
the impact. What other crate but a Hally could stand up under such punishment like that? She was proving a real old
work-horse for us. . . .

So now we'd get back into harness. The holiday was over.
We both hurried in to the comparative warmth of our hut.
For the past week it had been as cold in Yorkshire as I could
ever remember it being in winter-time back home. There'd
been some snow but it didn't stay very long on the ground.
Along with the snow came plenty of freezing rain mixed with
a little hail for good measure. Our runways from what I had
seen of them were ice-covered in many places and generally
treacherous if an aircraft braked unexpectedly or harder than
usual. But it wasn't only ice-covered runways that were keeping us off the operations board. Now that we seemed to be
winning the war the squeeze was getting tighter and tighter
on Germany. From this it followed that available heavy bomber air targets were growing less and less, with many of the
old familiar ones already in Allied hands. Added to this the
lousy weather conditions for the past week apparently all
over Germany and our inactivity in the air was pretty well
explained.

I lay there on my bed trying to fall off to sleep for an hour
or so, listening to Dave's steady breathing from his bed beside
mine. Something was eating away at me, making me very
nervous and restless. Wasn't it true that I didn't want to admit to myself that Prue was at the bottom of it? That after
two further meetings with her it was getting harder and
harder to pretend that our relationship had any real future
chance beyond one on a strictly friendly basis. Harder and
harder. Go on, smile at your own lousy joke. But it wasn't
funny, McGee. Rather it was torture having to be close to

her for several hours or longer at a stretch, and have to keep
telling yourself, hands off, no physical contact allowed. I
wondered how much more of this I could take before I threw
in the sponge.

As I remember it I was in the middle of a fairly confused
dream when I felt myself being shaken roughly awake. It was
Dave, of course, looking down at me a little anxiously.

"Apparently Tannoy sounded off again fifteen minutes ago.
I was dead to the world myself. If somebody hadn't yelled
down the hall I'd still be asleep. Briefing's at 1315. That's ten
minutes from now. Better shake your ass."

I shook it good and Dave and I arrived all out of breath at
the dispersal hut with a full minute to spare. A steady stream
of air crew was following along behind us as we went into
the large Nissen hut, one half of which was the briefing room
and the other half "B" Flight's office. The wheels of the
night's operation had started to turn and we were going along
for the ride whether we liked it or not.

The long narrow room was crowded already with blue bat-
tledress. There was the usual high buzz of easy-going conversation. I finally spotted some of our crew half-way from the
front. Pete saw us and waved. It turned out they'd managed
to save two folding chairs for us.

"Glad to see such a real keen group," I quipped as I
worked myself in beside Max.

"Up yours, Sutcliffe," Max said good-naturedly.

"How about a little respect for rank, sergeant?" I asked
him as I sat down.

"Kiss my rosy red," Max continued, "sir."

"That's better, sergeant. I can see you've got things in the
right perspective."

Walt, who was sitting next to Max, leaned across.

"What do you make of all that, Bill? It looks to me like
another dandy coming up."

He indicated the huge map hanging up behind the
briefing-room platform, on which was shown England,
France, the Low Countries, and Germany. Red tapes ran
from Yorkshire south-east across the Channel, moving first
into Germany between Wilhelmshaven and Groningen, then
almost due east to beyond the Rhone. Another south-east leg
led on to Leipzig, with a final south-west leg to the target almost at the Czechoslovak border. The returning green tapes

ran a straight northwest course skirting Kassel and Hanover, to exit over the North Sea at approximately our point of entry.

"That looks like a bitch of a long haul," was my reaction. "Any idea what the target could be, Dave?"

"It has to be either Chemnitz or Dresden. What else is down there that we know of? But we'll have the gen soon enough."

We didn't have too long to wait. Not five minutes later Wing Commander Wickes, affectionately known as "Big Wick," strode into the room while we rose to our feet in rather ragged fashion. He moved briskly up the aisle between our chairs and sat down in the front row. We all resumed sitting with a lot of shuffling and scraping.

That was the signal for the Chief Briefing Officer, Squadron Leader Lewis, to move up onto the platform. He went directly to the war map, holding a long wooden pointer in one hand.

"Gentlemen, most of you may remember that we hit Chemnitz the middle of last month. You may also remember the cloud cover that made accurate bombing pretty well impossible. So we're going back there tonight and this time we're going to do one hell of a lot better. The target here," and he indicated it with a tap of his pointer, "is an important rail junction with many railway repair shops. Smashing it hard will disrupt the enemy's lines of communication with his rapidly disintegrating eastern front."

"A diversionary flight of training Wellingtons is to fly a pattern along the south coast east of the Channel to keep Jerry guessing. Our night fighters will be out in strength to attack his fighter stations. You will take off at 1635 hours and orbit to the left at 1500 feet. At 1700 hours you will set course 130 degrees magnetic so as to cross the East Friesen Islands southwest of Wilhelmshaven."

He paused to make sure we were all paying attention, then pointed to the red tape on the map.

"Once you are over the Channel reduce altitude in order to fly just above the water. When you reach the German coast start climbing to your assigned height. One hundred miles inland you will turn left to 092 degrees and fly due east of Hanover. Beyond the Rhone you will head south-east skirting Leipzig. Your final leg will bring you downwind over Chemnitz. After the bombing run turn north-west on a heading of 300 degrees to bypass Gottingen, Hanover, Bremen and Groningen."

"And," he concluded, "if any of you are worrying about it, flak should be light with no heavy fighter opposition expected. Any questions?"

There were no questions. The Squadron Leader had made things very clear. Someone coughed, a chair scraped. The Met Officer now took the platform. He advised us quite glibly that there were heavy clouds up to 15,000 feet between base and target and 3/10 cloud over the target itself. The wind was expected to shift to 030 degrees at 20 knots over the target. He went on with several more observations about the weather, closing with the promise that the base should be fairly clear for landing.

That was all for the Met gent. The usual b.s. The weather in this part of the world was about as dependable as the war news you read in the English papers. He knew it, we knew it, the brass knew it. Still, they had to play their little game of the weather.

There was left only our Squadron commander. Big Wick looked much older than his reported twenty seven years. As he faced us on the platform he seemed the perfect picture of the Six Group veteran with his D.S.O., D.F.C. and bar, and twin silver tour of duty wings.

He wasted no time getting right to the point.

"The Group Captain wanted to be here today but was called up to Headquarters at the last minute. So I'm glad to be here and able to talk to you Muskrats as well. All I want to say to both squadrons is that, while you've got a long trip, you've also got good flying weather and an important target. But let's not have any bright boy trying to get home early by making his own flight plan. Just the other day one of our Group Lancs was shot down flying over London where he had no damn business being in the first place. Stick to those flight plans and don't give me any more grey hairs. Now let's paste them good this time and get the war over with. That's all, gentlemen."

He strode briskly down the aisle and out of the briefing room as we stood at attention. The Chief Briefing Officer took his place immediately.

"Be ready at the flight huts by 1600 hours. We'll now synchronize watches. The time will be 1300 hours in nine, eight, seven, six, five, four, three, two, one, NOW." As he said "NOW" I pushed in the stem of my wrist watch with everyone else in the room.

"That's it, boys. Now it's all up to you."

There was the loud noise of numerous chairs being pushed back. Fred and Pete as gunners were now free to go. Max as engineer would merely have to see the Engineering Officer about engine handling and he was finished. The rest of us all had considerable paperwork to do, Dave especially.

"Bastard Chemnitz," Walt grumbled as Dave and I moved along with him to the far side of the room. "These long ones give me the heaving shits. Only good thing about it, we're off those bloody daylights, eh, Bill?

"For this hop at least," I agreed. To me one was as bad as the other now, each in their different way.

I spent the next ten minutes at one of the tables presided over by a junior Intelligence Officer, getting flight routes, more information about the target area and other gen. This I scribbled down in a notebook which I'd probably never refer to, but it looked good all the same. Then I waited for Dave to finish getting the last word on navigational problems. Finally he picked up his carrying case and joined me by the door.

"I don't feel that hungry," I said, "but it's going to be one hell of a long night so I'd better get something in my stomach, even if it's only spuds and bangers."

"Keep talking and you'll convince yourself into a second helping," Dave kidded, as we hurried along the slippery pathway leading to the mess. There was a cold damp wind blowing now from the west, chilling me all the way through. I even found myself shivering once or twice. Good old balmy England.

"Not bloody likely," I corrected him. The mental picture of three or four sausages swimming around in their grease beside a small mound of mashed potatoes and another of leeks or turnip had already taken the edge off whatever appetite I'd been able to muster.

"Maybe you're going to eat sausages, but I'm going to have a small steak, medium rare, with onion rings, chef's salad smothered in Thousand Islands dressing. The dessert may be a problem," Dave said. "Perhaps peach melba or a French pastry."

"That's what I like about you, Dave," I told him, "you're living in a world all your own. But it's still nice of you to share part of it with us now and then."

"Any time, old pal," Dave said. "Oh yes, and Viennese coffee. With brandy in the lounge to finish up with."

"No cigars?"

"Why not?"

Why not indeed, I thought as we came to the two Nissen huts joined together roughly in the shape of a T that was the officer's mess. A sense of humour wasn't all you needed to get you through a war but it helped.

"Here goes nothing," I said as we went inside. But the meal turned out to be not bad at all. I even managed to scrounge a second lemon tart from our buxom WAAF waitress. I'd probably regret it before the evening was over, but at the moment it seemed worth a few gas pains, the kind that could double you up at 14,000 feet. Why not take a chance with a lemon tart when you took one with everything else? It sounded very logical if you didn't think about it too long . . .

The Halifax in front of us took off with an ear-splitting roar. We turned, braked, hearing our own motors rev up as Walt advanced the throttle. Then that sudden feeling of released motion came as Walt let go the brakes and "Y" for "Yellow" started to roll. As the speed increased we could feel the tail of the aircraft going up very gradually from our sitting positions back in the mid-fuselage. Suddenly a gentle swaying told us we were clear of the runway, airborne at about ninety miles an hour.

"Next stop, Chemnitz," Joe announced as he got to his feet. "Something tells me this trip is going to be a breeze."

"Tell me that tomorrow morning over bacon and eggs and I'll believe you," I told him, also getting up from the floor.

"You've got a bloody nerve talking about bacon and eggs while I've still got a gut-load of sergeant's mess garbage stuck in my craw," Pete moaned as he started to move out to his rear-gunner's turret.

"What the hell do you think they serve us, T-bone steaks?" I asked him. "Don't worry, I hear we've got Spam sandwiches for the trip back."

"Up your arse." Pete's cheerful answer came from out near the tail. When I heard that I knew we were in good shape for this attack.

I moved along with Dave up forward toward the nose. I shared Dave's dinky little navigator's compartment below Walt's cockpit. You went down a few steps and entered a small section with a navigator's metal table down one side and the H2S equipment down the other. A curtain in the nose end hid the even smaller compartment where I'd go into a huddle with my bombsight and other instruments when we got reasonably close to the target.

While Dave spread his maps and instruments on the table, I busied myself warming up the navigational radar set known as Gee. This was very accurate over England, but once we neared the enemy coast it would pack up due to jamming by enemy radar beams. Then I'd have to switch to the set next to it called H2S, a newer invention whose signal emanated from the underbelly of our own aircraft and therefore couldn't be interfered with. Right now, however, I had plenty to do watching the oblong Gee box for the blips moving from left to right from our Master Station, and the blips from our Slave Station moving from right to left. If the instructions were followed carefully Gee could get you within a few hundred yards of any desired spot. We'd proven this many times in our practice hops over England.

Once we were orbiting at 1500 feet Dave gave Walt his first heading. At 1700 hours we'd be on our way. I had my earphones plugged in now and could hear our control tower talking to aircraft still taking off. I'd never quite ceased to marvel at the fact that at this very minute over the other stations of the Group Halifaxes and Lancasters of the various squadrons would be orbiting now. Before long we'd leave England behind and cross the Channel in one swarm of machines, each aircraft flying through the darkness entirely independent of any other, observing total radio silence, even our red and green navigational lights extinguished once we reached the south coast of England. We'd been told at briefing that Group was putting up an almost total effort on this one—two hundred heavies—the old reliable Halifaxes and the newer, larger Lancasters. Crews from Goose and Thunderbird squadrons at Linton, Snowy Owl and Alouette at Tholthorpe, Lion and Bison at Leeming, Tiger and Porcupine from Skipton-on-Swale, Moose and Ghost from Middleton St. George, Iroquois and Bluenose from Croft, and of course our own Algonquin boys and our base rivals the Muskrats.

Now that we were airborne again I was strangely aware that I'd missed flying for the past week. Which was another way of saying that flying had become almost second-nature to me now, a habit like eating and sleeping and thinking about girls. It sounded corny but I felt a part of this awkward-looking aircraft still cruising slowly under the power of its four Hercules engines. It was in the same lumbering lady that we'd gone to Essen almost two weeks ago in mid-afternoon to flatten the Krupp works. A milk-run that, hardly any fighters anywhere in Happy Valley. And the next day to Kamen, which was completely obscured by cloud, making accurate bombing impossible, and where we lost a Muskrat crew. Three days after that we'd done the last op of the month to Mainz, a daylight which produced smoke from our bombing which Pete could see from his rear-turret vantage-point a hundred miles after leaving the area. Again no enemy fighters had challenged us. Now very shortly we'd be on the way to another target, but this time in a night operation, which was the way we'd really been trained to fight . . .

I shook myself loose from my thoughts and re-focussed my eyes and all my attention on the rectangular Gee box, watching the blips move back and forth. The kind of concentration where time almost ceased to exist. It must have been close to half an hour later that Walt's voice came on the intercom, relaxed yet very business-like:

"O.K., gang, we're at ten thousand now, in case any of you have managed to keep awake. Let's get plugged in on that oxygen. Get ready for a check in half a minute."

Reluctantly I pulled the rubber mask over my nose and mouth. I'd never become used to wearing one, probably never would, but at high altitudes in a bomber oxygen was an essential ingredient you simply couldn't do without.

After the oxygen check things became silent again in our little world until Dave came in on the intercom to talk to Walt.

"Course alteration in five minutes, Walt. We're bang on within half a minute."

"Hot shit, Dave," Walt's voice came back. "Let's keep it that way, shall we?"

That meant we were close to the Channel and before long the Jerries' radar would jam up the Gee. After that I'd have to switch to the round set housing the H2S radar. Watching the blips on the Gee wasn't too bad but the H2S was something else again. You had to concentrate completely or you could lose your bearings before you knew it. Once that happened it was very difficult to pick up your proper position again on the set.

The course alteration came up next.

"One six zero, skipper," Dave said. "You can start turning any time. Are we at fifteen thousand yet?"

"Fourteen five. Pilot to crew. Enemy coast coming up soon, boys. Let's be really sharp, especially you gunners. Just because we haven't been jumped by Jerry so far doesn't mean the bastards won't be out tonight. Sing out loud and clear even if you only think you spot something. O.K., Pete?"

"O.K."

"Fred?"

"Got you, Walt."

"All right, gang, here we go. Hang on to your seats."

The aircraft strained as Walt banked to port. We were now on our first long leg, with two more course turns to be made before we ran in over Chemnitz.

As if to verify the fact that we were moving closer every minute to the enemy, the Gee began to be jammed less than five minutes later. I leaned across the navigator's table that I shared with Dave and touched him on the shoulder. He looked up from his paperwork and I pointed to the set, now a mass of white wavy lines. He nodded and went back to work again.

"Bombardier to pilot," I said into my throat mike, "Gee now u/s. I'm switching over to the tube, Walt."

"Have fun," he cracked and that was that. I'd really reported the jamming more than anything else to let Joe Petosky, our wireless expert, know that I was going on H2S. Of course it told Walt and the rest of the crew that Jerry knew we were coming and to really watch out from here on in. But we all knew that there were two or three diversionary attacks in the works at the same time that would keep his controllers guessing, so this didn't bother us too much.

For Joe in his wireless spot behind the pilot's cockpit my message was also his signal to warm up what we called "the fishbowl", which was nothing more or less than a miniature extension of my H2S set. He'd be able to pick up a secondary image from the centre of my larger scope. This image would reach out several hundred yards around our aircraft. In his scope he'd see a pattern of blips maintaining the same position and speed. Those blips would be the crates of our own bomber stream flying all around us in the pitch darkness. If, however, Joe saw a blip that seemed to change course rapidly or was passing the other blips, it was a good bet we had a Jerry nightfighter for company. If he got too close Joe could call for evasive action, and as soon as the gunners spotted him they'd open up with all they had.

I switched on my circular, larger H2S set. As it warmed up I could see what had to be the German coast-line at the Rhine estuary silhouetted like a map, the pale green fluorescent picture showing up a remarkable contrast between land and water. Once we left the coast and the Channel behind, the radar picture in front of me would become one large circumference, with our aircraft at the centre. By checking with my maps I could identify the fairly large yellow blobs that would appear from time to time as the cities we were avoiding because of their flak concentrations. The H2S was very sensitive to steel-constructed buildings and railway yards, so the larger and more industrialized the city the more brightly it showed up on the pale green screen.

Now the first yellow blob appeared about a quarter of an inch from the right edge of my radar screen. My map said it had to be Bremen. We were fairly well inland now. It wouldn't be too long before we'd be deep in Germany. I wondered what was happening in Chemnitz tonight. It was almost three weeks since our last visit. If, as they claimed, we hadn't done too much damage, things could be pretty well back to normal there, at least as much as they could be with the Russian armies closing always nearer. Would they be expecting another attack? If they weren't and the weather was good, we could really clobber them. If not too many of the people were in air raid shelters when we struck about midnight it would be a real slaughter. I knew enough about air bombing now to know that most of our bombs, even with the best of intentions, usually fell very wide of any military targets we were supposed to be hitting. Most of the time they landed on working-class areas near the factories and rail yards which were our stated targets. What bothered me were the reports of the raids on Germany appearing in the English newspapers. They talked about this military target and that military target as if night bombing was a bang on the nose proposition. As if only the Germans bombed indiscriminately, as in the Blitz, or now with their V-1's and V-2's. Even on our daylight attacks bombing was usually well scattered, and that meant only one thing, a lot of civilians would die. But this was the kind of war it was, dirty, strictly knock-down. The only important thing seemed to be the number of dead bodies one side or the other could pile up. Bomber Command, of which we were a part, was doing very well right now in this department.

I shrugged my shoulders mentally and forced my whole attention back to the radar. Already the yellow blob that was Bremen had disappeared off the screen and it was then that we swung due east into Germany.

Hanover was the next large German city to appear on my screen to the right of centre, moving slowly across the tube as I picked up Brunswick on the left. I knew that before long we'd turn onto the second last leg of our course taking us straight to the target. So far it looked like another milk run; there hadn't been any flak or any sign of enemy fighters. I didn't mind that in the least and I knew the rest of the crew shared my sentiments to a man. While we wouldn't run away from trouble, we certainly weren't out looking for it.

Then almost before I realized it we had made our last course change onto the final leg and Dave was announcing fifteen minutes estimated time to target over the intercom. That was the signal for me to get down to my real business on the op. I moved up out of my seat, gave a short wave to my partner on the other side of the navigating table, and moved forward into the moulded perspex nose of the aircraft, which formed a small, isolated compartment. I pulled the night curtain across the opening behind me and was all to myself with my bombsight and other tools of the air bomber's trade. Automatically I plugged in my oxygen feed line again and made sure I was breathing comfortably before I did anything else.

By this time my eyes had grown accustomed to the comparative darkness in the compartment, a darkness relieved only by the luminous shine of the instruments and selection switch panel. I soon became aware of how much colder it was in the nose even compared to Dave's cubby-hole next door. Perhaps the single red light he had burning there made it seem warmer; up here it felt at least ten degrees colder. Of course a Hally was always a deep-freeze proposition even at the best of times. There were supposed to be pipes giving off heat throughout the aircraft, but this was a laugh. I found my hands and feet were always cold by the time an op was half over. You simply had to learn to live with it.

It was high time I checked my equipment over. I knelt behind the Mark Fourteen bombsight, pulling up the large canvas heating-hose between my knees. This would help to keep my hands warm when I had to take my gloves off to set up the switches accurately. I could feel the extra weight at the front of my flying suit with my chest pack parachute now in place.

Every time bombardiers got together the talk always turned sooner or later to what new wrinkles someone had thought of to keep any loose fragments of flak which might be driven up through the nose from de-balling the defenceless air bomber kneeling at his bombsight. I'd heard all kinds of stories but didn't believe most of them. Some guys were supposed to have steel plates they placed strategically on the floor of the compartment. I couldn't be bothered myself, even though I valued my manhood as much as anyone else. The whole business was so completely a matter of luck that it didn't seem to me worth worrying about.

We were due to approach the target down wind as usual. As an experienced crew now we were bombing at twelve thousand feet at the bottom of the stack. I turned the entire panel of bomb selection switches at my right to the "on" position in series, then threw on the arming switch. I was able to drop bombs either in one load or straddle the target in line with a one-second delay between the first bomb and each one following. Tonight "Y" for "Yellow" carried a full load of incendiaries. Clearly the intention was to put the torch to Chemnitz.

I was ready now to turn on the bombsight. With that done I made sure the repeater compass attached to it was in good working order. Both the wind velocity and direction were set

up to feed ingeniously into the bombsight. Lastly I checked
the altimeter. All ship shape. I was now as ready as I'd ever
be. The head of the bombsight in front of me swayed back
and forth with the motion of the aircraft, a little like a cobra
under a snake-charmer's spell and every bit as deadly.

I leaned back on my knees, trying to relax a little. It was a
lost cause. Even though I could do the bombing drill in my
sleep, each new time out was always much like doing a repetition of our very first op. My hands always sweated, and I
could feel the rest of my body sweating under the flying suit.
I suppose it was partly because the lives of six other guys had
to be placed on the line each and every trip in order that I
could drop my bombs accurately and without any hitch.

Now far ahead I could make out a faint red glow reflected
on the clouds. That had to be either the glow of fires down
below or sky-markers from our Pathfinders. As if to settle
this the Master Bomber broke radio silence at that very moment:

"Red Dog One to Oboe. You will bomb on fresh sky-markers. Hold your release until you're bang on the aiming-point."
His measured, very calm voice rose to a pitch as he concluded with, "Give it to them good, lads!"

Bombing on sky-markers. Christ, it looked more and more
like 10/10 cloud all around us now, the very same conditions
as our other trip here. Chemnitz really had the golden
horseshoe for luck.

Now it was Dave's turn to do the talking.

"Five minutes to target, Walt."

"Right, Dave," Walt answered, then cut in right after him.
"Those markers look pretty good tonight, Bill. And I think
we've got plenty of fires going to help you out. Say when.
O.K.?"

"O.K., Walt, will do," I answered. He was referring to my
taking over the aircraft for the actual bombing run. That was
still a few minutes away. Now there was a definite pinkish
glow on the clouds all around us. One good thing about it,
Jerry couldn't use his searchlights even if he wanted to, and
his flak batteries couldn't do much more than put up a blanket barrage and hope they caught one or two of us in it. But
the cloud cover wouldn't keep their night-fighters off our tails
if they ordered any up.

There. A slight thudding noise against the undercarriage

and I knew we'd started to run into flak. Fire away, you bastards. Just don't get any wild ideas that you're going to shoot down this crate.

It was time now to get the show on the road.

"Ready when you are for bomb doors, Walt," I called over the intercom.

"O.K., Bill, they're open," Walt came back with very shortly after.

"Ready for bombing run," I told him next.

"All set?"

"Now," I said. And the aircraft was mine. At the same time my eyes began focussing through the bomb-sight on an orange-coloured cross which seemed to be moving across the sky below but was really only an illuminated extension of the bomb-sight's hairlines. As the vertical line of the cross moved to the right of the target ahead I called "left" to Walt over the intercom. He swung the aircraft five degrees, then leveled out. The target was coming up rapidly now, but still a little left of centre. I called out "left, left," and Walt swung two and a half degrees to port. He was pouring the coal on now as we made our run. It felt as though he was doing 300 m.p.h., and that was possible with the Mark Seven's top speed rated at 312 m.p.h.

The glow in the clouds was almost a pale crimson as we came over the target area. I could see the red and blue patches of the sky-markers, also many small black clouds all around us which I knew were flak bursts. Now, as near as I could judge, the vertical tip of the bomb-sight cross was dead-centre at the bottom of the aiming-point. As the glow of the sky-markers moved down the vertical line, I held the release tit firmly in my hand until the horizontal arm of the cross moved to the centre of the aiming-point, then pressed it. I watched the red lights on my selector panel flash off one by one. I counted twelve flashes. That signalled twelve canisters of incendiaries dropping one per second. There was nothing to see below. I imagined the spaghetti-like groups of bombs falling in clusters. A late evening surprise for the good citizens of Chemnitz.

I roused myself out of my moment's daydream.

"Bombs away," I almost shouted through the intercom to Walt.

Walt's voice came back, again very cool, very business-like.

"Right, Bill, good show. Dave, did you get the time of the bomb release?"

"Roger," Dave cut in. "Our next heading will be 345 degrees north."

I knew that while Walt was listening to us over the intercom he had his eyes glued on the little light on the instrument panel which kept flashing on and off. This told him the camera recording the bomb drop was working. Until the light went off, showing we'd run out of film, Walt had to hold her hard and steady on our present course. Jerry had a steady stream of flak coming up now, centering around the sky-markers. Once our aircraft shuddered violently and I thought we'd been hit for sure. But a Hally could take a lot of punishment. We thundered on, apparently undamaged.

Without warning "Y" for "Yellow" gave a sudden lurch as Walt gave her full throttle now the bomb-bay doors were closed. We swung north on our return heading. Thank Christ for that.

I put everything back in order in the bombing compartment. I deliberately took plenty of time, trying to release some of the tension that had started to build up from the moment I'd stepped into the compartment and had gradually increased as we came closer and closer to the actual bomb run. I even tried to forget that there were still Jerry flak bursts clustered around us, although the sheer noise of them alone shouted for some kind of attention.

Then I happened to glance out the perspex nose and my heart almost missed a beat at what it saw. There, strung out as far as I could see over what was obviously the first leg of our homeward flight, were the eerily-glowing red ball-like flares of the German night fighters. What bothered me now more than anything else, and this included the fact that they made sitting ducks out of us, was the first notion you had that Jerry must have known somehow of our flight pattern even before we'd left England. Then you realized that what they'd done was simply follow one of the lead bombers out of the target area, lighting up the sky with flares after him. Still, seeing it now even for the fourth or fifth time was disturbing enough to give me that uneasy feeling deep in the pit of my stomach. I imagined Walt up above me at the controls wouldn't be feeling much better.

As if reading my thoughts his voice came over the intercom.

"Pilot to crew. The bastards have those fighter flares going again along our course. So heads up, everybody. You gunners, keep those eyes really peeled. Don't let them get the jump on you or we're dead. O.K., Pete?"

"O.K."

"Fred?"

"O.K., Walt."

I finished doing everything I had to do up front. Then I pulled back my dark curtain and came out in the navigator's compartment. Dave's spot was cheerful by comparison, the one dull red light that illuminated it slightly reassuring.

Dave was busy plotting our new course. I sat down at the table opposite him while he showed me where he estimated our present position was. He wouldn't be more than a degree or two out, and from that I could find our exact position again on the H2S. I had just turned the set on and was waiting for the screen to warm up and show its delicate green shade of colour when Fred's voice broke in frantically on the intercom, "Port go, port go." Almost at the same instant the aircraft shook like crazy as both mid-upper and rear turrets opened fire, the next moment bucking like a scared horse as Walt pulled a sharp five degree turn in the bargain.

Then Fred was shouting something to Pete but I couldn't catch it over the infernal racket of the guns. The next thing I knew there was a tremendous echoing jolt from the rear of the aircraft and Fred was yelling breathlessly over the intercom, "Direct hit on rear turret." Then there was a bewildering deathly silence as his guns suddenly stopped firing. He came on again still breathless. "Check it out fast, Walt. Something's burning back there."

Immediately Walt's voice sounded over the intercom with most of his usual coolness missing.

"Pilot to rear gunner."

No answer.

"What's happened back there, Pete?"

The second longer silence over the intercom sent a chill leaping down my back.

"Pilot to crew. We're going down, gang. If that bandit makes an underside pass at us we're screwed. Hang on now."

Walt didn't waste any time. The Hally plunged into a steep

dive that almost took my breath away. When I thought we
were never going to pull out of it Walt leveled her off beautifully. I glanced across at Dave. He was trying to hold his
maps and papers down with one hand while holding on to the
table with the other, much the same as I was doing. That was
some evasive manoeuvre.

"We're at nine thousand five," Walt's voice came on again.
"Bill and Joe, both of you get back there fast and see what's
up. Don't forget your oxygen bottles and fire extinguishers."

I grabbed up a portable oxygen bottle off its cabin bracket
and the extinguisher next to it. Then I climbed the steps and
hurried back through the fuselage. Joe moved in behind me
and we worked our way along to the rear turret. The turret
door was slightly jammed but I managed to pull it open. Immediately smoke poured out from a small fire inside. I
couldn't see Pete at first until I'd poured half the contents of
the extinguisher through the door. Then I made him out
slumped over behind his guns. It looked like his chute had
caught fire and had caused the smoke. There was a small gale
blowing through a big jagged hole in the turret just above the
guns. A cannon shell from the Ju. must have scored a direct
hit.

I dropped the fire extinguisher now. Then I pushed my
way into the turret and over to Pete. One look at him and I
knew he was dead, very dead. Half his helmet was torn off or
burned off. There was blood still running down over his flying suit. I took a closer look and almost wished I hadn't. A
big piece was missing from his face under one eye. A splinter
from the cannon shell must have caught him squarely on the
oxygen mask.

"Pete's dead, Walt," I heard myself saying over the intercom. "The turret's completely u/s. The fire's out. Looks like
a part of the tail is missing or damaged. We'll carry Pete forward now."

"O.K., Bill. Make it as fast as you can. Fred, keep your
peepers open. If that bastard comes in again I want you to
nail him good."

"Got you." Fred's voice seemed very subdued. Even some
of the authority seemed to have gone from Walt's voice,
which was easily understandable.

I pulled off my oxygen mask. So did Joe. It would be
tough enough trying to carry Pete forward even without them

on. Walt had said we were around 9,000 feet, so we should be all right.

"Well, let's get at it," I said to Joe. "I'll get his shoulders, you try to ease his feet out."

Pete was tall and lean, but with his flying suit and boots he turned out to be a fairly heavy weight. Being half-wedged in behind his guns didn't help either. But slowly we worked him out of the turret, then managed to carry him amidships. There were a couple of grey airmen's blankets lying there and we wrapped Pete roughly in these. I must say I felt a whole lot better when we had his face covered and I didn't have to look at that hole in the side of it. Most of the bleeding seemed to have stopped, though. Joe had several big patches of blood on his flying suit and I noticed I had much the same on mine.

There was nothing more we could do for Pete. Nothing anyone could do for him. We left him there on the fuselage floor. I looked at Joe. We didn't need to say anything. There was only one thing both of us could be thinking at that moment. Then we moved back up through the aircraft, Joe returning to his wireless set and "fishbowl." I went on to the cockpit.

"We've got him wrapped in a couple of blankets in the fuselage," I told Walt.

"Fine, Bill. Hold on to your rabbit's foot. Let's hope that bastard's lost us."

I walked down the steps to Dave's compartment, suddenly feeling half-sick at the stomach. I sat down heavily across from Dave still hard at work at the navigator's table. My breathing seemed all right but I put on my face mask and plugged in the feedline. Maybe the air around was still a bit rare. That didn't seem to help much so I took it off again in a couple of minutes. If I was going to be sick there wasn't much I could do about it.

Dave had taken his mask off now so at least I could break the silence a little.

"Pete's a mess, Dave. I guess the poor kid never really knew what hit him. Which is a blessing, I guess."

"This bloody war. Now it's finally got to us," was all Dave said. And that expressed it as well as anything.

I realized that I had to snap out of my present mood, but fast. Pete was dead, we couldn't bring him back. Maybe we'd all be dead any minute. There wasn't too much we could do about that either. Nothing but get back to work. Get your mind on the job. This is still a team effort, something kept telling me.

"What do you figure our position is now?" I asked Dave, and he pointed it out on the map. I went back to the H2S, which I hadn't turned off, and forced myself to get all my attention back on that coloured screen and glowing tube. Our course was taking us toward the North Sea, avoiding Bremen. If any fighters didn't jump us on this leg we had a damn good chance of making it. No doubt the Ju.88 who'd got in the first big hit was still hunting us if he hadn't run out of gas by now. After one smell of blood he'd want to be in on the final kill if at all possible.

As if echoing my worst fears Fred's voice came excitedly now over the intercom.

"Thought I spotted something dead ahead of us, Walt. Could be our Ju. friend though I didn't get a real good look."

"Nice going, Fred. Stay with it. Say, Bill, how about you breaking out that pop gun in the nose? We sure could use that extra fire-power."

"Hell, Walt, I've never even fired the stupid thing," I said.

"So now you're going to get your big chance. Get it ready, Bill, and right now, eh?"

The tone in Walt's voice told me he'd made up his mind. He was the crew captain. What he said went. If I'd been in his shoes I'd expect the same. An order was an order.

"O.K., Walt, right away."

I went back into the nose, leaving the curtain open this time to get whatever light there was. The pop gun or Vickers gas-operated .303 machine-gun was mounted on a swivel and stuck out through the perspex nose. I took a pan of ammunition from the box on the floor and placed it in position. I recalled now the short instruction lecture we'd received on the V.G.O.; the R.A.F. sergeant telling us that the gun was famous for jamming. All you had to do was look at it the wrong way and it would plug up on you.

I got behind the thing, sighting through the gun to get the feel of it. A real World War One production. I hadn't fired a machine-gun since Bombing and Gunnery School at Mountain View late in 1943. That had been a Browning, not a relic like this. If Ju. should suddenly make a pass I really couldn't tell how I'd make out at all. But I'd sure give it my very best try for old Pete.

Straight ahead I could make out the Jerry fighter flares still lighting up our flight path. Why one of their boys hadn't jumped us by now in our battered state I'd never know. I figured we had a good hour still to go before we hit the coast. Those flares would probably stay with us all the way. As long as they had us lit up bright as a Christmas tree we were potentially in big trouble.

Now that the tension of the last ten minutes had eased a little, I found myself going back to Pete's death whether I wanted to or not. That was the one thing I'd tried to erase from my mind from the first shock-stunning moment of seeing him slumped over his Brownings in that shattered turret until I'd covered his face with the blanket back there in the fuselage. It was the first time I'd looked on violent death right after it had happened. I'd seen some dead, charred bodies at B & G School, at A.O.S. and O.T.U., but never the faces, and then it hadn't been anyone I'd really known or been close to. You tried not to think of dying because it wasn't a natural thing for young men to brood about, and besides it could undermine your fighting ability like nothing else. We knew that some of us were going to die every day, but there wasn't very much we could do about it. We had all volunteered for the air force and for aircrew, so we couldn't say anybody had pushed us into it. Perhaps the risks had never been fully explained, but we'd seen enough British and American war movies to know that death was one of the principal ingredients of war in the air. It was only that I'd never seen a war movie where they showed you a close-up of the hero with one side of his face blown off or horribly burned. So I'd been slightly unprepared when it had happened right on my own doorstep. Now that it had happened, though, and I'd handled myself not too badly through it, I could almost think about death objectively, unemotionally. The hell you can, a voice said within me, but I shrugged that voice off. The truth was all very clear now. So clear that it made me uncomfortable to even think about it. But I had to face it just the same. I was sorry that Pete had had to die so tragically, but also glad that he was the one who was dead and not me. I knew that it could have just as easily been me, and I wanted very much to stay alive. I wasn't ready to die for him or anyone else in the crew if it was simply a case of either me or them. It was easily the most selfish thought I'd ever had before in my life. But it was true that we were all on our own when it came to dying. I also knew that living as we did from day to day now wasn't really life or living in any true sense of the word. Frantic, fragile existence, maybe, but not living. That was the best you could say for it. Still, there was something very precious about it. You had that feeling when you first woke up every morning, even though the feeling had pretty well melted away before the day was very old. Just the same it was something that you weren't willing to exchange for anything else.

Tell us all of it, that inside voice said. The big trouble with you is that basically you're a yellow belly, a lousy coward. Admit that you're afraid of death. Perhaps the look of death, I told the voice, but not really death itself. How can I know until I've personally met it face to face? Poor Pete had never had that chance, had he? He'd never known what had hit him. Of course that was the most merciful way. All of us might not be that lucky.

Christ, but my mind was churning around. I wasn't making too much sense, either. I shook all thoughts out of my head. At the same time I tightened my finger around the V.G.O. trigger as if to get back in touch with reality. I stood staring out ahead through the nose while we thundered along, the sky around us still lit with enemy flares. I stood there, chilled all the way down inside my flying suit, and waited. Waited for death to swoop perhaps out of the clouds. To come at me in a lightning-like explosion of cannon shells. . . .

"Pilot to crew. Dave says we're skirting the Bremen flak belt in five minutes. So everybody hang on in there, and you'll get your spam sandwiches before you know it, you lucky people. Bill, you might as well leave off on the pop-gun now. See if you can get us a good fix on the tube."

"Swell, Walt," I answered. For the past hour the only words I'd exchanged had been when Dave gave our captain the heading changes as they came up. It sounded wonderful to hear how close we were to the coast. If we could keep clear of the last flak belts and miss any night fighters prowling around we'd have it made.

I left the bombing compartment and joined Dave again.

Before long I had Bremen, then Oldenburg showing strongly on the tube well to our right. Wander over into that backyard and you could be in real trouble.

Now Walt asked Joe Petosky to get onto base and request a priority landing. Joe came back on the intercom in a minute or two, swearing mad.

"We're bloody well socked in again, Walt. I wish all weather men would go shove their balloons. The bastards in the tower say we're diverted to Mildenhall, some bloody R.A.F. base."

"Everybody hear that, gang?" Walt asked, the disgust very plain in his voice. "Isn't that the rotten luck? Got to spend another goddamn night with the Limeys, and I'll bet my last bob their bar'll be closed when we get there. And we'll have to hand Pete over to them. This is getting to be one hell of a war, boys. O.K., now I'm all through bitching. Can you give me a heading on Mildenhall, Dave?"

"Have it in a minute, Walt," Dave answered. He tried to smile at me across the navigation table as he went back to his maps.

"You'd almost get the impression the skipper didn't like Limeys too much, wouldn't you?"

"Just a slight impression," I said. I knew that actually he didn't feel that bad about them, none of us did. The R.A.F. had fought this air war since 1939, and they were going at it stronger than ever now in 1945. They'd lost thousands of aircrew while we'd lost hundreds. It was only that man for man we thought our Canadian crews were a little better. And everyone knew that one quarter or one-fifth of R.A.F crews were Canadians, I forget which it was. Trust the bloody Canadians to know how they could get killed off the easiest. Canadians were good at dying. Look at Dieppe. We'd certainly walked into a slaughter there. And now it was Pete's turn to die. Maybe some of us or all of us would get it next time round. No doubt people would read about us in another twenty years and wonder what the hell we died for. Right now I didn't have too much of an answer. All I knew about for sure was that Pete was back there in the fuselage covered with a couple of dirty, blood-soaked blankets, half his face shot off. He hadn't had time to think of any reason for dying. No time at all. One cannon burst and it was all over. . . .

Forty long endless minutes later we came into the Mildenhall circuit. Even here it was partially closed in, I gathered from Walt on the intercom as he talked to their tower. But we had almost no gas left so we had no other choice than to touch down now and take our chances.

"Everyone get set," Walt warned us as he came around into his final approach. "This could be one of Uncle's poorer landings, children."

It certainly was. Because of the turret being shot to pieces and with possible tail damage as well, the aircraft didn't handle well at all on the touch-down. We could even feel it wobbling seated back there in the fuselage. Then, as we hit the runway, Walt had to go hard on the brakes for some reason, and my heart jumped into my mouth again. But luck was with us tonight. Walt brought her under control right away. Thank Christ for that.

At the dispersal area where we came to a final stop an R.A.F. ambulance was waiting for us. I was the first one to open the hatch.

An R.A.F. sergeant was standing there below.

"We're here to take the body out, sir," he said.

"Thanks all the same," I said, "but we'll bring him out ourselves."

The sergeant shrugged his shoulders.

"Suit yourself, sir. We don't want the job that much, you know."

I guess he was right. I was being a bit stupid about the whole thing. Pete was dead, his body was lifeless. But he was one of our crew. He was our dead, not theirs.

"Come on," I said to Joe who was standing behind me at the hatch opening, "let's get him out. We can't be any more messed up than we are now." I didn't want to stick Dave or any of the others. It wouldn't bother Joe much now; it would probably bother me a lot more.

"Why not?" Joe said. "As you say we can't get any more messed up. Besides, I think Pete would want us to."

I was glad he felt the same way I did. It made the job a lot easier for both of us. Pete's body was a grim weight we somehow managed to carry the short distance to the hatch. We lowered it gingerly down to the waiting ambulance boys. I was glad now we'd done it ourselves. It was one of the last things we'd ever be able to do for Pete Yarish.

Then I went back slowly up to the navigator's compartment to get my carrying case and chest pack. Well, I was still alive, back once again on the good solid ground of England. But I felt almost like someone different now. I had the funny feeling that after this night I could never be quite the same person again.

12

I didn't know why I'd come to Betty's Bar particularly. I wasn't even in the mood to enjoy the good pint of beer sitting on the table in front of me. But I'd had to get off the base, I couldn't have stood it another minute. I had to get away from anything that suggested the air force, at least for the next few hours.

It was the day after the Chemnitz nightmare. We'd flown back from Mildenhall that morning and were in time for lunch after a speedy de-briefing. That is, if you felt like lunch. I certainly didn't. My gut felt as if it had a lead weight dragging it down. I even had to force myself to drink a beer when the bar opened up.

All the talk in the mess was still about the raid. Our squadron had lost one aircraft, the Muskrats another. Apparently other squadrons had been harder hit. The best information was that more crews had been killed on take-offs and landings using the iced-over runways then the combined force had lost over Germany. I heard a Squadron Leader say it was one of the worst nights in Group history.

The R.A.F. had brought Pete's body up from Mildenhall early in the afternoon. Burial would be on Sunday, Walt said. The whole crew was excused duty to attend the service.

Even though nobody could expect us to fly again that evening, they still kept us waiting around the dispersal hut until four o'clock when the 0800 stand-down was announced. By then my nerves were worn pretty thin.

Now I sat in Betty's and stared at the long mirror behind the bar on which dozens and dozens of signatures had been scrawled. It would be interesting to know how many of these signatures belonged to men no longer still in this world—infantrymen picked off by machine-gun fire in Italy, troopers blown to bits by a direct hit on a tank in Normandy, airmen

trapped in a flaming bomber making its last crazy dive somewhere over Germany. There was no way of knowing, so it
was pretty useless speculation. But at the time they'd signed
or printed their names on the mirror they'd been alive, laughing, drinking, wenching, enjoying all the male pleasures of
life. They hadn't thought of death, they were going to live
forever. Maybe one of these nights after one too many I'd
have the urge as well to be immortal—no, just to be remembered—and my half-legible signature would be squeezed in
somewhere among all the rest. But not tonight. Tonight I was
cold sober, I'd seen death strike too close to me for comfort,
and the whole idea seemed damn childish.

By a quarter to eight, when I left Betty's, I was glad I had
a date with Prue. I was looking forward to talking with someone after sitting in there alone for an hour. It was strange
that somebody hadn't come in that I knew, but perhaps just
as well tonight. I didn't think I'd make too good company. I
certainly wasn't in the mood for small talk. Perhaps Prue
would snap me out of it. I certainly hoped so.

To my surprise Prue was waiting for me when I reached
the shop. As I helped her on with her coat she explained that
for some reason business had been very slow today.

"Thank goodness for that, too, I suppose. Mom and Dad
had to go up to Darlington, so I've been doing double-duty
here. Say, you look rather glum, sir. Anything the matter?"

"I'll tell you about it a little later. You know, I feel better
already. It wouldn't surprise me if you have something to do
with it."

"Glad to hear it. Say, are you in the mood for a flic?
There's a rather good one at the Odeon, so I'm told. That is,
if you haven't seen it already."

I hadn't, and it proved to be very enjoyable. One of those
crazy English comedies that the British can do so well, but
which Hollywood falls flat on its fanny even attempting. I
found myself laughing, real honest-to-goodness gut laughter,
and it did me good. I could feel the tears running down my
cheeks and I hardly bothered to wipe them away. Prue
laughed as hard or even harder than I did, no doubt catching
some of the more subtle stuff, which I had to admit passed
over my head. We sat in the back of the dress-circle, I held
her puppy-soft hand in mine, and it was an hour and a half
of pleasant enjoyment in the warm darkness. I was almost

sorry when we had to leave our seats and make our way down to the lobby.

"I think I could use a drink," Prue said as we came out into the cool street air. "How about you?"

"Wonderful. We've got better than forty minutes before closing time if my watch is right. Anywhere in particular you'd like to go to?"

"Not really. There's a nice enough place about a block from here."

The saloon bar in question was fairly posh and very crowded at this time of night. I had a job getting someone to take our order. Finally, though, we had a gin and orange and a pint of mild and bitter for company at our table.

"You were saying before that your mother and father had to go up to Darlington. Anything wrong?"

"You could say that. My father's brother is very poorly. He had a second heart attack last night. They thought they might cheer his wife up if they stayed there a day or two. I must say when you showed up tonight I thought I was going to have to cheer you up as well. You really had a long face on you. Did you know that?"

"I suppose I did. And I had a hell of a good reason for it."

I went on to tell her about the Chemnitz raid, omitting none of the details. Even when I was only half-finished I felt much better. It was almost as though I was a child again and had decided to tell my mother about something I had done wrong. You always had a strange sense of relief after doing that. As if in the telling everything was turned around again and you had a fresh start.

"All the time I was back there in the aircraft with Joe trying to get Pete out of that turret I had the funniest sensation," I went on, "as if the two of us were acting out the whole thing in some kind of a play, and that any moment the scene would shift and we'd find ourselves somewhere else with something entirely different going on. Like one of those dream sequences in the movies—you've probably seen them. That's how unreal the whole business seemed at the time. Now it's all clear and I know damn well it happened and no mistake about it."

Before Prue could answer me the man behind the bar was calling out "Time, gentlemen, time," and it was too late to order another drink.

"If I hadn't talked so much we could have had another round," I said. "Trust me to keep babbling on."

"I'm glad you told me," Prue said. "It's made me realize the war is still really on. Not that that's a very welcome thought, because it isn't, but we shouldn't try to fool ourselves. Even though we're tired to death of the whole business here. I suppose while Hitler and his gang are still alive we can't count on anything being over."

"That's about it. We've got to smash them once and for all, Prue. Come on, I'll take you home and I've got a big surprise for you."

"What's that?"

"I've finally got the car heater working. It's positively luxurious, as they say in the ads."

"If it's that comfy I may not want to get out."

"That's one of my little trade secrets. I trap more pretty young girls that way."

"I'll bet you do, too."

"You don't know the half of it."

It was very enjoyable driving out to Tadcaster. My mood was fairly cheerful now. Thanks to Prue I'd decided that I might as well be happy while I could. All the long faces in the world wouldn't bring Pete back now. Nothing could do that. Eat, drink, and be merry, for tomorrow we may die. That wasn't such a bad motto for the air force. Or for me either. It was simple and realistic. You couldn't build a life on it. But maybe you could manage to survive around it. As long as it was survival with honour. That was where you had to draw the line.

When I'd parked the car and walked her up to her front door, I wasn't as surprised as I thought I'd be when she invited me in. It was as though the evening now was going too well for both of us to want it to end at all suddenly.

The inside of the house was about what I had expected it would be. It had an old-fashioned, lived-in look that I liked right away. The rooms were large, the furniture solid and comfortable. All this I noticed on the way to the kitchen, where Prue produced a bottle of gin from one shelf and a large bottle of tonic water from another. We sat at a huge kitchen table and sipped at our drinks. There was plenty of gin in them, not too much mix. I was used to having ice in a drink like this but you couldn't have everything. The way the first one was going down after a couple more I could leave the car behind and fly back to base.

"I've only felt this way three or four times in my life before," Prue said very solemnly, "but tonight I feel as though I want to get drunk very much. Does that sound strange to you?"

"It's not very complimentary, I'll tell you. I didn't think my company was that deadly."

Prue smiled.

"It's nothing to do with you, it's simply bewildered, befuddled me. I suppose I'm merely feeling sorry for myself. It's one of my major vices."

"The others being?"

"Oh, I'm selfish, vain, thoroughly spoiled. Shall I go on?"

"That'll do for now. You know, I could say much the same things about myself without too much trouble. A hell of a lot of other people could, too."

"You don't really know how mean I can be," Prue said. "I've been mean to you, for instance."

"You have? I wasn't aware of it."

"Yes, I have. I've never even given you a goodnight kiss. And yet you keep coming back for more. I can't understand it."

"I think it should be fairly obvious to you by now, shouldn't it?" I asked.

"That you love me? No, because I don't really think you do. You may be puzzled, even fascinated, but it's not love."

"How can you be so sure?"

Prue raised her glass and swallowed the rest of her gin before replying.

"A woman knows. Believe me, she does. And don't ask me how." And with that she got up from the table.

"Finish your drink and I'll make you another," she said. "After I have another myself I may change my mind about you altogether. Who knows?"

"I'll drink to that," I said, draining my glass and handing it to her. The gin was starting to go to work in me now. My stomach had a beautiful warm glow that was beginning to spread out along my arms and legs and into the rest of my body.

Prue refilled our glasses and suggested we move to somewhere more comfortable. She led the way into the huge living room and excused herself for a moment. There was a large old-fashioned chesterfield that looked very comfortable and proved to be exactly that.

Prue returned very shortly. She'd combed out her hair and put on some fresh lipstick. She looked very beautiful to me in the dull light of the living-room.

"I see you've found the most comfortable spot," she said. "We keep wanting to get rid of this old relic but always manage to change our minds at the last moment, thank goodness."

She sat down close beside me and held out her glass.

"Cheers."

"Cheers."

We clinked glasses solemnly and then took long sips from them. Prue made a face almost instantly which must have brought a wide grin to my face.

"Go on, smile. So I am a horrible bartender."

"Let's say it isn't lacking in gin and leave it at that. About ninety-five percent at a conservative estimate. Rather high for a Collins."

"The first mouthful is the worst," Prue said. "After that your palate is completely burned away and you can't tell the difference."

She took another long sip of her drink and carefully set the glass down on the rug. Then she reached over, took my glass and placed it down beside hers.

At that exact moment what could only be the front door knocker was struck very vigorously four times in rapid succession. The noise crashed and re-echoed against the deep silence in the house. The first stroke gave me a distinct start, the others brought me bolt upright on the sofa in a second. Either my nerves were a hell of a lot worse than I knew about or my reflexes were working overtime.

Prue seemed almost as startled as myself but she recovered a lot faster. She jumped up off the sofa, bending over almost in the same motion to pick up our two drinks on the floor.

"Sorry, Bill," she said calmly but quickly, "but I'm afraid I'm going to have to ask you to step outside at the back for a bit. You can stay in the garage if you like—the door's open. I'll call you when the coast is clear. I'll explain it all then. All right? That's a dear, now."

Before I really knew what I was doing I'd buttoned up my

tunic, picked up my hat and greatcoat and followed behind Prue through to the kitchen. There I went down two or three steps and out a door leading into the garden. Without another word Prue quickly closed the door behind me.

When my eyes gradually became accustomed to the darkness I made out the outlines of the garage she'd mentioned. It was well at the back of the property. There was a small door leading into it that was supposed to be unlocked.

I worked my way slowly across the back grass and went inside. It was stone-cold in there. I might as well be standing outside as in here, I thought. But there was a sports car of some ancient vintage occupying one half of the garage, and the door of it wasn't locked as well. I put on my greatcoat, buttoned it up, and slid into the front seat. At least it was more comfortable than standing.

I lit the first of several cigarettes and tried to relax a little. How long would I have to wait? Not too frigging long, I hoped. I also hoped I'd hear Prue calling me the all-clear. I'd left the garage door open and the car window was down, so there shouldn't be any problem.

Now that I could look back on the events of the last five minutes, the whole incident had a cloak-and-dagger element to it. The things you read about in spy stories. The hero forced to hide out on the hotel window ledge ten storeys up above the busy city street while inside the hotel room the heroine tried to get rid of an unexpected caller. It also brought back out of a far deep corner of my mind the teenage memory of slipping out the side French doors of a girl's home at the same moment as her parents were coming in the front entrance. Only that had been a much more innocent time than tonight.

I decided it couldn't be Prue's parents at the door. They were up in Darlington. It was apparently someone she knew who always woke up the dead with their heavy touch on front door knockers. Perhaps a neighbour. What the hell. Why worry about it? After all, Prue had promised to explain everything. There was no doubt a very simple and logical explanation.

I was well into my third cigarette and beginning to feel my feet becoming half numb from cold in the thin oxfords I was wearing, when I heard Prue's voice call, "Bill, are you there?"

I was there, all right. I butted out my cigarette in the car ashtray and got out of the rather cramped front seat. Right away I could feel my bladder aching. My feet felt very strange to walk on the first few steps, as if they were only vaguely connected to my body. I closed the garage door and walked up toward the house. I could make out Prue standing in the centre of a small pool of light by the back entrance.

"You poor man, you must be half frozen," she said as I came up to her. "Sorry I had to keep you out there that long, but he was so long-winded I thought I'd never get rid of him."

I walked up into the kitchen and Prue followed behind me. She switched on the kitchen light.

"I need the bathroom and a stiff drink in that order," I said.

There was a two-piece bathroom next to the kitchen. When I came back from it feeling slightly better Prue had two drinks waiting on the kitchen table and had sat herself down in front of one of them.

"You're not the only one who needs a stiff drink," she said as I joined her at the table. "What a bloody time for him to call around!"

It was the very first time I'd heard Prue swear and it didn't sound quite natural. I hadn't thought of her as a girl who ever needed to use strong words. Maybe there was a lot I still had to learn about this intelligent, vivacious, beautiful girl seated across from me.

"But I promised I'd explain, didn't I? Well, his name is Dankworth, Major Tony Dankworth of the Royal Medical Corps. We grew up together here in Tadcaster. His parents lived two doors from here. His father was the local doctor. I suppose you'd call us childhood sweethearts. Anyway, he went away to the Middle East in '41 and I forgot all about him. Six months ago he came back and he still thinks we're sweethearts. He got himself moved up to the military hospital outside York and he's been making himself quite a nuisance. What I mean to say is, he won't take no for an answer."

"I can't really blame him too much," I said. "So what was the purpose of the call tonight? Checking up on you?"

"You could say that. He chewed me out about having liquor on my breath. I told him it was absolutely none of his business. That really got us at each other's throats. At one point I was almost prepared to throw things. Then all of a sudden he left in a big huff."

"And won't be back, I hope?"

"Not tonight, at least. Oh, he'll phone first thing tomorrow and apologize."

"Sounds like quite a guy." I took a long swallow of gin. It was beginning to get in my blood stream again and warm me up. Even my feet felt like they were returning to my body. "What would he think if he knew I was here?"

"He'd be bloody mad. If he caught you here he'd probably try to pick a fight with you. Although he's very much the gentleman, when he gets a bee in his bonnet he's like a mad-man."

"And you can't discourage him?"

"Honestly, Bill, I've tried everything."

"Has he slept with you?"

Prue threw back her head and laughed.

"It's really none of your business, you know, but no, he hasn't. Not that he couldn't have several times, but he doesn't believe we should have sex before marriage. He thinks it degrades the blessed union."

"What do you think yourself?"

"I've never really thought too much about it, seeing I haven't given marriage with anyone a serious thought. Say, are you ready for another drink? We're both getting too damn solemn to suit me."

"Wonderful idea," I said.

She was pouring mostly gin and very little lemon mix into our glasses now, I noticed. One more of these and she might have to help me get up from the table. But maybe we'd stop drinking before then.

"You know," Prue said in a voice that suddenly seemed very playful indeed, "just before we were so rudely interrupted in the parlour I was going to ask you to kiss me. Does that sound as if I've had too much to drink?"

"Not in the least. It's a very attractive suggestion. Is your offer still open?"

She leaned across the table. Her lips were red and full. There was an almost laughing look in those beautiful eyes of hers.

I'd wondered many times what that first kiss would feel like and when it would happen. I'd never expected it to be across a kitchen table. Well, you had to start somewhere. I found out her lips were softer, more-deeply-yielding, more dryly-moist than I'd thought possible.

"Like that?" she asked me quite casually as our lips came apart.

"I certainly liked the sample," I said. "I'd like to try the whole line as well."

"I'm still too sober. Don't you think I'm too sober?"

"Disgustingly." I raised my glass. "Here's a toast to all the sober people. May we leave them far behind."

"I'll drink to that, sir."

We clinked glasses solemnly and polished off the rest of that drink with the aid of another hastily improvised toast.

"My sitter's getting very tired of this kitchen chair," Prue decided after the next drink had been poured. "Seems to me we'd be a lot more comfortable somewhere else. We were so comfy back there when we were so rudely interrupted."

"We certainly were," I said. We both got up and picked up our glasses. But half way across the kitchen Prue turned to me and said, "I really can't stand that parlour, Bill. Come with me, I know something much better."

She led me out to the front stairs, holding my free hand as she guided me through the darkened house. Half way up the stairs changed direction, and Prue stopped me on the tiny landing.

"I want to ask you something, darling," she said.

"Fire away," I said.

"Do you think I'm a tramp?"

The question floored me for a moment. But I recovered quickly. I couldn't afford to lose out now.

"You're a wonderful girl," I told her, "a sweet, wonderful girl. Whatever gave you that idea?"

"You can say it, you know. You don't have to pretend. I'll like you just as much."

"You know, you're a very funny girl, a very silly girl. If you say anything more like that, I'm simply going to have to take you into your room and give you a good spanking."

She didn't say anything more. She gave my hand a squeeze. We went on up the rest of the stairs.

13

"Hey, Bill, where's that bloody wandering roommate of yours got to this time?"

It was Walt who had put the question as we climbed into a compartment of the London-bound Edinburgh Express a week later on the start of a seven-day leave.

All the crew were present except Fred, who was heading in the opposite direction, bound for Edinburgh and his Scots lass. He had an engagement ring with him and meant business. We'd miss not having him with us in London. At the same time we wished him all the luck in the world up in Scotland.

"Christ, how should I know?" I grumbled, "I'm not his damn keeper." But who was kidding who? I stepped down out of the compartment and hurried along the platform into York Station looking for our elusive navigator. I figured I had two minutes at the most to spot him.

I found him where I'd expected he'd be, sitting very casually in the Station restaurant, a cup of tea in front of him.

"Hi, Bill, the big train in yet?" He asked the question as if the Royal Scot was expected in during the next ten minutes or so.

"It could pull out any damn second, you fat-head," I exploded. "Better gulp that tea and shake your ass. This is one train that won't wait even for you."

"No sweat, I'll be right with you. Sorry if I got you in a flap."

"You should be, you clod."

Dave and I were barely settled in the compartment with the others when the train whistle blew the first of two warning blasts. Very shortly after our coach gave a sharp jerk and began to move slowly forward. Another leave was under way.

I settled back in my seat and tried to relax a little. Sleep seemed out of the question, for the time being, anyway. The crew were in too high spirits to permit me that luxury. But I'd crowded so much living into the past few days that I'd reached the point where I needed desperately some time to simply look back and let some of that time rewind, play itself back through my mind. A little time to sort and resort some of the impressions, the emotions still very fresh and alive in my memory. . . .

It had all begun the previous Saturday morning. Along with six other sleepy members of our crew I'd taken my place in the C.O.'s personal car, no less, and we'd been driven to the Group war cemetery on the other side of York. There, in the wind and cold of an almost sunless March day, we'd stood beside a freshly-dug grave at the end of what seemed like countless rows of small gravestones, and paid our last respects to Pete. The padre conducting the service had said all he had to say very quickly, the coffin was lowered, and we soon found ourselves walking slowly out of the cemetery. It was my first Air Force funeral and I fervently hoped it would be my last. Ed Barber, our new rear-turret gunner, was along with us, of course, and I wondered what thoughts might be going through his head. He was nineteen, the same age as Pete, and apparently full of the same joy of life and living that Pete had possessed. This ceremony couldn't help but have some kind of sobering effect on him. But probably not for very long. That was one advantage of being young. Nothing bothered you very much or stayed with you, not even the thought of sudden violent death.

I had hoped for that evening off to spend with Prue. It had seemed a short eternity since we'd kissed good-bye very feelingly, both half-awake, at six o'clock the previous morning at her place in Tadcaster. After which I'd gone out into the greyish-white of a Yorkshire morning to drive back to camp, still hardly believing that I'd actually spent the night with her.

Instead we found a stand-to at the base when we unloaded from the C.O.'s car. Later, at 1820, we cleared the runway in "N" for "Nan", destination Hemmingstedt and the Heide oil refinery. The sky was fairly clear of cloud, a good night for a raid. But over the target area it was a different story. Ground haze had set in, and even when the Master Bomber called us down to six thousand feet we still couldn't identify the oil

plant. A general ball-up developed, with the glare from the il-
luminating flares making it difficult to pick out the yellow target indicators around the aiming point. I released on what I
thought was dead on the button but somehow didn't feel too
happy about the whole attack. On the homeward leg the gunners had received permission to shoot up any searchlights
they could spot. As this was a rare chance to use their guns
over enemy territory the operation took on a slightly carnival
atmosphere. Walt had offered to buy the beer if the boys had
any confirmed hits. But although they blazed away a number
of times with the aircraft shaking violently, all the time babbling over the intercom like a couple of cowboys at a shoot-
out, apparently it was largely a wasted effort. Several times
Walt made stomach-churning downward swoops without
much warning, and that was pretty well the main excitement.
When it was all over we had to agree that any Jerry search-
light batteries along our route would be free to do their prob-
ing another night.

Sunday the day of rest brought no relief to us. We had a
four-thirty briefing for another night attack. That was the bad
news. The good news was that promotions had come through
for all of us, Ed Barber excepted. Joe, Fred and Max were
now Pilot Officers, Dave and I had made Flying Officer, Walt
was a Flight Lieutenant. Now at last the old crew was on an
equal footing. It was too bad about Ed, but that was replace-
ment's luck. What burned me up when I thought about it was
how close Pete had come to getting his commission. So close
and yet so far.

"That's a real son-of-a-bitch, isn't it?" I grumbled to Dave.
"Can't you just imagine him strutting around in an officer's
uniform! He'd really look sharp with that build of his. And
I'll bet the orders for his commission were cut the same as
ours well before he got the chop." That was one irony of the
war that I didn't appreciate one little bit.

"It's a bloody shame," was all Dave said in reply. It was
one of the few times, though, that I'd heard him swear when
he was cold sober. I'd probably wait a long time before it
happened again. But coming from him now it sounded perfectly right to me.

The objective that night was the Blohm and Voss shipyards
at Hamburg. Apparently the attack started out bombing on
ground markers, but by the time we'd begun our run thin

cloud cover over the target caused our Pathfinder boys to switch to skymarkers. I could make out what appeared to be numerous fires below but little else. After I'd returned to my seat in the navigator's cabin Dave told me we'd come very close to having another fatality. Joe Petosky had the added job on an attack of tossing out bundles of aluminium foil called "window" as we approached the target area. This was supposed to bugger up the enemy radar. As he was throwing the stuff through the open hatchway door the aircraft apparently had dipped slightly and he'd come within an inch of falling out. As Max jokingly said later back at de-briefing, that really would have fouled up the Jerry radar. Everyone laughed but Joe.

Monday we received a welcome day off and I'd had a fine evening with Prue. We seemed to be perfectly relaxed in each other's company now. The fact of us having slept together no doubt had something to do with it. The mystery of her body still largely remained, but I knew something of its delights and I was content to bide my time to sample more. I still had the feeling that although Prue had given me her body, she hadn't yet given me her love. It was still withheld, waiting some further development. But her goodnight kiss inside the big front door of the house in Tadcaster was long and achingly held. I felt it would only take a little more time and she would be mine completely. Major Tony Dankworth knew what he could do.

Tuesday we'd flown a daylight to Essen in Happy Valley. The Briefing Officer had tried hard to whip up some enthusiasm by telling us it would be a record attack; eleven hundred heavies taking part, two hundred from Six Group. I didn't think he succeeded. Most of us simply wondered what in hell was still worth bombing there. So it was over Essen at three o'clock, a routine run over the target using skymarkers, no flak, and bags of brown smoke billowing up through the clouds. The only excitement had come on our way home. Fred had spotted a V-2 trail and we all had a quick glance at the huge smoke-spiral blasting up to disappear through high cirrus clouds.

Walt had summed it up for us perfectly over the intercom: "Another killer headed for London. Those bastards, they never give up, do they?"

Seeing that rocket had brought us squarely back into the

war. It might have been a milk run for us over Essen today, but Jerry still had a few ugly counter-punches to hand out. The V-2 was the ugliest and most devastating yet.

Wednesday had brought yet another daylight, this time to Dortmund to blast the steel works in the area. It seemed strangely like a repetition of the previous raid—same cloud conditions over the target, little flak, good skymarking, identical black and brown smoke pouring upward. This time, though, we hadn't spotted any V-2's: the one surprise of the day was waiting for us after we'd completed de-briefing. Our flight O.C. told us we'd been granted a week's leave effective 0800 hours Thursday.

Prue had taken the news very calmly, I thought, when I'd seen her that evening, which wasn't too flattering to me. Our affair seemed to have cooled slightly. By hints more than anything definitely said I was given to understand that our relationship was still based on friendship rather than on physical attraction. I hadn't tried to promote any active sex play and she hadn't indicated in the least that she'd welcome it if I did. I still had the memory of that one glorious night in the house at Tadcaster, but I was beginning to feel I needed something more than a memory to go on. I was as hopelessly in love with her as I'd ever been, perhaps even more so. One look at her and everything started to flutter inside me. It looked as though I was doomed to follow along wherever the trail of our relationship led us.

"You should have quite a time with all the crew together up there," she remarked. "Watch out for those London girls, though. They're the very devil, I understand, and they make a speciality of unsuspecting Canadians."

"I'll try to be careful. I must say you don't sound very jealous. As far as I'm concerned it's going to be a long long week away from you."

"That's very romantically put, Bill. You really deserve a lot nicer girl than me, one who can really appreciate your feelings. You must think I'm a very cold fish."

"Have you had any complaints? I'm quite happy with the way you are, thank you."

"All right, darling, but actually this leave will be good for us both in a way. It'll give me a little time to think things over. I still have my problem with Tony, you know. I keep putting it off but it's got to be settled fairly soon. So who knows you may find a whole new Prudence waiting for you when you get back."

"Or no Prudence at all."

"Please don't even think things like that. I want you to go away to London without a care in your head. You've earned every hour of your leave, you know."

"I won't worry. And I'll find the same old Prue when I come north again."

"That's very sweet. Now give me one of your special, deluxe goodnight kisses."

It was that kiss I must have been reliving over in my mind when I felt someone shaking me. As I came out of sleep I thought, I'm going to see Dave's face and he's going to tell me that there's a briefing in another hour. . . .

It was Dave all right, but what he said was, "Come on, dream boy, we'll be in King's Cross in a couple of minutes."

Then it all came back. I was on leave, seven whole carefree days of it. For a week I could forget the war, the Air Force, the whole bloody business. London was ahead of us, the dream of every serviceman. Waiting to be taken, to be crushed and squeezed dry by our sheer strength, our spirit of youth. I watched the backs of endless tenements flashing by, the blur of outer stairways, the dull colours of washing on a thousand clotheslines. It was London, all right, but suddenly it seemed strangely like coming into Montreal on the train. But that had been almost two years ago, in a far distant country. Canada, I remember it being called.

14

Everyone knew that finding hotel rooms in wartime London was almost as hard as flushing out virgins. In point of fact, much more so. I fully expected to spend the first night and maybe more in one of the airless dormitories of the Officer's Club. Coming down to London at almost a moment's notice there simply hadn't been time to write ahead for reservations.

However, luck was with us for once. That and the fact of having arrived before the weekend rush. At the first hotel we tried, the Metropole in the Strand, we bagged three double rooms without any trouble. Not on the same floor, of course, but we couldn't expect miracles. Walt made us all pay the full week's deposit down straight away. This way he figured at least we'd know we had a bed and a roof over our heads all the time we were in London. We might starve to death but we'd do it in style at the Metropole.

Dave and I shared a room on the fifth floor which looked out on the Covent Garden Market. After washing up and changing into our best blues, we emerged into the busy Strand with the sun shining and most of the afternoon ahead of us. Dave was going up to Cheltenham in the morning to visit some relatives, so this might well be our only time together. We decided to do a little sightseeing while the weather was good. First we walked down to the River to get a good look at London Bridge. London Bridge is falling down, falling down kept going through my head—but it wasn't time, today at least—there it was, very much in order, with the Thames far below very wide, dark and slow-moving as we crossed and re-crossed it. Then on to the Houses of Parliament. We both experienced close to a childish delight simply hearing Big Ben chime out for real. Our last stop was Westminster Abbey. What impressed us the most were the elaborately-carved tombs of kings, dukes, and their families. It was

94

almost six before we arrived back at our hotel, foot-sore and weary, but agreed that it had been a fine afternoon. We lay on our beds up in the room chewing the fat until supper-time. Finally we couldn't wait any longer. The dining-room had better be good.

We ate very well indeed. Our hotel at least had found out how to beat wartime rationing. It could only be that there was a large, efficient black-market operating in London. After all, you couldn't expect the war profiteers and their friends to queue up for almost everything they ate like the ordinary man in the street. Well, for one meal at least we were eating with the very best.

We'd arranged to meet the gang in the basement bar at eight for an opening round of drinks, the prelude to a full evening's pub crawl. It was five after when we left the hotel dining-room, full of beefsteak and kidney pie and a fancy Italian dessert with a wine base. "Almost as good a meal as we'd get back in the mess," Dave said as we went down the stairs to the bar. With a sense of humour like that he deserved to be shipped off to Cheltenham in the morning to stay with two maiden aunts for part of the week.

We hadn't taken half a dozen steps into the noisy crowded room where your first impression was that there were at least two girls for every male present, when I heard Max's fog-horn voice bellowing out over the loud hum of voices. The boys had a strategic location right in the centre of the room. As we moved over toward it two girls got up from the table. They both brushed past us and I could see that their very carefully made-up faces were anything but happy.

"Hi, Dave, hi, Bill," Walt greeted us as we came up to the table. He was smoking a long fat cigar and already looked beyond any pain. "Too bad you weren't here sooner. You'd have had a chance to meet a couple of real nice girls."

"Very nice indeed," Max added. "Dolores and Charmaine. They wouldn't say what their real names were. Having a bloody drink with us. Real nice girls. Don't think either one is over sixteen. Asked them for their rock-bottom price on a gang shag. Five quid apiece. And they wouldn't do it for a penny less."

I sat down next to Max. He looked like he had a bigger load on than Walt. But he was still obviously in very good shape. The table was littered with beer bottles. It looked as if they all had at least an hour's start on the two of us.

"Bloody bitches," Max continued. "Seemed to take offence when I told 'em we only wanted to rent it for an hour, not take a ten year lease on it. Say, what are you guys drinking? Both of you look too damn sober to suit me. How about you, Walt?"

Walt agreed and a waiter speedily brought another round of beer. As I'd expected Walt thanked me for buying the round as the waiter stood over us waiting for payment. He carried it off so well, however, that you reached for your money, your only regret that you yourself didn't have the same smooth, effortless technique. Moochers like him were born, not made, and thank God they were a chosen few.

While I downed my ale, Joe, who was sitting on the other side of me, introduced me to the room's unique, built-in entertainment feature. The floor below us was literally one huge transparent shiny mirror. Once you realized that, and had the fact brought home to you that many of the young ladies present didn't appear to be wearing panties under those low-cut dresses, there wasn't too much left to the imagination. Whenever a red-head or a blonde went by who'd been born unmistakably a brunette, our whole table rocked with laughter. The girls themselves didn't appear either to mind or to notice. It was probably terribly old hat to them.

After that round of beer someone suggested we hit the road. We scrambled out of the bar, up into the damp night air of the Strand. It would have been much easier and much more sensible to stick to the pubs in the neighbourhood, but Max and Walt both had the brainy idea of utilizing the Underground. We ended up riding the trains one stop at a time; then we'd pile out at a station, climb up to the street, and search out the nearest pub. As the evening wore on and we moved up the subway line, we noticed that the platforms at each stop were filling up more and more with men, women and children getting ready to bed down for the night. They seemed cheerful enough as they stretched out on their bedrolls.

"Poor bastards," Walt had said after we'd picked our way over reclining bodies at one station, "I only hope the Jerries are getting it worse at their end." We couldn't argue very much with that. The V-1's and V-2's were apparently coming over in droves every night now. It was a little like the London of the Blitz all over again.

It must have been a few minutes past ten o'clock closing that a big-bosomed, thick-armed pub owner's wife stood over us a little sternly as we sat at our table still with four or five half-emptied glasses in front of us, and growled out not too pleasantly, "Time, please, gentlemen, for the last time now. I'll have the coppers around any minute if you don't finish up, I will."

"Walt," Max said, "I get the decided impression that this charming damsel wants us to leave. How do you read it?"

"Loud and clear, Maxie boy."

"We can take a hint, can't we, fellows?" I asked, and raised my glass. That was the signal for a general raising of glasses. Then after some good-natured banter with the pub mistress we moved out in column of route.

While weaving our way toward what we thought was the direction of the nearest Tube station, a cab happened along without a fare and Joe hailed it down immediately. We piled in and before we knew it were back at our hotel. My key miraculously fitted into our room door first crack, and within ten minutes Dave and I had poured ourselves into bed.

It seemed as though I'd only been asleep for a very few minutes when a shattering explosion electrified the air right outside our bedroom window. I jumped at least three inches off my mattress, while Dave seemed to throw off his bed clothes and leap out onto the floor all in one terrified reflex.

I saw it was one-thirty by my watch when I finally thought to look at it. By this time we could hear frantic footsteps and very excited voices outside in the hall.

"Doodle bugs must have started for the night," I said to Dave, trying to sound a lot calmer than I was. "That one sounded pretty close. You going down to the shelter?"

"It might be a good idea. How about you?"

"Bugger it. Besides it's a hell of a long shot that anything's going to land right on us." I was talking pretty big at the moment largely to convince myself. I wasn't any hero. I wanted to stay alive. But my bed had soft clean sheets and a solid mattress, the best thing I'd slept in for months.

"I'm with you, Bill. Let's go back to bed then. Maybe there won't be any more come over that close again."

"Good boy." I was a little surprised that Dave took it so

calmly. But then he always seemed cool as hell up there in his navigator's cabin even when the flak was breaking out all around us.

We were hardly settled back into bed again before we heard the pulsing throb of a V-1 approaching. The Jerries made all their motors different from ours, so it had a distinct sound all its own. The throb increased. Then the sound suddenly cut out. That meant the bomb was on its way down. Another loud crash, further away this time. The noise had hardly died away when another explosion ripped the night, this one much closer, much louder. There had been no warning chug from that baby.

"A V-2," Dave said quietly across the dark of the room. "Looks like a busy night. I heard one hit a pub last evening with half a hundred Yanks in it. Not a trace left of one of them."

"The bastards can't win but they still won't give up. I wonder how much more this city has to take?"

"Until we either bomb out or capture their launching sites they'll keep pouring them over. It's a lovely war, isn't it, Bill?"

It was a beauty, all right, and I tried hard to take my mind off it and fall back to sleep. It didn't work for a long long time. First I tried counting buzz bombs the way you'd count sheep—I started with them rising from their launching pads across the Channel. Stubby V-1's which only rose a few thousand feet and then straightened out like aircraft. Sleeker V-2's which climbed in a gentle arc to a height of a hundred miles before stalling and then dipping noiselessly for the dive to earth. English earth. When that didn't work I tried hard to think of Prue under this sheet with me, Prue a little drunk, Prue choosing her words carefully, Prue biting my ear, Prue with her tongue busy, Prue with her fingers moving along my back and over my chest and slowly across my stomach. Prue giving a little moan that made my whole body shiver. . . .

The chug of another V-1 moving closer pulled me back to the present in a hurry, to this room in the Strand with my navigator in the bed across from me, both of us sitting up now as the engine-throb grew to a loud crazy roar very near, the engine cutting off with the feeling that this time it could be right overhead. With the thought pounding through my head at the same moment, this is it, this is it, your last second in the world.

But no, it exploded dully quite some distance away. I took a deep breath, felt my whole body relaxing all at once. I was strangely half way between laughing and crying, not wanting to do either.

"No wonder people go down into shelters with all this crap flying around. It's too damn hard on the nerves," Dave said in the darkness.

"I thought that last one had our number on it for sure," I told him. "After this I feel a whole lot better about letting my bombs go."

There were a couple more V-1's after that but nothing that sounded even close. It was funny how you soon got used to them. But the V-2's were a different matter, something fiendish straight out of hell.

Bugger the war, I told myself. You're officially out of it for six more days. Let them all kill each other off in the meantime.

I lay there in my bed wide awake for the longest time, trying to keep my body perfectly still, listening to Dave's steady breathing. Finally I felt the room moving slowly, slowly away from me. All at once I relaxed and let it take me with it.

15

Dave had expected to stay in Cheltenham two or three days visiting his old aunts, but it wasn't until the second last day of our leave that he arrived back at the hotel. Although it was almost noon I was still in bed in our room, hung over yet from the night before, but vaguely beginning to feel like getting some food into my stomach.

He pushed back the curtains and began to change his clothes.

"Well, pal, how was Cheltenham?"

"Wonderful, Bill. You really should have come along. London seems so damn dark and grimy by comparison."

"Don't tell me you spent five days just visiting with a couple of aunts."

"Sure. Of course it turned out they had a couple of nieces so that helped to pass some of the time. Very nice girls, Bill, and both real lookers. It was a bit of a problem with the two of them."

"I'll bet it was, sport. But you seem to have survived. Hope you didn't knock either or both of them up."

Dave looked over at me long enough to register his disapproval, then went on changing.

"Anything exciting happen down here while I was away?"

"More buzz bombs every night if you want to call that exciting. And Walt's getting pretty close to having the D.T.'s. It's a damn good thing this is his last big night. Max isn't too much further behind him, come to think of it."

"Why don't you get out of the sack and I'll buy you some lunch?" Dave said when he'd finished changing. "I'll wait for you down in the lobby. Don't be all day, though."

"You deserve a break after such a rough time down at Cheltenham. Give me twenty minutes."

Half an hour later Dave and I were walking out the front door of the hotel.

"How's business today?" I asked the big doorman on duty.

"Very brisk, sir," he said. And winked at me as an American G.I. came out almost right behind us with a heavily made-up woman wearing an elaborate fur coat. The doorman signalled for a cab and one promptly pulled up at the curb. As the cab drew away I saw the shade being drawn on our side. From what the doorman said the cab would circle the block very slowly a couple of times, then pull in at the hotel entrance again. The couple would get out and go in the hotel; five minutes later the same woman would come out with another G.I. on her arm. It was almost instant sex. And much cheaper when you could hire a cab for five minutes instead of a room for the night. You had to hand it to the Americans. They were resourceful as hell. And they had taken over everything they wanted in London in much the same way. No wonder the Jerries were losing the war. They were up against an even more thoroughly efficient machine than their own.

"I'm sure glad the Yanks are on our side," I told Dave as we moved down the Strand to a restaurant we'd discovered where the prices were moderate and the foot eatable.

"They make the rest of us look like amateurs, I suppose. But they seem to make as many enemies as they do friends."

"Most of them I've met are good guys. I guess they have a little too much money to spend. Speaking of money, you were serious about buying lunch, weren't you? I'm down to my last quid and change."

"I said I'd buy, didn't I?"

"And you're a man of your word, I know. Here's the hash palace now."

We had a good lunch and afterwards strolled along the Strand. It was a fine day for London, the sun breaking through the clouds now and again, the air still cool and a little damp. It wasn't too much different from a March day back home; a hint of spring somewhere about even though it was only a first promise.

Back at the hotel I hit the sack again, wanting to be in good shape for my last evening in London. Dave started to run the water for a bath, but I must have dozed off even before he'd finished.

A loud knock on the door brought me rapidly back to earth. Dave was still muttering about people banging doors from his bed as I groped my way through the now dark room to the door.

"Sorry, didn't know you were having a snooze, Bill." It was Jake Rosen, a fellow bombardier with Muskrat Squadron, up on leave since Monday. I'd met him a couple of nights ago in the bar downstairs and we'd spent an evening drinking and trying our luck at the Covent Gardens dancehall. He was sharing a room on the floor above us. A big, good-natured Jewish boy from Montreal, he had half his tour completed the same as us.

"Come on in, time I was up anyway," I said. "What's on your mind, Jake?"

"Just wondering if you felt like doing a pub crawl. We really had a ball the other night, didn't we?"

He was right. We had had a ball together. It was the best evening I'd spent in London. A lot of beer, a lot of laughs, and some wild dancing at the end of it.

"Why not? Hey, Dave, how about coming along and lap up a few beers? Do you the world of good." I knew there wasn't a chance in the world of him joining us, but I thought I should ask. And then of course I was going to have to bum a few quid from him.

Dave's voice came sleepily from the bed. "You guys go ahead. This bed is so darn beautiful I may stay here the rest of the war. Bill, if you want a loan, just reach in my tunic pocket and help yourself."

Dave was one lovely guy. So uncomplicated, so relaxed. I envied him for both those qualities. But every now and then you felt he needed a stick of dynamite under him to shake his ass a little. Not that it did much good. He actually enjoyed a quiet time. Which at his age was a little hard to figure, that was all.

"O.K., Dave, pleasant dreams," I said. I took two quid from his pocket on my way out. That should be enough to last me for the evening if I tipped very lightly and made sure I got the right change every time.

Jake and I got under way at once by hopping the first double-decker bus that came down the Strand. It didn't matter where it was going, we wouldn't be on it long enough to matter. Our plan was a simple variation of the Tube pub-crawl, using double-deckers instead. Once we'd spotted an interesting pub, we'd hop off, grab a quick beer, and catch another bus. The big thing was to keep moving and drinking without having too large an interval between catching a new bus and finding the next pub. Jake, as I'd discovered already, had a fine natural singing voice. Even better than that, he had an endless variety of songs with all the words to match. *Alouette, Home, Home On the Range, Lili Marlene, The Big Rock Candy Mountain,* Jake knew them all. Tonight the singing started right after the first pub. Jake was in very good voice. I followed along the best way I could, faking the words where necessary, making plenty of noise if nothing else. As we left the bus at one stop on our tour, an old lady solemnly stood up and thanked us Canadians for the entertainment. Jake, the perfect gentleman at all times, took off his hat and made a deep bow in her direction. The rest of the passengers raised a mild cheer at that. We felt a little like goodwill ambassadors on an important mission as we navigated our way up the street to our next pub.

I found myself comparing Jake with Pete Yarish. They both had a lot in common—big, young, good-looking boys from around the Main in Montreal—both practiced girl chasers, both almost fanatical about *Les Canadiens* as the greatest hockey team in the world. They'd have had a ball together in London, those two—instead Jake was stuck with a rather sober-faced Anglo-Saxon from Toronto. It seemed almost a shame in a way.

Surprisingly enough, it was me who suggested as closing-time inched near that we should give the Covent Gardens dancehall a second break. Why not, Jake said, and that was that. Things were in full swing when we arrived. It was a huge ballroom with three balconies and a revolving dance-floor, no less. The management apparently believed in the unusual. While a male orchestra played waltzes an all-girl band rocked the place with up-tempo numbers. Hundreds of dancers swept around the dance-floor while almost as many more crowded around it. For all we knew it could be the world's largest stag-line.

The second girl I danced with, a cute little peroxide blonde by the name of Cathy, seemed to be worth spending the rest of the evening with. I spotted Jake a couple of times; he wasn't having any trouble at all. When I left the dance around eleven with Cathy he came by dancing close with a very striking blonde. We exchanged good-luck waves. It looked like he'd need a lot more than I would.

As we stood in the crowded Tube most of the way out to South Kensington, we held hands and kissed like two kids on our first date. She was a lovely girl. She shared a small flat with her sister and worked in the Air Ministry as a stenographer. Her sister was a clerk in the Admiralty. Both parents had been killed in the Blitz.

The flat was very small, but to compensate there was a good supply of liquor, which Cathy made no attempt to explain. After a drink we chose the couch in the living room. She snuggled up to me like a warm little bear. Just as things were moving to the intense stage a key turned in the lock and her sister walked in on us with a Canadian P.O. fighter pilot in tow.

There was no embarrassment, it was very very civilized. After introductions all round we sat down together and had several drinks. I didn't even find out where the fighter ace hailed from. Then the sister and her boy friend disappeared into the single bedroom.

"Haven't seen him before," Cathy commented, after we'd returned to the couch. "He's rather cute, don't you think?"

"If you like the type," I said, "which apparently you do."

"I know what it is," she said, "you bomber boys just can't stand the fighter pilots. I suppose it's only natural."

"Let's face it, we hate their guts. Every one of us started out wanting to be fighter pilots, but we ended up nursing bloody old bombers. But most guys would never admit this, of course."

"Let's forget all about it, shall we? All I'm interested in right now is you. You're on a week's leave, didn't you say?"

"That's right." What I hadn't told her and wasn't going to tell her was that this was my last night in London. No use spoiling my chances.

"Like another drink before we settle down?" she asked.

"No thanks. I'm flying high as it is. Now where were we when we were so rudely interrupted?"

We tried to find out where it had been but never did make it all the way back. On top of which the two quick drinks I'd had now really began to go to work on me. I'd felt tired half way through the evening. Now I couldn't keep my eyes open.

My head settled on a soft cushion and I was finished. I fell asleep with Cathy's passionate kisses still fresh on my mouth.

I woke to find myself alone on the chesterfield. The smell of coffee suddenly drifted through into the room.

I looked at my watch. It was only seven. My stomach felt heavy, my mouth very sour. I stumbled up off the couch and found the bathroom. After I'd rinsed out my mouth and bathed my face with cold water I felt better.

I found Cathy busy in the tiny kitchen off the living-room. She had hot toast piled up on plates, lots of coffee perking on the stove. She looked up as I came in and planted a cool kiss on my mouth as I stood beside her.

"Hi, Bill, did I wake you? We're working girls here, you know. If I didn't get up first my sister wouldn't stir until noon. Which reminds me, I'd better get the love birds up right now."

"Sorry I flaked out on you last night. That was a mighty poor performance."

"I think I was even more tired than you were. And I had a little too much to drink. Don't worry, we'll make it all up tonight."

"I don't know how to tell you this, but I have to be straight with you. I can't see you tonight. I have to leave for the North this afternoon. My time's all up."

Just for a fraction of a second I thought she was really going to blow up at me from the look on her face. But she seemed to regain her composure almost instantly and that old familiar smile came back on her face again.

"Then we'll have to do something about that right away, won't we? When do you absolutely have to leave here?"

"Noon at the latest. What did you have in mind?"

"I could telephone in sick. I haven't had a day off in ages."

"Why don't you do that little thing?" I told her, and pulled her firm little body in to mine. At the same time bending down to meet those moist lips of hers. While all the time the coffee pot perked merrily on.

"Now I'll get those two up," Cathy said, pushing herself finally away. "And you get ready for a good breakfast. You've got a lot of hard work ahead of you this morning."

16

The Royal Scot left for York and parts north at one forty-five. At twelve-thirty that afternoon I came back on the Tube from South Kensington to pick up the crew at the hotel. Walt had been up only a few minutes and was shaving, Max was packing his duffle bag. Dave, Joe and Ed had already gone downstairs for lunch. I joined them for a coffee.

"Where the hell did you get to last night, Bill?" Joe asked me. "We really had ourselves a time. The best night of our leave, eh gang?"

"Jake Rosen and I did a pub crawl. Then I met this cute little number at the Covent Gardens and one thing led to another. You know how it is, fellows," I told them. "So what was so big about last night?"

"Well," Ed Barber said, "here the four of us were sitting around in the bar downstairs last night feeling pretty sorry for ourselves. We barely had beer money left and had to nurse even that. It looked like a lousy evening all round. Somehow we got talking about sports. First it was hockey and the Stanley Cup. Then we switched to baseball and I mentioned the Leafs were opening this year against the Buffalo Bisons. Right away a Yank at the next table asks me what I know about the Bisons. He's a young kid with pilot's wings up and he's with two other young guys, also pilots. Well, I reeled off some batting averages from the year before and told him how they'd moved their right field in to the 310 mark at Offerman Stadium so a good long fly ball was a home run now, and before I know it he's invited us all over to their table and was buying us drinks. Turned out one of his buddies was from Rochester, so we dissected the Red Wings in short order, then went on to the Leafs and the Royals. Max, Walt and Joe didn't know what the hell we were talking about, but they were too busy drinking the free beer to worry too much. Then the fighter boys suggested we move upstairs to their room where they had something better to drink. After three second's hesitation we accepted the invitation, and before we knew it were sampling some black market Scotch. But the real surprise of the evening was yet to come. Apparently the boys had hired two girls for the whole week and installed them in a room down the hall. They're real nice girls and will do anything to please, my friend from Buffalo said. If any of you guys would like to take a crack feel perfectly free. How's that for a deal, Bill? Aren't you sorry you strayed from the fold?"

"Sounds as though I missed quite a night," I admitted. "How were the girls, by the way?"

"I can't speak for the others but I found it pretty nice going. Due to my somewhat inebriated condition I don't think I was at the top of my form, mind you."

"What he's trying to say is that he was plastered," Joe explained. "Ed's right all the way, though, it was some night."

"You didn't tell him how we sneaked four bottles of gin out of there," Walt smiled through his red-rimmed eyes. He'd just come into the dining-room and sat down at our table. "It was a dirty trick but they'll never drink all that booze in a hundred years."

"Well," I said, "let's shake our butts, shall we? That bloody train won't wait for anybody."

That afternoon as the express thundered north one of the bottles of gin was opened and passed around. Even Dave had his share. The first long swallow made you almost gag, the second went down much easier, the good warm glow lighting up the stomach more than worth it. We needed the gin that afternoon; a grim sadness had fallen over us as we finally had to admit to ourselves that our precious leave was over.

"Back to the salt mines," I said to Dave. "I still can't believe the week's shot, though, and that we're going back."

"You'd better believe it. But you know, I'm glad in a way. All these places like London seem really great when you're a couple of hundred miles away from them. But once you get there the magic wears off pretty quick, for me, anyway. Don't get me wrong, though, I'm in no hurry to get back to flying. But I figure we might as well get the war over with. Things sound very good in the papers. The Germans are just about finished. The Ruskies are beating them to a pulp."

"Don't believe the papers too damn much," Max warned. "They're put out strictly for the civilians. But we're the guys that have to fight off the 262's. There could be plenty of war still left for us."

"This next one we fly is going to be the big one for us," Walt said. "Number thirteen. Once we've got that bastard behind us we can coast the rest of the way."

Number thirteen. It was hard to believe we had done twelve ops in such a short space of time. I closed my eyes and tried to remember the names. They all came back, one after another, with a couple of hesitations. Chemnitz, Wesel, Monheim, Worms, Essen, Kamen, Mainz, Chemnitz again, Hemmingstedt, Hamburg, Essen a second time and Dortmund. I counted them up on my fingers. That Worms night attack had been the worst. I hoped I'd never see heavy flak like that again. And the searchlights had almost made a fix on us a couple of times.

O.K., boy, forget the war for today. Tomorrow you can worry about it, bitch about it all you want. But today think of something more pleasant. I thought right away of Cathy. Cathy with the small, compact willing body unleashing a flood of passion I'd scarcely believed possible. Maybe she did it the same way as I did, substituting the face and the body of someone else loved and gone as we lay in her bed, much as I'd had Prue's face and body behind my eyes as I responded almost savagely to her every hint, every mood. I'd left that tiny flat feeling drained physically but full of a new kind of strength and hope. I wondered if it would be any different with Prue and I when I got back. If my going away had meant anything to her or had merely widened the gap that had opened up between us. Perhaps like me she didn't feel anything one way or the other at the moment. The first time we were together again would probably tell the story. With that rather sombre thought I dozed off in my seat.

Arriving at York Station late in the afternoon felt almost like a home-coming. That familiar female voice with the strong Oxford accent calling out departures and arrivals over the echoing loudspeaker. The sight of my old Standard Nine, the stale smell of the upholstery as we all piled into her, the quick cough of the engine changing to a steady hum. And perhaps best of all driving to Betty's for a pint or two before we faced up to West Moor. Today for some reason I paid for the first round very good-naturedly, even though it left me with only a pocketful of small change.

Then we piled into the car again, and all the way out to the base it was:

"There was flak, flak, bags of bloody flak,
  In the Ruhr, in the Ruhr,
There was flak, flak, bags of bloody flak,
  In the Valley of the Ruhr."

And the inevitable refrain following after almost like a benediction:

"My eyes are dim, I cannot see,
 The searchlights they are blinding me,
 The searchlights they are blinding me."

17

———••◆◆◆••———

As we were driven back to Flights Walt finally told us. "We were lousy up there today, old chums. Maybe it was number thirteen and all that nonsense, but that's really no excuse. If we don't smarten up next time we may all end up dead."

The long silence that greeted his remarks must have told him we agreed with him one hundred percent. We had performed badly and for that there were no excuses. We'd been damn lucky that it had been an easy do, a milk-run daylight, no fighter reaction, only moderately heavy flak. Lucky for us we'd gone to Rheine instead of a really hot target. I shuddered to think what it would have been like if it had been a night attack.

I phoned Prue up a little after six. She was busy with a customer and I had to wait several minutes before she came back on the line.

"Hi, stranger. How was London and all the fleshpots?" Her voice sounded unusually cheerful. I thought perhaps she might be making a special effort.

"A nice change and all that. But after three or four days it all began to have a certain sameness, if you know what I mean."

"I think I do. Were you planning on coming in tonight?"

"I'd love to, but I've just come in off a trip and I'm really dead. I guess I'm out of shape or something. All I want to do is to crawl into bed. I must sound like an old man of seventy."

"Then you do just that. Make it tomorrow night if you can. Wednesday night I have a special meeting at the church that could be rather late."

"Tomorrow night for sure. Say, do you know I missed you very much while I was away."

"It's sweet of you to say so. I guess I've missed you too, Bill. I'll expect you about eight, then. Good night."

When I was rudely awakened the next morning at eight with the good news of a nine-thirty briefing, I was glad I'd logged that extra sack time. It looked as though the brass had been waiting for our crew to get back off leave to step up the air war into high gear again.

Shortly before noon we were off to batter Dorsten on the Lippe and its railroad junction. It proved to be another uneventful op. The crew was a lot sharper and Walt was all smiles as we went to de-briefing. Eleven more ops and we could hang up our skates for good.

That night Prue had the chemist's shop all closed up when I arrived shortly after eight. I wasn't nearly as tired as I had been after yesterday's daylight, but the strain of watching H2S and then taking over for the bombing run still wore you down even on a milk run like today. And I still had a warm lazy feeling hanging over all my body from the coffee and rum supplied at de-briefing.

Prue's welcome somehow didn't seem half as warm as she'd sounded on the telephone the day before. When I suggested a movie she agreed without too much enthusiasm.

The inevitable happened in the cinema. It was crowded and felt very warm and stuffy to me. The feature picture couldn't have run more than ten minutes before I found myself fighting to keep awake. And finally surrendered not long after.

I woke up to Prue's gently shaking of my shoulder, not sure for a moment exactly where I was.

"I thought I'd at least wake you up for the cartoon, sleeping beauty," Prue whispered. I lifted my head from her shoulder which had proved a very comfortable pillow. Mickey Mouse was about to go into his antics. I was suddenly wide awake and able to laugh along with the rest of the audience.

"Let's go," I suggested as the Gaumont-British newsreel came on. "If we hurry we have time for a quick drink."

It was cold in the Standard Nine and we were glad to warm up soon after in our favourite pub on the road to Tadcaster.

"How's your father and mother?" I asked as our drinks came.

"Mom's her usual bouncing self and Dad's about the same, no better, no worse. I've got a couch now at the shop and I'm trying to get him to take a lie down when he's not busy, but it's hard to sell him the idea."

"It's always tough to get older people to change their routines. Sometimes you get the feeling they'd almost die first rather than give in."

"That sounds like Dad, all right. But now I've got Mother on my side and that's a help. He has to listen to her whether he likes it or not."

The talk for some reason drifted on to my flying and from there to what I wanted to do after the war.

"I suppose I'll try university," I said, "although I don't know whether or not I'd be able to last out three or four years of studying after this life, which makes you so damn lazy and aimless. But I'll have enough credits to see me most of the way through, so I guess I'd be crazy if I didn't take the chance."

"You'd be a fool not to give it a try at least," Prue agreed. "I don't believe our boys have anything nearly as good as that."

"Even so I've found it doesn't pay to look much ahead in this business," I told her. "The best thing is to live one day at a time and let tomorrow take care of itself. That's not very original but it's the best thing I've found so far. Right now I have eleven more ops to go. They all should be fairly easy but you never really know. One day you think the Germans are finished, the next day they can bounce back up there to haunt you."

Seated back in the car we lit cigarettes. It was dark on the side of the inn yard where we were parked. I leaned over to kiss her but she drew away.

"I've had something on my mind all evening," Prue said, "but I didn't want to spoil things by bringing it up. Now I think I have to."

"Do we have to be serious right now? After all, I haven't seen you for over a week. Can't it wait until another time?"

"No, it really can't, Bill. So I'll try to make it short and sweet. It all boils down to this: I think we should stop seeing each other after tonight."

I looked over at her, puzzled. Her face had a very serious,

very determined look on it. Not happy, not unhappy. You couldn't read it at all. I knew I was in for trouble right away.

"Remember when we first started going together? We agreed then we'd only be good friends, we wouldn't get serious. Well, we have gotten serious, haven't we? We've even slept together."

"What's so wrong about all of that?" I said. "We started out as friends, then it became something else."

"I should have told you this a long time ago, Bill, it might have made things a lot easier for both of us. When I was a young girl about ten years old my mother took me over to a friend's place. The lady was having a baby. A midwife was there but the baby wouldn't come in the usual way and finally they had to rush to get the doctor. My mother put me in the next room and all I heard for the next two hours was that woman screaming her head off. Ever since that day that's the image I get when someone mentions having a baby—a woman writhing in pain on a bed, shrieking in agony."

"That was a bad experience," I agreed, "but surely you've gotten over that. Women usually don't have a quarter of that trouble nowadays."

"Perhaps not, but I can't get the feeling out of my head that the same thing could happen to me. And I'm not very good when it comes to bearing pain, I'm a real baby."

"So you're afraid that if we go on seeing each other we'll be sleeping together again, and you could become pregnant, is that it?"

"That's exactly it, Bill. I don't know what got into my head that night my parents were away. I suppose I had too much to drink, for one thing. And I do like you a lot, and I know how a man must feel about a girl he's been going with for some time. But it's plain now to me that I can't let it happen again. And there's only one way I know of to make sure of that."

"You mean, you're never going to get married? I can't imagine that happening to you. You're a beautiful, intelligent girl, Prue, and you must know it."

"Marriage is something I've never considered. Yes, I did once, to be truthful. But I haven't thought about it for a long time."

"Can I ask you one more thing?"

"Certainly."

"Where does the Major fit into all this? Or does he?"

Prue looked at me and smiled ever so slightly.

"I suppose he's bothered you all along, hasn't he? Well, he needn't have. I've never had any intention of getting serious with him. As a matter of fact, we had our final parting of the ways the night before you came back. So put your mind at rest. You're not losing out to anyone else. I'd have told you right off if it had gone that way."

There didn't seem to be anything more to say after that, not right at the moment. And Prue's cigarette was finished, mine was too. I started up the car reluctantly. I needed a few minutes to think, to try to work out some winning argument. Prue sounded as though she meant every word she said. I had to talk her out of it somehow.

That fifteen minutes on the road to Tadcaster was one of the longest times of my life. Finally after what seemed like an endless drive I pulled up across the street from her house. The lights were all out inside except for one feeble bulb burning in the hallway. I offered Prue a cigarette but she shook her head. Well, I sure as hell needed one. I lit up and we sat in silence for a minute or two. I could only stand that silence so long, however.

"When I was down in London," I said, "the only real excitement was the buzz bombs coming over every night. One evening rather late I lay in bed, my chum in the other bed, and we listened as they came over. This night for some reason or other I'd said to hell with going down in the shelter, so Dave agreed to stay too. It was pretty scarey lying there, so I had to try to get my mind on something else. I ended up with you in bed with me, making love, I suppose, and not caring at all for bombs or anything else."

Now that I'd broken the silence between us Prue seemed to be a little less sombre.

"I don't know whether or not I'm very flattered. It could depend a lot on the position. If you were simply using me as a shield against falling plaster. . . ."

"I like that shield idea, it never occurred to me. You would be lovely protection in a situation like that, come to think of it. No, I'm afraid I was shielding you. Not with any falling plaster in mind, though."

"There, you see, Bill, we always get around to sex sooner

or later, don't we? That's the impossible part of our relationship. It doesn't really give us a chance. We're both too healthy to have it any other way. Don't you agree?"

"I suppose so. But can't we talk this over some more? Do we have to make it final tonight?"

"I can't see any point in dragging it on, Bill, really I can't."

Then we didn't say anything more until we were standing at her front door. I butted out my cigarette. It was now or never.

"I love you, Prue, you know that, don't you? I don't want this to end. Why not think it over for just a little longer? Then, if you still haven't changed your mind, all right. But this seems to be rushing things so damn fast."

"It may seem that way to you, Bill, but I've given it a lot of thought. All the time you were away and even before that. No, I've made up my mind and I don't think I'll change it now. But I do want us to remain friends. If we meet anywhere I want to be able to say "hello" and not feel badly about it afterwards. Can we leave it like that?"

"If that's what you want," I said.

"It's what I want, and I'm sorry, too."

"Not half as sorry as I am. All right. We're still friends."

"It's not the end of the world, Bill. You'll find someone else without even trying. Someone else who'll give you all I can't give."

"I hope so. But I'm not so sure. Well, goodbye, Prue, it was nice while it lasted."

"Goodbye, Bill, and take care. Please stay alive."

"Don't worry about that," I said.

Prue put her key in the lock and turned it. The door opened and she went in. As she turned I saw her face for a moment. There were tears running down her cheeks.

"Prue," I said, but the door closed at the same moment. The light inside went out almost immediately. It was all over.

I walked slowly back to the car. I still couldn't believe it. Tomorrow I'd wake and find it had only been a bad dream. I had lots of bad dreams these days. This was a bad one, all right, but it was still only a dream. Tomorrow I'd phone Prue up at the chemist's shop. She'd answer and before long her laughter would come rippling across the wire. Every time she laughed like that I felt good all over.

18

———••—⊶⊷—••———

Luckily they gave us the next day off. If they hadn't I would have been lousy company at briefing, in the change rooms, and especially in the air. This way I was able to stick pretty close to my room all day and have a largely uninterrupted session of feeling sorry for myself.

But after a beer to two in the mess bar after supper my mood lifted a little, and when Walt blew in suggesting the gang hit the high spots in York, I was agreeable enough. Five of us, the maximum load possible, crowded into the Standard and away we went.

Joe, Walt and Max shoved off to the Palaise de Dance at nine, leaving Fred Waters and I alone over our beer. I simply wasn't in the mood for dancing or playing it cute with sixteen-year olds. Fred had always been pretty good company, so I was perfectly content.

"I haven't had a decent chance to ask you how it went up there in Edinburgh," I said after a lot of small talk.

"Wonderful, Bill, wonderful. Mary and I are engaged now and we're going to get married on my next leave. I only hope our flying is all over by then."

"It should be with any luck, touch wood. At the rate we're going now we should knock those ops off in another three weeks."

"If they keep coming up with targets we'll do it. By the way, did you have a good time in London?"

"So so. Of course it's almost enough just to get away from the base for a week. Maybe I'd have been smarter if I'd ditched the crew as well. Sometimes seeing the same people all the time can begin to get on your nerves, no matter how much you like them. The big thing in London right now, of course, is the buzz bomb. After hearing them come over night after night you realize why we've still got to hammer

116

away at Jerry. He's not going to give up until he's completely crushed."

"I guess you're right, but you begin to wonder if our raids really do any good."

"Maybe they don't do that much all by themselves. But don't forget the Yanks are hammering away as well day after day. It's bound to pay off pretty soon. But the hell with the war. I have to hand it to you, Fred, you really moved in on that girl of yours. You must have been sure of her right from the start."

"I was. It was just as though I didn't have to make up my mind at all. As if she was waiting all her life for me to show up. Now I feel as though I've known her all my life, and we've hardly had two weeks together. And her parents are fine people. I feel almost like one of the family. It's also given me a different outlook on the war. I have a lot more to fight for than I had before, if you know what I mean."

"I think I do, Fred." I was touched by his very serious manner. He was a real solid person, one of the best. You felt good knowing you had a guy like that in your crew.

"Say, can I ask you a favour?" he asked me a little later in the conversation.

"Sure. As long as it isn't a loan."

"No fear. It's just that I have a small parcel in my flight locker addressed to Mary. If anything should happen to me and you were still around I'd like her to be sure to get it. I'd feel a lot better if I knew you'd take care of it for me."

"No trouble at all. But the chances of you going for the chop and not having all of us along for company are pretty remote, don't you think?"

"Could be, Bill, but you never know. Look at all the crazy stories you hear. Take Pete, for instance. Why didn't I get it instead of him? It could have happened that way just as easily."

"The luck of the game, I guess. Maybe that 262 pilot was trying for the rear turret, not the mid-upper. Or he could have simply let it go in our general direction. Pete crapped out, that's all."

"Did he ever. But you know, even now I get this wild feeling that he still isn't dead. That he's on some kind of special leave, and some night we'll be sitting around having a beer and he'll walk right in and say, How's it going, you bunch of bullshooters, did I miss any real hot ones? I mean ops, not dames, of course."

"He was an only child, too, Fred. That's what bothers me so much. I'll bet it's broken his parents' heart. You know how close those Armenian families are."

There was a distinct pause in the conversation while we finished the rest of the glass of beer in front of us. I wondered if Fred was thinking the same thought that had suddenly flashed through my mind: eleven more lousy trips—will I make it or won't I?

"Let's have one more for the road," I suggested. "It's on me. We should make it nicely before closing."

"Don't mind if I do."

After we'd both sampled a fresh glass, Fred leaned across the table. His face had taken on a more serious look.

"I hope you won't laugh, but I've got an important personal question to ask you."

"This sure is our night to be serious, isn't it? But fire away. Only don't expect any brilliant answers. My brain's pretty foggy tonight."

"Fair enough. It's simply this: do you believe in sex before marriage?"

"That's an easy one to answer," I said. "Fred, old boy, I believe in sex at any time."

"Seriously, Bill, please."

"I'm serious as hell, believe me. If you've got a problem, though, let's hear it."

"It's about Mary and me, of course," Fred went on. "As you know, when I met her up there in Edinburgh she completely knocked me for a loop. I placed her on a pedestal, I guess, and wouldn't have dreamed of even suggesting sex to her. Not that we both didn't do a lot of heavy necking and got fairly worked up at times, believe me. It's just that we went so far and didn't go any further by a sort of mutual agreement. I'm sure if I'd worked on her seriously she would have given in eventually. But I was so damn happy the way things were going not to care that much. Being with her seemed enough at the time."

"This leave it started out the same way. Until one night her folks went out for the evening. We sat around in the parlour and she told me she'd been doing a lot of thinking about the two of us. As far as she was concerned we were as good as married, so why shouldn't we sleep together if we felt like it? If anything ever happened to you, she said to me, I'd never forgive myself for not having given you that at least. And you know, Bill, I was so touched by the way she'd said all this that I actually began to cry. And of course she was very sympathetic. Before very long we were very lovey-dovey on the sofa, and almost without realizing what we were doing began to make love together. I mean, it came so beautifully and naturally. After that night we made love whenever and wherever we could, which only amounted to a few more times. Back here looking at it all from a distance I wonder whether we did the right thing or not. I guess what I'm afraid of is that we may have somehow cheapened the whole act of love, which I'm sure should be one of the most wonderful experiences in a person's life."

As I listened to Fred I realized that I wasn't the only one who'd been having problems of the heart. He had certainly been having his share. But his Mary was cut from a far different cloth than my Prue. Certainly he had a problem, but it seemed nothing at all compared to mine. At least his solution was simple. There hadn't been one for Prue and me except to break up. For a moment I was tempted to tell him about the two of us, but my troubles didn't have much relationship to what was bothering him.

"Let me ask you this," I said. "Did you feel cheap at all while you were doing it? That's what you really have to ask yourself."

"I can't honestly say I did, and I'm sure Mary didn't."

"Then that should settle it. It's got to be right for both of you. I wouldn't worry any more about it. Just thank your lucky stars you've got such a wonderful girl."

"No doubt about that. Well, I hope you're right, Bill."

"I know I am."

A call of "Time, gentlemen, time" brought an end to further conversation. Ten o'clock. The evening seemed over before it had really begun. But it had been a good one for me. Fred didn't know it but he'd really helped me probably a lot more than I'd been able to help him.

"Come on, I'll drive you back," I said. "Want to bet we don't have a daylight tomorrow?"

"I'll bet you on the Stanley Cup but not on that. By the

way, who do you like this year? And for God's sake don't tell me the Leafs."

"Who else is there to like?" I asked him with all the built-in superiority, the absolute sureness of the native Torontonian.

"That answer is going to cost you money, chum. Two quid New York takes the bundle."

I would have bet him ten gladly if he'd suggested it. You simply couldn't back down on a bet where the home town team was involved. As it stood, however, the Leafs would knock off the Rangers or whoever without any trouble, so actually it was like taking candy from a baby.

"Let's make it a fiver at least to keep it interesting," I said. "That is, if you still think New York has any chance at all."

"It's a bet," Fred said, "but I sure hate to take money from my friends."

"Sure you do. Isn't it the truth?"

On the drive back to the base Fred talked away like a blue streak, mostly about his beloved. It was very obvious by now that the guy didn't have anyone he could talk buddy-buddy with, so now it was all coming out in a mad rush. The more he talked about his girl, of course, the more I thought about Prue. By the time I drove up to my parking spot beside Number One hangar I was feeling pretty sorry for myself. Instead of walking up to the billets with Fred I suddenly made up my mind, said goodnight to him, got in the car and drove a hell of a lot faster than I should have back into York.

At first I had the vague idea in the back of my mind of simply trying to find Joe, Walt and Max and raise some kind of late-evening hell. But something else was eating away at me, and I knew there was other business I had to attend to first. Like a man in a trance I drove through town and out the Tadcaster road.

I parked the car around the corner from Prue's house and walked back to her street. When I saw a sports car with a British military licence parked across from her place I was surprised I didn't react more strongly. Obviously I had been expecting to find some kind of a car there all the time. There wasn't any other explanation that made much sense.

I didn't know what my friend the Major drove but I'd bet a week's pay this low-slung sports job was his. Besides, Prue had never mentioned any other military friends. So it had to be this son-of-a-bitch.

All of a sudden I remembered her words of the night before. Something about her and the Major breaking up just before I'd come back off leave. Now it all began to add up to one word. Bullshit.

I stood there in the street trying to decide if I had enough nerve to go up close to the house and take a look in. The dim-out was on and the blinds were all drawn but I might manage to see something. Upstairs the house was in darkness, but downstairs lights were visible in what I knew to be the kitchen, dining-room and living-room.

I decided against being that snoopy, even if my curiosity was burning a hole in my pocket. Instead, I walked back to my car and got in. It was a quarter to eleven. The Major or whoever he was should be leaving fairly soon. His car would have to pass mine coming out and I'd have a good look at him. Why this was so important my mind refused to tell me.

I sat there until eleven, almost ready to drowse off from the beer I'd drunk earlier with Fred, but forcing myself to keep awake. Then all at once it seemed to get bloody cold in the car, so I started up the engine. When the engine was warmed up I turned on the heater full blast. But for a long time I couldn't feel any warmth at all.

By eleven-fifteen I was fed up with waiting. I turned off the engine and got out of the car again. I walked back to Prue's street again and looked down its short length. The sports car was still parked outside. So whoever it was in there was taking his own sweet time leaving. I went slowly down the street until I stood opposite the house. There were no lights whatever showing now, the house was in total darkness.

For a minute or two I was so mad I could have picked up the nearest rock and thrown it right through a window. But a voice inside me kept repeating, you've had it, chum, you've been had, so give it all up, why don't you? There are plenty of other fish in the sea. Fish in the sea. I listened to that voice all the long drive back to York. It didn't help much, but it was all the sense I could make out of things at the moment.

Still not really knowing why I headed down to the Palaise. Maybe the boys would still be there. The place closed at eleven-thirty if I remembered rightly. If I knew my crew mates at all they'd have something lined up for themselves once the dance was over, some young things they figured on the make.

I parked the Standard across from the dancehall and went upstairs. There was no ticket-seller on duty, so I knew the dance was almost over. But the orchestra was blaring away off the lobby as though things would go on all night.

As I stepped into the crowded ballroom the band finished playing what I vaguely recognized as *One O'Clock Jump* and immediately swung into the strains of *Auld Lang Syne* in fox-trot tempo. I'd timed it exactly right. Now all I had to do was find my three boozed-up friends.

I sat down at the nearest empty table and spotted them one by one as they came into view on the crowded dance-floor. The whole room was one gigantic hot box. Sweat glistened on the faces of the dancers as they glided by.

Then the band came to an abrupt stop and the dancers started to pour off the dance-floor. Max, who had a young blonde with him, noticed me and waved. A minute later he came over to the table.

"Never thought I'd really be glad to see you, pal," he said by the way of greeting, "but then you never know, do you? Point is," he went on, slurring his words now and then, "Walt and I have two young bitches in heat who also have two girl friends available after midnight. Joe is game for a blind date, how about you? Or are you above this sort of thing?"

"If Joe is agreeable what have I got to lose? Where are the two friends at the moment?"

"Still at work, apparently. They come off shift at twelve. Munitions factory or something. Big-breasted, fat-assed, you know the type. Just the thing for a cool winter night. Hope you can cut the mustard, Bill old cock."

"Don't worry about me, star. I suppose you want me to provide transport? Probably the only reason you're dealing me in."

"How'd you guess, chum? Now, come on over and meet the little ladies. And no horning in or I'll kick your balls off."

I hadn't realized how big a load on Max had. Now I knew he was really flying by the way he was talking. It was a poor time to argue with him.

"The jail bait is all yours," I assured him. "By the way,

how's the booze situation? Anything left or have you and Walt guzzled it all?"

"All in good time. We've got a mickey saved. Sometimes these broads need an extra drink or two to lower their pants."

He led the way over to a table where Walt had his arm around a sixteen-year old made up to look like twenty-two. The girl that Max had wasn't any older but looked very sexy, even with her slightly long nose. Joe looked uncomfortable sitting there at the table as odd-man-out, and seemed to brighten up considerably when I arrived.

After I was quickly introduced we left the almost empty Palaise and drove toward an older part of the city. Walt, his girl, and Joe sat in the back seat, Max and his charmer were up front with me. His girl must have had a drink or two already by the free and easy way she very quickly and openly placed one hand on my knee. Her action didn't seem to bother my driving any and Max wasn't any the wiser. He and Walt must have killed at least a crock between them; they both swore like troopers and talked pretty wildly. Both girls didn't seem to mind in the least.

Apparently our passengers, who now turned out to be sisters, had to arrive home before their father left to go to work on the graveyard shift at the Municipal Water Works. Their mother was dead, so they did what they pleased when he wasn't around. They were good friends with two older girls who very conveniently lived next door. These two had parents who arrived home from the pub every night at ten-thirty and poured themselves into bed. The thought came to mind that our blind dates might turn out to be the best bets for a change.

We got the girls home with five minutes to spare. They lived on an old street with ancient row housing down both sides of it. Before long what had to be their father emerged carrying his lunch pail and disappeared around the corner. We piled out of the car and the girls let us in with a great deal of horseplay. Mabel and Sally should be home very soon, Joe and I were assured. They usually stop in here for tea. They'll get more than that tonight, I said, and both girls tittered.

As it turned out we didn't have too long to wait. And a good thing at that, the way Max and Walt were fooling around with the sisters in the kitchen. We had tea and a drink all round to warm up to the business at hand. I paired off with Sally, who looked at least twenty-one and still smelled slightly of sweat. She had a charming Yorkshire accent and I soon found out she'd been in the Land Army until she was kicked out for getting pregnant.

This and much more she told me as we held hands in the kitchen, sipping a second cup of tea. I was playing it cool and not rushing things, the whole night was ahead of me. The other three couples were distributed through the house by now, the only signs of life from them being a few nervous female giggles that made both of us smile.

"Come on, love," my girl said finally, "let's find us a lie-down, I've had a bloody long night of it on my feet." We had to settle for a slightly saggy couch in a corner of what looked like the dining-room. The house wasn't that warm, so we used both her cloth coat and my greatcoat for a kind of combination blanket. That was, of course, after she'd slipped out of her dress and I'd parked my pants and tunic over a chair. She had an unusually slender waist for such well-proportioned thighs and buttocks, and my hand wouldn't begin to reach around one of her breasts. I was primed like a bull by now and made the most of it with her caressing fingers and her earthy whispers in my ear. Once locked in I fought the good fight to burst finally to freedom in one straining, glorious upheaval. . . .

After that we must have slept like two children in each others' arms. I awoke with darkness still in the room and her telling me softly it was six-fifteen and we'd all have to be out of the house before seven. I can be up in no time at all, I whispered in her ear, and to convince her turned her over on her back again.

When it was all over, when we were breathing heavily from the good, honest work of it, she asked, "Who's Prue, love? You yelled and yelled the name out in the middle of the night. Damn near scared the wits out of me, you did."

Good thing it wasn't something else, I was tempted to wise-crack, but I really didn't feel that light-hearted at the moment. So I'd called her name out in my sleep, had I? I'd have to watch that little thing in future. It could get me in a hell of a lot of trouble some day.

19

Briefing at five-thirty in the morning! I looked at the luminous dial of my watch in the dark of our hut and still couldn't believe it. Four bloody o'clock. It was still the middle of the night. What a time to wake human beings up.

Dave stopped my grumbling as we began dressing with the light on. Human beings? We're Air Force, remember? What really bothers me is missing chapel on a Sunday morning, I said. I wasn't the only one who had lousy jokes up his sleeve.

At five-fifteen Dave and I joined a disgruntled, half-asleep mass of aircrew in the Briefing Room. The morning before it had been bad enough, being called out at six with a seven-thirty briefing for a milk-run to Gladback. But five-thirty was something else again.

It turned out we had a new target today, Munster, a city a little north of Dortmund and due east of Nijmegen according to the war map up front.

"Looks like another set-up," Max whispered to the rest of us as the C.O. gave us one of his usual pep talks. "It's turning out to be a lovely war after all."

It certainly looked that way. Little or no fighter opposition expected, moderate to light flak, good weather over the target. Walking over to the flight hut I kicked the loose stones with my best soccer follow-through, feeling fairly cheerful in spite of the early hour.

"You're in a lively mood this morning," Dave remarked. "You must have sneaked in an extra bowl of porridge at breakfast."

"You mean that slop we had to eat was porridge? My Scots grandmother would turn over twice in her grave if she could hear you, David, my boy. No, I feel good for no real reason I can think of."

"Bully for you, chum."

125

The rest of the crew must have shared my mood that morning. They horsed around in the flight hut and then in the lorry taking us out to dispersal. Even after we got to our area and Walt, Max and I were looking over good old "N" for "Nan" to make sure our ground crew hadn't slipped up on the obvious, the rest of the boys got so childishly playful that Walt finally had to tell them to knock it off. But it was still a good sign when a crew could behave like that after fifteen ops over Germany, milk runs or no milk runs.

As we took off at 0702 the sun came bursting up over the horizon. I thought of all the several hundred other Group Halifaxes and Lancasters taking off this morning, the Hallys bound for Munster, the Lancs part of a bigger Bomber Command show laid on for Hanover.

This was the earliest we'd ever flown in daylight. Before long we picked up our usual fighter escort. Then a large formation of Liberators passed above us to the left. With the bright sunlight glinting off their fuselages they resembled a school of giant silver fish swimming in perfect order. There was one other bonus. The fine weather gave me my first chance in a long time to map-read over England.

We droned on across the Channel to the Dutch Coast. Then began that continuous zigzag that was supposed to keep us out of range of the numerous Jerry flak belts.

I'd scribbled down the bombing strategy for Munster and now I looked over my notes. The gaggle was to feint an attack coming in south-east of the city, take a ninety degree turn to the north, then a final ninety degree turn to bring us in downwind from the north-west. It sounded perfect on paper.

Dave had asked me on the trip over if he could come up front in the nose and watch the target. It's a little frustrating sitting back there at the plotting desk all the time wondering what the hell's going on when the action starts. Just once I'd like to see what an attack really looks like. It's fine with me, I'd told him, if Walt says yes. I've already asked him, Dave said. Great, come up as soon as I take over the aircraft, I said. You'll see all there is to see when we go into our bombing run. But please try to keep out of my way, will you? I have enough trouble as it is on my own, I concluded.

"You're sure it's all right? I don't want to foul up anything."

"What the hell. Glad to have a little company."

Almost too soon it seemed to me we'd drawn opposite Munster at around twelve thousand feet, still ten miles west of our target. Walt was banking to the left in a large "S" turn to come in on our pre-arranged heading. It was cold as an old bitch in the bomb-aimer's compartment where I was already kneeling before the bombsight, checking things out for the final time. At the completion of the turn I talked with Walt, took over the aircraft from him. As Dave came through into the compartment I looked over to my left. There, at our exact height and upwind on what was a perfectly clear sunny day, I saw a huge continuous black cloud of billowy dark smoke now several miles wide and mushrooming larger and larger as I continued to watch it in complete disbelief. So our approach hadn't fooled the Jerrys one bit. Probably the two gaggles flying ahead of us had tipped them off and given them time to adjust to our move. There had to be a lot of flak batteries down below to produce all this concentrated fire. At the moment it looked as though they were sending up an all-out curtain barrage. So we'd walked right into the trap. Now that their guns had us predicted it was too late to do anything about it. Unless of course we turned back. Which of course was unthinkable. I couldn't watch that black cloud any more. I turned back to my bombsight.

"Christ, Walt," I heard Max's startled voice over the intercom, "look at all that crap piled up over there. That barrage must be a mile thick. You'd think somebody sent on our headings to the bastards. How the hell are we ever going to get through all that garbage? It's bloody murder."

"Pilot to crew," Walt's voice sounded next, perhaps trying to rally us a little after Max's near-panic outburst, "hang on, boys, Max is right, we may be in for quite a ride. But we'll make it without any sweat. Now I want everybody right on their toes. We're flying a pretty tight gaggle. If you see somebody coming too close, sing out loud and clear. Got that, gunners?"

I was busy with my bombsight now, getting ready for the run in to the target. I'd felt cold all over inside my flying suit five minutes ago, now I was beginning to sweat in it. I was crouched over the device with Dave somewhere close behind me, waiting for the aiming point to come up.

Suddenly Dave grabbed me hard by the shoulder.

"Look at that poor son-of-a-bitch," he blurted out over the intercom, his voice high-pitched, almost hysterical.

I looked up, slightly irritated at being interrupted in the middle of readying the bombsight. No matter what else was happening I still had to get through my last-minute preparations. Nothing else really mattered. But I glanced up, stirred by the fear in his voice.

There, not more than a hundred yards ahead of us, the "H" of its silhouette showing it to be unmistakably a Hally, one of our squadron aircraft was on fire. Even as the two of us watched breathlessly one wing was falling off. A direct flak hit. Now the whole aircraft seemed to buckle, to disintegrate all at once. God. I counted one, two, three parachutes, then a fourth as some of the crew tried to jump for it.

Then all at once we were in the middle of that huge black endless cloud ourselves. Flak fragments started to hit us right away, their sound heavy, ominous, every shell-burst rocking us more and more. The hits felt like huge chunks of coal shovelled with all of someone's might against our undercarriage. Now they seemed to rain against it. God, I thought, this could be it. We'll never get out of this. My heart began to pump like crazy. My whole body inside the flying suit seemed to be swimming in sweat. I was scared worse than I'd ever been in my whole life before, I suddenly realized. Right to the bloody marrow. O God, get us out. Please. Nan, old girl, hold together. I felt both my hands shaking.

I heard a loud splash behind me. I turned just in time to see Dave whip off his face mask and bend over awkwardly. His face was chalk-white; he was puking his guts out on the compartment floor. I pushed my mask back.

"All right, Dave?"

He nodded. The smell of the vomiting almost made me want to be sick. But I took hold of myself, shook myself out of it. I slipped on my mask again, made sure I was still plugged in O.K., and turned back to the bombsight. I'd make the bloody run if it was the last thing I did.

The target was coming up swiftly below. A target which by now was only one huge whirling sea of dust and smoke. With all the time flak still thudding, crackling away at the undercarriage beneath me.

"Steady," I called finally to Walt, after a couple of corrections, then "bombs away." As I pressed the release tit it was as though a huge weight had suddenly lifted from my shoulders. I straightened up and looked around. Dave had left the compartment. I turned my head back. We were still hurtling through a sky filled with dark flak bursts. But that black wall of hellish black smoke was behind us. Still, it felt like an eternity waiting for the signal that all our camera pictures were taken.

Then Walt's voice broke over the intercom, somehow managing to be crisp and cheerful. "O.K., boys, we're going home. Can you get me a heading, Bill? I'm afraid Dave's still being sick up here at the escape hatch."

I pushed myself to my feet, and half-stumbled back into Dave's cabin. My legs felt rubbery, as if they really didn't belong to me. Our first return heading was on Dave's pad clipped to the navigation table. I gave it to Walt and he swung "Nan" around, engines all out now, diving a little to pick up more speed. We'd made it. We'd come through. We weren't dead. No more flak. No more dying. All of a sudden I wanted to laugh, to shout out loud. Then almost as quickly I felt tired, drained of all energy. It was a real effort to return to the nose, watching out for the mess Dave had splattered over the floor. Our ground crew would love cleaning that up when we got back. My body felt at least a hundred years old under the flying suit. But the sun was pouring into the nose, brilliant, blinding yellow sunshine. It forked at my eyes, making them blink crazily in the glare. And all around me clouds, white fluffy islands of them, gliding so peacefully along. That was it. Everything was suddenly peaceful. The evil darkness was gone from the sky. The threat of death also gone.

But all I could really see at that moment was the picture burned into my brain of that Hally from our squadron on fire straight ahead of us, then the wing breaking off. The parachutes one, two, three, then a final fourth. No more. Four out of seven. The rest of the crew hurled into nightmare oblivion. And I but for the grace of God one of them.

20

That night I drank as much beer as I could hold at the mess but still it didn't help me sleep very much. Added to that I had a brand new nightmare: the Hally breaking right up in front of me on the bombing run. Toward morning I must have unloosened somehow. It was ten-thirty when I woke up. Dave was still pounding the pillow, which was unusual for him. I took a short trip down the hall, came back to the room and promptly fell back to sleep again.

Dave moving around in the room about noon woke me up again.

"Feel like a little chow? I've just been over to the hut. Our keen-ass Flight Commander has us down for a practice flip at 1335."

"Christ, we made it yesterday, didn't we? How sharp do we have to be?"

"You'd better ask him that. Come on, shake a leg and get something in your stomach."

"After yesterday," I kept on, "all the practice we need, Dave, is how to drop our bombs at least ten miles from the aiming-point and get away with it."

"Very funny. I'm glad to see you haven't lost your peculiar sense of humour."

"Anyway," I said, " I guess from now on you'll be spending all your spare time up front with me." As soon as I'd said it I wished I hadn't. Me and my big mouth.

"I'm sorry as hell that happened, Bill. It was too much of a shock seeing that Hally, I guess. I know Walt was plenty sore at me blowing a bird right beside the cockpit. I really didn't think I had that much to puke up."

"Forget I ever mentioned it. And screw Walt. I felt like doing the same thing, to tell you the truth. I was just lucky I could keep it down. Who got the chop, by the way?"

130

"A freshman crew. I guess they never knew what hit them."

"They sure didn't. Well, some of them got out, so it could have been worse. Now, let's get a little lunch. I hope it isn't bangers today."

It wasn't, which made me feel a little brighter. Down at the dispersal hut all the talk was about Munster. I'd already named it Black Sunday for my own future private reference. Group had lost three Hallibags in the raid, all the casualties in a force of a hundred and seventy five. Nobody knew for sure, but I was willing to bet all three had been in our third and last gaggle.

Walt was there, looking, I thought, a little more serious than usual.

"You know, Bill, if they'd ordered us out on another one today I think they'd have pretty much of a mutiny on their hands. As it is, this practice hop's a lot of balls. Not only did we get up before the crack of dawn yesterday but we had that diversion to Croft. That meant another landing and take-off. We were on the go for over twelve hours in a row. So we get H2S, bombing, F/A and A/Sea for a couple of hours as a reward. I'll sure be glad when this bloody tour is over."

At one-fifteen the covered lorry we rode in to dispersal picked us up in front of our flight hut. We were a pretty gloomy crew that climbed aboard. All of us viewed this practice run as really unnecessary, cutting in on what should have been a lay off after the fairly tough grind of the past week. Max and Joe tried a little horseplay to try to lighten up our mood, but we weren't buying it today. This extra duty was just about the last straw.

"For Christ's sake," Max said finally in exasperation, "snap out of it, you guys, or I'll call my birthday off and you can all buy your own beer tonight."

"No kidding," I responded, "you were really born, were you? I always thought you were pushed up out of the pavement at Portage and Main."

"Very funny, Sutcliffe. Keep it up and you'll get yourself a thick ear, no charge, either."

"Any time you think you're big enough, chum."

But it was only a half-hearted exchange in which none of

the others in the lorry took the slightest interest. The crew had certainly struck bottom today.

We drew up at the dispersal area where "C" for "Charlie", our aircraft for the day, was waiting, It suddenly struck me how unattractive a Halifax looked from the side, the straight-back line of her unrelieved, except for the slight curve of the undercarriage. She looked business-like enough, but in no way graceful. You had to see her head-on or following behind to see what truly trim lines she could show. I wondered how long our riggers would take to put "Nan" back into shape after the beating she'd taken yesterday. "Twelve flak holes" I'd written in my log book; each of them were bit enough to stick your head through. But I'd come to regard her as an aircraft with an especially charmed life. Flying any other ship made the odds a little tighter.

"Bloody aircraft's more battered than old "Nan" is," was Max's comment as we began a quick walk-round check of "Charlie." "Good thing we're not flying this crate out of England."

"That's a hell of a wind," I remarked a minute later, as I came out from under the bomb bay doors after making sure our practice bombs were fused and properly placed, "almost right out of the north. Could be rain later on. You know, if it isn't the fog it's the rain or the wind," I went on. "If Jerry had to fly out of Yorkshire he'd have given up the air war long ago."

"Which reminds me," Walt said, "I think the goddamn flight plan calls for using runway 270. That stupid jerk of an Operations Officer. I'll get onto the Tower as soon as we get inside. Doesn't he ever check for a wind change, especially on a day like this?"

Five minutes later, with our four engines now running up to the minimum temperature, I heard Walt call the Control Tower over the intercom. I was seated on the floor back in our regular spot in the rear fuselage along with Dave, Joe, Fred and Ed Barber.

"This is "C" for "Charlie". Please re-confirm we are to use runway 270. Repeat, strong north wind blowing. Runway 010 indicated."

The answer came back so quickly that the idiot in the tower couldn't even have had the time to let Walt's words

sink into his thick skull. He was obviously upset at having a
written order challenged; his voice sounded deeply irritated.

"Control to "C" for "Charlie". Repeat, you will take off as
directed. Regard this as a direct order, Flight Lieutenant."

So that was that. I wondered what kind of clod they had in
charge up in the tower today. He was the world's prize fat-
head, no doubt about that.

While I was still wondering if Walt would fight the order,
our aircraft began to move slowly forward. That meant Walt
was taking her out of the dispersal bay onto the perimeter
track and along to the runway. It looked as though he was
going ahead with it after all. Unless he deliberately chose to
disobey the order and refuse the take-off he didn't have much
choice under the circumstances. I'll bet he gives that nob in
the tower a real talking to when he gets back if he doesn't
punch his nose in first, I thought.

"That wind's worse than ever now," I said to Joe seated
beside me. "Uncle Walt's going to have to be awfully good
on this one."

"Don't be a worry wort," Joe answered. "We've had a
damn sight worse weather than this and we never worried.
Walt can make it if anybody can, chum. Have a little
confidence, eh?"

I didn't say anything more. What was the use? But because
I'd soloed as a pilot and flown Wellingtons at O.T.U. and
Hallys once or twice at H.C.U. I knew a lot better than Joe or
the others what Walt was faced with here. But perhaps it was
better that way. We'd soon know one way or the other.
Worrying about it wouldn't help one little bit.

The time seemed endless to me until we turned onto the
runway. The narrow ribbed fuselage around us seemed to
press in on me somehow, much the same way as my narrow
perspex nose sometimes did. I could hear the wind buffeting
the sides of the aircraft, then the whining roar it made gust-
ing past. Then the wind noise was totally drowned out as
Walt revved the powerful Hercules XVI engines up for the final time.

All at once we seemed to be hurtling down the runway,
throttles wide open. I could tell we were gaining speed, but it
somehow didn't feel exactly right. Suddenly I knew with a
sinking feeling inside of me that the aircraft was being pulled

off its course. Walt was fighting that wind with everything he had but was losing the battle.

At that instant a flash picture lit up in my brain of old Slim Cochrane sweating to get our Wimpey back on the runway at Topcliffe the day the starboard engine quit just as we were airborne. With me beside him as co-pilot, utterly useless, half-paralysed with fear, watching with an almost insane fascination as the R.P.M. indicator unwound like a clock in reverse. Then we were coming down in a hurry, and while I braced myself as the runway came rushing up, Slim was cutting magneto switches, pulling up the undercarriage, closing off petrol cocks as he fought the wheel with his other free hand. . . .

Christ, I wanted to shout out, get the bloody undercarriage up and grease her. Do it now, Walt, right now, or we're cooked. Now or never.

But instead we were roaring faster than ever down the bloody runway. Walt was still going for it. He was taking the big gamble. You crazy nut, something hollered inside of me, you'll never make it now, not in a hundred years.

I couldn't sit there a moment longer with my hands clasped behind my head, legs outstretched, head forward between my knees in the approved manner, the way the rest of the crew were doing. Waiting almost calmly for the inevitable crash. Fear suddenly gripped my body in a way I'd never known it before. I felt trapped, waiting without a hope for death to come along any second now. As I sprang to my feet we seemed to leave the edge of the runway. Then the aircraft began a terrible, bump-grinding ride over the farmland lying off the runway. You could feel "C" for "Charlie" starting to break up under the beating it was taking.

"Get down, get down," Dave screamed, and grabbed at my legs. With one tremendous effort I twisted free and pulled open the hatchway slightly to the rear of where we were sitting. A blast of cold air struck me at once, almost knocking me over. But I somehow stayed on my feet, clinging to the side of the fuselage. The country outside the hatch was going by in one frightening green blur now. The aircraft was now rocking, plunging, bumping, dragging, still carried along at almost the same speed, like something out of control. Out of the corner of my eye I saw Dave trying to get to his feet, no doubt with the idea of pulling me down again. What a crazy guy. Fear engulfed me completely. It was now or never. With a last wild effort I flung myself out of the hatch door, plunging against the killer wind roaring insanely through the hatchway. I was conscious of floating entirely free for several seconds, of more green blur, then something snapped and blackness poured at me, swallowed me whole in one tremendous gulp.

21

As I opened my eyes I was conscious of three things all at once: that my forehead was bathed in sweat, that my left side and shoulder ached almost unbearably, and that a pretty female face was looking down at me.

When my eyes focused better I saw that the face belonged to a young woman dressed in the white, blue-trimmed working dress of an Air Force Nursing Sister.

"So you decided to wake up, did you?" she asked very pleasantly, a slight hint of relief in her voice.

"I knew you'd expect it," I said. My eyes looked away from her face for a moment and around the small, white-painted room. There was another bed next to mine, made up with a red hospital blanket lying across the foot of it.

"Do you know where you are?" she asked me.

"A hospital."

"Yes. West Moor Hospital. You've been here since one-forty this afternoon. Remember—your plane crashed."

I suddenly remembered. All of it came rushing back. "C" for "Charlie" charging hell-bent down the runway, then rampaging off onto farm land. My wild jump out the hatchway. Then darkness.

"What time is it?" I asked the nurse.

"Five thirty. You've been lost to the world all that time. You must have taken quite a knock on the head. By the way, my name is Nursing Sister Gordon. Can I get you anything? A drink of water?"

I realized then that my mouth was bone dry. I was actually very, very thirsty.

"Please, I'd like that."

I gulped down the glass of water that she brought, then had to ask right away for the bedpan. Before I'd got it into position I experienced several small agonies shifting ever so

136

slightly in the bed. I could tell now that I had some lovely bruises on my right hip, thigh and shoulder.

After she'd gone away for the second time and returned, I asked her what had happened to my aircraft.

"Sorry, but I'm not supposed to say anything. Your Flight Commander is coming in as soon as you can see him. Then the M.O. will want to look you over again. They'll answer all your questions. So please be patient and relax."

"You can't even tell me what happened to my crew, Sister?"

"I have to follow my orders, Mr. Sutcliffe. You understand, don't you? Now, can I get you something to eat? It will have to be pretty light for the moment. Some custard or ice cream? After the doctor's been in you can probably have a real meal if you feel you can manage it."

"I'm not hungry, thanks. And please, Sister, if you'd get word to my Flight Commander that I'd like to see him as soon as he can make it."

"I'll phone him right away for you. Now you be a good boy and lie quiet for a while."

I didn't have much choice. It was too bloody painful to move much. The news about the crew didn't sound too good, the way the nursing sister acted. Old Bowman, my Flight Commander, was probably elected to tell me the bad news. The whole gang could be banged up worse than I was. There was a hell of a whiplash in any kind of crash like that. If Max and Walt were in hospital they'd be in agony right about now being unable to get to a bar and have a couple of pints.

My Flight Commander didn't arrive until a good hour and a half later. In the meantime another nursing sister, a Miss Thibadeau, had taken over from Miss Gordon. She said that according to my chart I had suffered shock and some painful bruises, but apparently nothing was broken. I'd probably have X-rays in the morning to double-check. While Miss Gordon had been pretty, Miss Thibadeau was close to being beautiful. She filled out her nurse's uniform very interestingly indeed.

From the first moment Ralph Bowman walked into my room I could tell from his face that the news was bad. He was a real nice guy, perhaps two or three years older than me, a pilot almost through his second tour with a D.F.C. I'd been told he was a pretty useful halfback on the Toronto

Varsity squad before joining up. He was obviously uncomfortable as he stood there beside my bed.

"How do you feel now, Bill? You don't look too bad to me. I wouldn't mind a couple of days in here myself with old Thibadeau on the night shift. Looks like a nice soft pinch to me."

I suppose he was only trying to be cheerful, to try to get me in as good a mood as possible for the coming let-down. I sure wouldn't have wanted to be in his shoes. But he was my Flight Commander and I expected him to give it to me straight with a minimum of bullshit.

"It sure looks like a beauty, Ralph, although I'm not sure yet she's the pinching type. I'll have to do a little more research first. But I'm sure you didn't come here just to talk about Thibadeau's backside. How're the boys doing? The nurses won't tell me a bloody thing. You'd think it was top secret or something. What the hell's going on, Ralph? I want to know and right now."

I knew my voice had started on a mild conversational tone but had gradually increased to a half-shout. I was sorry, sorry as hell, but I couldn't help it. I didn't want to roast Ralph Bowman, but someone was going to have to pay, even if it was only a little.

"Cool down, Bill, for Christ's sake. You think this is easy for me? I'm just sorry as hell I'm the one elected to tell you. They all bought it this afternoon, I'm afraid. I've never seen a worse mess in my life." And his voice shook a little as he said it.

There it was. God, there it was. Bought it. Killed. Smashed all up. Now it suddenly struck me that I hadn't accepted for one moment what my mind had wanted to believe. That bull about them only being injured. I'd really known all along it was a lot of balls. You knew, deep down, didn't you, that they'd gone for a shit. It was written right in the nurses' faces. So you're the lucky survivor. You made the lucky jump. The rest all got banged to hell. "C" for "Charlie" had carried them all the way to wherever. They'd all stayed with the ship but me. They'd put their lives on the line all together and had crapped out. Even old Walt hadn't been able to pull the rabbit out of the hat this time. Old Walt, gentle Dave, boozy Max, Ed Barber the Silent One, poor Fred, easy-going Joe. Gone. Wiped out. The whole bloody works. All those dead faces. All those lifeless bodies. My crew, my buddies, my friends.

And all because of that crud in the control-tower, that stupid bastard. That prick. That murderer. The son-of-a-bitch not listening to Walt at all when he'd called in from the runway. You will take off as ordered. I'd never forget the smug, assured sound of that voice for the rest of my life. The stupid turd.

"Hey, Bill, say something. Don't just sit there." It was Ralph's voice now in my ear.

"Fuck you, Ralph. Fuck them all," I heard myself shouting now. "Fuck the nurses, fuck the doctors, fuck the whole fucking Air Force."

That must have shook Ralph up. He half-grabbed my shoulder. And now he was shouting too.

"Snap out of it, Bill. This isn't Sunday School. This is war, this is killing. Shit. I've lost two crews myself. I know what you're going through. But you've got to pull yourself together."

That brought me around a little. I realized that all this wasn't fair to Ralph. I was only putting him through the wringer.

I tried hard to calm down. I even tried to talk calmly again.

"I'm O.K. now, I think." I wasn't really, but I had to make a start somewhere. "Sorry, Ralph. No hard feelings, eh? This is my problem, isn't it? Now do you mind telling me what happened exactly?"

"Apparently the aircraft took out a storage Nissen hut right after you jumped, caught fire, blew up very soon after. The firefighters never even got to her. Three airmen in that hut went for the chop as well."

"Oh God," was all I could find to say. Not only six but nine. All snuffed out in a few seconds of hell. It was too much to understand. But I was beginning to learn a little. The Air Force was one huge killing machine. Our job was to kill the enemy, the Germans, as quickly and as neatly as possible. But sometimes the machine back-fired and killed some of its own. And of course the enemy was allowed a percentage. As long as he didn't go beyond the set figure nobody worried very much. As long as there were always new bodies to fill the empty beds and sit in the empty chairs at the mess.

As long as there were new faces to replace the old ones, so
that after a time all the faces looked somehow alike and one
was as good as another.

Now there was something I had to say to Ralph and then I
hoped he'd go, fast.

"You know, Ralph, they never had a snowball's chance in
hell. The wind had shifted almost due north but the stupid
bastard in the tower wouldn't change the runway. Walt argued with the son-of-a-bitch but it was no use. He ordered us
to go. Walt should have told him to fuck himself and refused
to budge."

"That explains a lot, Bill, and you'll have a chance to put
it all down in writing just as soon as you're able. But let's face
it, even if you do report it, that won't make that much difference, will it? It won't bring any of them back. God, how I'm
starting to hate this war."

"If it only keeps that crazy bugger from killing some other
crew it'll be worth it, won't it?"

"Of course you're right, Bill. Now I'm going to get out of
here. Remember, don't let all this throw you. You've still got
to keep going somehow. That's all I want to say. I'll try to
get in tomorrow if you want me."

"Sure, Ralph. And thanks for everything."

That was one swell guy, I decided after he was gone. So
he'd lost two crews himself. Then he must know how it felt a
lot better than me. But I guess he hadn't let it get to him too
much or he couldn't have kept flying day after day. I suppose
you had to keep it all at a distance whether you liked the
idea or not. He was a beautiful guy, really. Maybe he had a
charmed life after forty-five ops. I hoped he had. The Service
had the habit of destroying too many of the good guys and
leaving the second-raters, the bastards, behind.

Then, without knowing really why, I started to cry. The
tears welled out of my eyes, streamed down my cheeks. I felt
I couldn't stop them and I didn't know if I wanted to that
much. After a couple of minutes when I wanted to stop, I
found I couldn't. It was a strange sensation. So I'd lost
control. I'd let go, given in.

Right in the middle of it Nursing Sister Thibadeau came
into the room.

"Get the hell out of here, will you?" was all I said, and she
went out without a word and closed the door behind her.

Thank God for that. I must have cried for another five minutes until I'd used up all my tears. I felt better then, a little silly, too, but more relaxed. Before I realized it I'd fallen off to sleep.

It was a deep, deep sleep and when I woke up it was dark in the room. Someone had turned on a night light beside the bed. I lay there, not caring about anything, not wanting to think or even shift my body. I had one hell of a headache. My mouth was very dry again. And I could tell from the way my stomach was acting that I was very, very hungry.

Someone knocked on the door a little later. I supposed it was one of the nurses.

"Come in, please," I said.

It was Nursing Sister Thibadeau. She had a very nice smile. How was I feeling now? Could she get me something to eat? You really should try. All this was said with her beautiful French-Canadian accent.

I felt like a heel. It had been very rude swearing at her like that. After all, she'd only been doing her duty.

"I'm very sorry for the way I spoke to you. Please forgive me, Sister."

"I understand," she said, "you really don't have to apologize, though it sounds nice. You've had a very bad day. Now, you're really not supposed to have anything solid to eat yet, but what they don't know won't hurt them, will it?"

"I suppose not." What else could I say to that when it had become a cosy little conspiracy between the two of us?

She came back very shortly afterwards with a tray. I had some chicken white meat, a slice of bread, a bowl of Jello, and a pot of tea. I felt a lot better almost right away.

I must have dozed off after that, falling into what turned out to be a very restless sleep. In which at some stage I was back in "C" for "Charlie". We were all huddled together in the fuselage as the aircraft started to bump and rock horribly, then began to make that horrible scraping noise. I was trying to get on my feet to make it to the hatch opening, but Dave had hold of one leg and Ed Barber the other and I started to punch out desperately at their faces, but I kept missing and they kept holding on. Then I got one leg free and kicked as hard as I could at them, at the same time lashing out with my fists. . . .

I woke with the light on in the room and Nursing Sister

Thibadeau bending over the bed, trying to straighten out the covers I'd managed to kick off. I could feel my whole body covered with sweat, the pajamas I had on soaked, clinging to my chest and legs.

"That was a good one you were having," she said calmly, after she'd wiped my face with a damp cloth, and I had more or less settled back in bed again. "Don't worry, half the boys in here have them. If you didn't we'd think there was really something wrong. Some have a lot worse. The ones who scream are something. One or two boys we've even had to strap in bed at night. How does your thigh and shoulder feel?"

I told her my shoulder was throbbing but the thigh bruises weren't bothering me too much.

"I think we'll give you a needle. That way you'll relax and get a good night's sleep."

She was right. Within five minutes I was dead to the world and as far as I know slept like a baby. Nursing Sister Gordon had to shake me awake in the morning. I was definitely hungry this time. I went through juice, hot cereal, bacon and eggs in short order and could have managed seconds on the bacon and eggs. As it was, though, I had only nicely finished my last sip of coffee when the M.O. came in.

I'd seen the Squadron Leader a few times in the Mess. He was very good at bending the elbow. A handsome-looking man, perhaps fifty, with some grey showing in his rather severe haircut. Rumour had it around the hospital that he and Nursing Sister Thibadeau were making it very hot and heavy together. If I'd been in the Doc's shoes I'd have been trying for exactly the same thing. Thibadeau was a lot of woman.

The M.O. looked me over, touched a few tender spots. There were a number of these.

"There'll be X-rays this afternoon, Sutcliffe. I don't think there's anything broken but we might as well make damn well sure. The bruises should be pretty well healed within a week. I want you to get up and walk around all you want to. As soon as you can dress without too much discomfort I'm gong to discharge you and send you on a week's leave. Then I'll look you over when you get back. After that you should be able to resume flying. How does that sound to you?"

"Great," I said, "especially the part about the week's leave.

Yes, I want to finish my tour if at all possible. I owe those other boys."

"That's the spirit. You know, I thought you were dead when I first saw you down there off the runway. I still can't figure out how you didn't get at least a skull fracture out of it. I suppose it was the freak way you landed and your flying suit that saved you. You're really a lucky young man."

"I know it. I just hope it stays with me for another month or so. Say, can I ask you a big favour?" I said as he started to move away from the bed.

"You can try me."

"I haven't heard when my crew's being buried but I'd sure like to be there if at all possible."

"I understand. I'll check with your squadron on that. Then if those X-rays are O.K. this afternoon I don't see why not."

"Thanks very much."

"Don't thank me. Thank whoever gave you that hard head."

Shortly before lunch I had a visitor. Jake Rosen, the bombardier I'd chummed around with on my leave in London, stuck his friendly kisser through the doorway.

"How are you making out, mate? Pretty posh digs by the look of it."

"Come on in, you old bugger, before you scare all the nurses to death."

"I really go for nurses. I think it's because they look so virginal in all that white. I think I'll have to log some hospital time myself."

"Just figure out an easier way to get here than I did."

"That was bloody rough about Walt and the boys. Just when you had your tour pretty well sewed up, too."

"Eighteen trips. And we had to crap out on a lousy training flight."

"That's the Air Force," Jake said. "Say, what kind of shape are you in?"

"A few dozen bruises. Good enough to get me a week's leave in a few days if nothing's broken."

"How the hell did you get out anyway?"

"I went for the side hatch before she hit some tool shed. Luckily for me I landed on my head."

"They say you'll be back flying?"

"What else? They'll have me back up there the day I get back off leave."

"Unless they send you to the Pool to pick up a crew. That way the war could be all over before you get sorted out again."

"No green crews for me if I can manage it. I figure something may open up in the squadron by the time I get back. I passed out as a straight A.G., I have navigation, and I even think I could fly a Hally if I had to in a pinch. But I'd be a lousy engineer. How many trips have you got left, hot shot?"

"Five. And just when I'd like to finish them off the brass seems to have run out of targets. We had another standdown today. It's waiting around that's harder on you than the actual flying."

"You'll get those five in before you know it. Nice safe milk runs. Then you'll have a free ticket back to the Main."

"And believe me, Bill, once I get there you'll have to drag me away the next time. I never thought I'd miss Montreal that much, but now I dream about it all the time. I've decided it's a pretty good town after all."

"Sure it is, if you're just passing through."

"You can come from Hogtown and still say that. What a phoney."

Jake left me in a very good mood. He was better than medicine. Too bad he couldn't come along on my week's sick leave. We could really have a ball together.

I had the X-rays after lunch. The results weren't long in coming. There was definitely nothing broken.

The M.O. dropped by again later on that afternoon.

"The funeral's tomorrow. If you feel you can make it over there it's all right with me. We'll give you a driver and one of our station wagons."

"Thanks again," I said. "Remind me to buy you a double when I get back."

"I won't forget it," he said. His eyes had a habit of twinkling that made you want to smile even when the conversation was deadly serious. "And I hope you have more luck with your next crew."

That last phrase of his lingered with me all the rest of the day. And was still on my mind the next grey Yorkshire morning as I drove over in a hospital car with a WAAF driver to the Group cemetery on the other side of York. It seemed a long time now since I and the rest of the crew had driven over exactly as I was doing today to see Pete Yarish put under. Yet it was only a lousy three weeks ago! March 8th, three days after the Chemnitz raid. Today was the 29th. So much to happen all within such a short time. Time that had been moved up to the speed of the fastest camera. Today I was the only one left to make the trip. By what right I didn't exactly know. No right at all, I suppose. Pure blind luck, the whim of chance. Nothing that made any sense.

There were a lot of boys from the squadron at the service presided over by the two padres, one Protestant, one R.C. Even a few guys from the Muskrats. Walt and Max, generally known around West Moor as "the two characters" had many friends, even among those whose inclinations were a lot less lively. Dave was the one I'd miss the most. He'd been the ideal room-mate, always making sure to hoist me out of the sack in time for briefings, always ready to lend me a fresh shirt or a pair of socks without holes for one of my mad last minute dashes into town. And then there was Fred Waters. I'd made a promise to him that would have to be kept. I wasn't looking forward to sending along that parcel to Edinburgh for him. Walt I'd miss because I admired his skill as a pilot and crew captain; in him I saw reflected some of the qualities I'd have liked to have myself but didn't. The rest of the crew I'd miss simply because they were the ones I'd lived through my baptism of fire with; their faces I knew would come back again and again in the future to pass hauntingly through my mind.

Several of the guys in "B" Flight recognized me as I stood near the two large graves waiting for the service to begin, my hospital blues showing under my greatcoat. They came over and said hello. They were really sorry about what had happened, but glad I'd made it anyway. It was all a little awkward but still nice.

The Protestant padre gave a short but moving address before the six coffins were lowered one by one. He reminded us that these comrades of ours had died tragically, denied even the airman's death in battle. But he refused to believe that these lives had been wasted or thrown away; rather they should serve as a reminder to us, their living brothers-in-arms, that there was still a fight to be finished against the forces of evil. Until we'd won that final victory their lives could be said in a sense to be held in the balance, part of an unfinished payment. And, he added, it was up to us as the generation that had had to fight this war to make sure that our sons and daughters never had to fight another. Our fathers before us had failed, and we were paying now the bitter price of that failure. We couldn't afford to fail as they had. If we did we'd have to live the rest of our lives with the realization that lives like these before us today, given so generously in the cause of freedom, had been a worthy but useless sacrifice. He closed by reciting the last lines of "In Flanders Fields":

"If ye break faith with us who die
 We shall not sleep though poppies blow
 In Flanders Fields."

I walked back slowly to the hospital station wagon. I didn't say one word to my attractive WAAF driver all the way to the base. She must have thought I was one strange Canadian and I couldn't have blamed her. But suddenly I'd had the certain feeling that something in me had changed: it was hard to believe from this moment on that I could go on exactly as I had before. Some part of me seemed to be missing. Perhaps it had died along with the others in the aircraft and had been lowered into place with them at the cemetery. Now, for all I knew, it would lie with them there forever.

22

The train I'd boarded at Waterloo Station that would take me to Bournemouth was very crowded. It had been a bad mistake waiting for an afternoon train. Somehow I should have gotten out of bed quite a bit earlier that morning and caught the one before noon. My body ached all over now and even my feet were sore.

I stood in one of the corridors tightly wedged against a window. By bending my knees and back at the same time I could make out the blur of stations and backs of houses flashing by. Then we were running through fairly open countryside and I gave up.

There was an American Army first lieutenant next to me. He was from South Carolina, I found out later. He had one of those Southern drawls which seemed a pleasant novelty at first but after half an hour became vaguely annoying. His outfit was the Quartermaster Corps, he informed me. He was in charge of a negro loading company on the docks at Southampton. Did I know anything about niggers? Not very much, I told him, we don't have too many negroes in Canada. You're damn lucky, he emphasized, where I come from there's fifty of 'em to each and every white man. Then he went on to explain that you couldn't get a day's work out of one of them unless you stood over them every minute of the time. I could almost picture him on the Southampton docks, working the ass off his men while strutting around in his faultlessly-pressed uniform with the big insignia at the shoulders and half a dozen ribbons up for making it as far as the European Theatre. I wondered how long he'd last before one of his boys couldn't take any more and went at him with a billy hook. I could only hope they'd have enough sense to

rip the bastard open after dark, so he couldn't pin it on anyone if he happened to live through it.

Maybe I was being a little tough on him. Maybe he
couldn't help being the way he was. Or perhaps I was simply
cheesed off because my week's sick leave had gotten off to
such a very poor start.

At Southampton the train emptied almost completely. I
had a whole compartment to myself for the remainder of the
journey. I stretched out comfortably and dozed off until the
train stopped with a jerk in Bournemouth West Station.

The last time I'd hopped off a train here I was one of a
draft of three thousand weary Canadians in Air Force blue.
We'd just finished spending six uneventful, cramped, card-
playing, dice-throwing, meal-vomiting, zig-zagging Atlantic
Ocean days from Quebec City to Liverpool on a Cunard liner
which had seen much better days. Then, with us all jammed
aboard, a snorting miniature model of a train had alternately
crawled and raced its way across Southern England before
coming to a grunting halt in this Channel city. We'd marched
through the streets to our billets in the fifty odd hotels requi-
sitioned by the R.C.A.F., sweating in our greatcoats under
the warm March sunshine. I remembered I'd had a sudden
surge of pride again in being part of this Air Force which almost a year of heart-breaking, monotonous training in
Canada had all but erased.

Today there'd be no marching through the town for me—I
was travelling first class by taxi. My destination, the Royal
Spa Hotel. I'd strolled by it a hundred times while girl-chas-
ing along the Promenade in those first three glorious weeks,
and wondered exactly what it was like inside. Today I'd find
out very shortly at first hand. I'd shot the bankroll and
booked a room already by phoning from the R.T.O. office at
the station.

I noticed a number of Canadian air force uniforms during
the drive through familiar streets to the hotel. No doubt the
Overseas drafts were still arriving. They probably still needed
a lot of men in Second TAF on the Continent as well as Six
Group and Coastal Command.

My room at the Royal Spa proved to be on the small side
but very clean, with a window looking right down on the
Channel. The mattress on the bed was firm but comfortable.

After admiring the blue ruffled waters rolling up almost to the Promenade below and distributing the contents of my rucksack in the appropriate places, I lay down on my bed, smoked a cigarette and tried to unwind a little. . . .

After a rather shaky start my leave seemed to be back on the track again. I knew now that it had been a mistake to go back to London, especially so soon after being there on leave with the crew. Even sitting in the train going south from York had been something of a strain. I wasn't alone one mile of the way. The whole gang was with me in the compartment, their faces shining with that look that only a seven day leave can bring out. Their laughter almost seemed to be shaking the window beside me, their talk exploding through the compartment as their favourite air force four-letter words flew around, their whistles piercingly shrill whenever a good-looking girl appeared down the corridor outside, or was seen walking across any station platform we'd pulled into.

And it had been even worse when I'd stepped off the train at Charing Cross and taken a taxi to our old hotel in the Strand. All six noisy bodies had jumped into the cab along with me, and on the way made sure the locals in the streets knew that more Canadians were in town. It was the same in the hotel, checking in at the desk, and even when I'd shut the door of my room behind me. I couldn't shake off my ghosts. I was stuck with them whether I liked it or not.

I'd ended a very restless nap about three o'clock by taking a walk along the Embankment under cool grey skies. The question on my mind had been whether to phone up Cathy or not. By six o'clock, after a couple of beers in a friendly Thames-side pub, I decided I was a fool to pass up another chance at her trim little body if she was still available. Her number rang and rang but no one answered. I couldn't tell whether I was relieved or not. I had something to eat in the same pub and joined a couple of Eighth Air Force lieutenants who were flying B-17-E's out of Cambridgeshire. They'd finished twelve missions and like me had to complete twenty-five. I matched them ale for ale until they left to meet a couple of girls at nine. I put through another call to Cathy's. Still no answer. So that was that. This time I was definitely relieved. I could forget her. I wasn't really in the market for any complications at the moment. I'd sat down again and stayed until closing time, leaving with my back teeth floating.

Either the Allies had broken through to their launching sites or the Jerrys had decided to take a night off, because I hadn't been kept awake by any buzz bombs that night. But I'd had my usual nightmare of the crash on take-off, followed strangely enough by a more pleasant dream in which I was back with Prue again and things were going beautifully. So well that my dream became purely erotic with the inevitable consequences.

Late the next morning, after several strong coffees to help put my head back together again, I'd realized that if I stayed in London another day and night I'd go out of my skull. I had to get away from it, anywhere. It was then that I remembered Bournemouth, those long sunny days at the Reception Centre. Why not give it a try now? It wasn't far away. And it couldn't be worse than London. . . .

I put out my cigarette and decided to get a little of those fresh breezes off the Channel into my lungs. The weather was warmer in Bournemouth, trench-coat weather. One look at the clear blue sky overhead and I'd forgotten about the oppressive overall greyness of London. I strolled up through the Pleasure Gardens. It was after four, and there were quite a few people walking about or sitting on the many benches. Most of the servicemen were American soldiers, flirting with young girls, most of whom didn't look more than sixteen or seventeen. I walked on up through the Gardens as far as the bus terminal, where I bought a London paper at a newsstand. I sat down at a nearby bench and glanced through it. The usual war news—Russian advances, German strategic withdrawals across the Rhine. The Russians had captured Danzig and were attacking Germans encircled at Breslau and Glogau. I had some idea where Danzig was, but the other two places didn't mean anything to me. I turned the page. More war news. The Austrian border had been crossed, German troops had begun to leave Holland.

Suddenly I heard my name called.

"Bill Sutcliffe, you old bugger you."

I looked up. Two R.C.A.F. sergeants with straight AG wings were standing on the path in front of me. I didn't know one of them for sure, but the one who'd evidently spoken looked vaguely familiar.

Then I remembered the face. Jack O'Donnell, the kid who lived around the corner from me in Toronto. Christ, I hardly recognized him. He'd shot up and filled out. He even had a toothbrush moustache. He still couldn't be more than nineteen if he was that.

"Hi, Jack. How the hell are you? Why don't both of you sit down and make your miserable lives happy?"

Jack introduced his buddy as Gary Stevens, also from Toronto.

"So what the hell are you doing here?" Jack wanted to know. He was a brash kid, plenty of mouth, but loveable all the same.

"A week's leave. I got tired flying. How about yourself?"

"Both of us came in with a draft a week ago. But I still can't believe it, you being here."

"It's a small world, that's for damn sure," I told him. Then I went on to explain what I was doing in Bournemouth, listening carefully to what I said to make sure I didn't sound too much like the old veteran looking for sympathy and admiration from his captive audience. After I'd told it I felt that at least I'd been honest with myself, no matter what it sounded like to them.

"From what you say then, there's not much chance of us getting into any action, at least not over here," Jack said.

"Not unless Jerry has another Air Force and Army hidden away somewhere. He's practically a dead duck as of now. I don't figure I'll get in much more time myself. And believe me, Jack, I'm not that anxious. This war isn't any ball game or basketball game, it's straight out-and-out murder. Don't believe a word of what they told you back on the training stations. That was all a lot of crap: and don't believe me either. I'm full of shit. Say, what do you guys do for excitement around here now? Do they still have the tea dances at the Pavilion? Do the Squadronaires still come down from London to play for you?"

"Everything's probably the same as when you were here, only a little better organized from what they tell me," Jack said. "There's a big dance tonight at the Rec Centre. Why don't you come along?"

"Jack didn't tell you but we're due about now to meet a couple of WAAFs as they come off duty at the Bowling

Green," Gary told me. "If you're interested we could probably line you up something nice for the evening."

"No WAAFs for me, thank you," I said. "I like the civvy girls much better. But I just may see you over there anyway."

"The dance starts at eight. We'll look for you, Bill. I guarantee there'll be some lovely stuff there."

"I'm sure there will be. And a couple of thousand pigeons after them."

I sat on the bench a while longer after they'd gone, finishing my newspaper. Then I walked slowly down through the Pleasure Gardens to my hotel. Christ, the kids they were sending over were getting younger and younger. Jack O'Donnell. It seemed only yesterday that I was pinning his ears back after he made one wisecrack too many about my then current high school girl friend. Now he too was caught up in the war, another small expendable cog in the meat grinder. But unless I was all wet in my theories, the war would be over before he'd finish his re-training. Although if they were very short of air gunners he might end up in a squadron a lot sooner than I could imagine. I hoped not. There wasn't enough war left that was worth his life. Much the same way as Pete Yarish's had been thrown away before it had hardly begun. That was the tragedy. War demanded the lives of only the very young. When the older ones died it seemed only incidental.

As I neared the Promenade I caught a glimpse up above through the trees of the Hermitage, a hotel commandeered by the Air Force. They used to have tea dances there, too, at a five o'clock, with the late afternoon sun shining through the windows, a warm breeze off the Channel and the sight of all that endless blue just below, with the dance music from the Armed Forces network sounding through the large panelled room, keeping the dancers very busy and very happy. It had been hard to believe there was a war on at that moment right across the narrow stretch of water out front. Perhaps there was a dance up there this afternoon at this very minute. If there was the new dancers wouldn't be any more aware of the war either. They'd go gliding on to the music, boy locked in the arms of girl, losing themselves in the music, in the scent of perfume, the soft touch of hands linked together.

Maybe I hadn't been too smart coming back to Bournemouth. Maybe I'd be buried up to my neck in nostalgia before I knew it. But at the moment it looked pretty good to me. And I was still only twenty-two. West Moor had been trying to make me old before my time. Perhaps here I could feel young again. At least it was worth a try.

23

The dance at the Recreation Centre was in full swing by the time I got there at eight-thirty. I'd eaten in solitary luxury in the hotel dining-room, then had a couple of drinks at the bar. I decided to look in at the dance, give it an hour at the most, then move on somewhere else if it didn't pan out. There were bound to be a lot of civilian girls at any dance given by the Air Force, so it might pay off. I was ready to make a night of it. All I wanted really was a few laughs. Believe it or not I still had to keep reminding myself there wouldn't be any flying in the morning.

The dance-floor and surrounding tables were very crowded, but I managed to find Jack and Gary. They were sitting with two WAAFs. One of them, a blonde, had a very pleasant face. She was with Jack, it turned out. I found myself a chair and sat down with them.

"Ladies," Jack announced, "this is an old friend of mine, Bill Sutcliffe. He's down here on leave from his squadron. Didn't you say you had a girl in mind for him, Mavis?"

"I don't think Midge is with anyone," the blonde said. "Let me see if I can find her."

"Thanks very much," I said, "but don't bother. I'll look around for a little while. I may not be able to stay very long. You know, Jack, this place hasn't changed one bit. Even the air in here is the same. No, I'm only kidding. It's fine. And they have a pretty good band up there on the stand."

"Nothing but the best for the boys. Well, excuse me, Bill, Mavis and I are going to try out this next number."

Gary and his girl got up to dance as well, so I was left at the table alone. It was very warm in the place. I could feel the sweat under my armpits sticking to my shirt. What I needed was a drink. I guess I had a big thirst on tonight.

Even a soft drink would be better than nothing. I got up and worked my way out to the refreshment stand.

There were so many attractive girls flitting about in the entrance hall that I almost stayed out there after I'd sampled a bottle of orange masquerading as a carbonated beverage. But I soon found out that most of the girls had come to the dance with steady partners. If a girl was unattached there was a fairly obvious reason for it.

When I came back in to the dance and over to Jack's table again there were three WAAFs seated with Jack, Gary and a new sergeant, a WAG. The third WAAF caught my eye right away; no doubt this happened to anyone seeing her for the first time. She had a very cute baby face with a lot of freckles around her delicately-shaped nose which seemed appropriate for her orange-red hair. She was a good head shorter than the other two girls and didn't look any more than fifteen.

She was introduced as Midge Wilkins. I found out later on that her real name was Madge but nobody ever called her that, not ever her mother. And at the same time she proved that she was nineteen and a half no less by showing me her I. card. But that was later in the evening.

So this was the WAAF they'd picked out for me. The last Air Force girl I'd gone out with had been back in Canada and it had been enough of a disaster to cure me of girls in uniform ever since.

Shortly before the band began playing the WAG excused himself and didn't come back. It wasn't clear whether the little redhead had been dancing with him or not. So it looked as though I was elected if I didn't move out as well.

But I found myself staying, perhaps more curious than anything else. For one thing I wondered how she'd look when she stood up. Would the rest of her be as miniature as the face, the arms, the hands?

When I moved out onto the dance floor with her a short time later I discovered that I'd have to bend over to talk to her. And that she was built considerably sturdier under the awkward uniform than you would have supposed, with actually a pair of nice legs showing below the regulation skirt.

"Jack said you were on leave. But he didn't seem to know why you were here in Bournemouth." Her pale blue eyes had a very attractive way of lighting up when she talked.

"Yes, I have a week. And I don't know really why I'm here myself."

"I don't like people who have to have reasons for everything," she said. "I'm a creature of impulse myself." As she spoke I was counting the freckles on her face and had already lost track. The thing was you hardly noticed them unless you got up really close. I suppose it was the shock of the carrot-red hair that threw you off the track.

"Good girl. Since I've started flying there doesn't seem to be too much point in worrying about reasons either."

During the second dance I found out that she'd only been stationed in Bournemouth since the first of the year, that she worked a little further downtown in the Equipment Section of the Reception Centre, and that she preferred Canadians to British or American servicemen.

"You boys are much more natural. Our fellows are inclined to be snobs, the Yanks are either boring or disgusting. But to be completely fair, perhaps I've only run into the wrong types. And I've only met up with Canadians since I've been here."

"There are some pretty rotten Canadians around, let me tell you," I said.

"What kind are you?" she asked me, with that little girl's smile of hers.

"The kind to be avoided at all costs."

"You don't look that terrible to me."

"That's how I fool pretty little girls like you."

"Am I really pretty?"

"That, and then some."

"But I'm too small, aren't I?"

"For what?"

That made her smile again. She squeezed my free hand a little tighter, or I thought she did. I made it my excuse to tighten my other hand against her slender waist. She didn't seem to mind.

When I'd decided to come to the dance I'd mentally given myself an hour there and then I'd move on if nothing interesting turned up. My hour was almost up according to my watch.

Midge noticed me checking the time. She didn't seem to miss much.

"Do you have to go soon?" she asked.

"Nothing like that. It's just that the pubs close at ten."

"You're feeling thirsty?"

"Dry as dust," I said. "I don't know why especially."

"It's very warm in here. I'm thirsty myself."

"Know any nice pubs close by?"

"I'm no authority. But a lot of our crowd go to the Lansdowne Arms. It's on a side street behind Lansdowne Square."

"I think I know it. It's not very far from here. Care to join me?"

"What about the others?"

"We don't want the others along, do we?"

"I don't, I just wondered about you."

"That's a good girl. Now let's get our hats and coats and get out of here."

Bournemouth was still under a dim-out, so it was very private and very pleasant walking along the street. We cut through the Pleasure Gardens. There were a lot of couples in the park, some on the benches, some back in the grass. It was a cool night, but there wasn't any wind to speak of.

"I have to be back at our billet by ten-thirty, which puts rather a crimp on things," Midge told me. "On the weekends we're allowed out to midnight."

"I went out a few times with a nurse in training back home," I confided. "She had to be in by ten during the week. But we made out all right."

"I suppose nurses are very practical girls."

"This one was, believe me."

"Do you miss Canada, Bill?"

"Sometimes. When I have a lot of time on my hands and start thinking about things, I tend to get a little homesick. But I've been too busy the last few months to think much about it. And I don't have any girl back there to worry about and write letters to. That probably can bother you more than anything else. Especially if your girl is pretty and you're the kind to worry about who she could be making time with while you're away."

"You sound almost glad in a way you haven't got a steady girl."

"You're absolutely right, I am. A week ago I was flying with six of the nicest guys you'd ever want to know. Now they're all dead, and why I'm walking here with you right now I couldn't tell you. It wasn't my time to die, I guess. But it could be my turn in another week or so. So why saddle any girl with grief like that?" And I told her about Fred Waters and the parcel I had to send on to Edinburgh when I got back to West Moor.

When I'd finished I said, "I'm sorry I pulled that story on you. You've probably got enough troubles of your own without wanting to hear mine. I promise I won't do that again."

"It doesn't hurt to be serious once in a while, Bill. I really feel sorry for all of them. They wanted very little out of life and they missed even that."

We didn't say very much more until we reached the pub. Luckily for us it wasn't very crowded tonight. We managed to squeeze around a small table in a corner of the very cheerful saloon bar. There was orange gin for the ladies. I settled for my usual mild and bitter.

"You never said where you were from," I told her, after we'd tried our drinks.

"London. Shepherd's Bush, if that means anything to you. My mother runs a rooming-house, very genteel and all that. It's actually our old home. After Dad died Mom said she'd have to keep busy or she'd go off her rocker. So she started taking a lodger or two. Now she has four steady boarders and puts up another four overnight at times. She gets a lot of calls from your Beaver Club actually. Bed and breakfast, half a guinea. Oh, my Mom's quite a person, she is. And so was Dad. A gentleman's bookie, I suppose you'd call him. He did very well at it too. Left both of us nicely fixed, as a matter of fact."

I told her a little about my home back in Toronto. She seemed very interested in everything I said. When she made a comment it was almost always very intelligent. She had just enough accent without sounding like someone from Oxford. That was one thing I liked very much about English girls. They seemed to use English so correctly and so naturally. It was a pleasure to listen to them. It almost didn't matter too much about the words, the sound of them was what counted.

Much too soon to suit me they were calling out the inevitable "Time, gentlemen, time."

"Why do they have to close pubs at ten?" I asked Midge. "It seems a shame to stop all the friendly feeling in these places so early. Eleven would be much more reasonable, don't you think?"

"I've never really thought about it," Midge said, "but I suppose there are good reasons or they'd change it. Perhaps this way everybody doesn't get tight. People can be very unpleasant when they've had one too many, as you may very well know."

"I've met a few of those, all right," And after we'd gone outside and were walking back toward Lansdowne Square I told her about Dave running wild at that Limey base we'd been diverted to after the Wesel attack last month. Re-telling it now, unfortunately, it didn't seem to be very funny. Stories about the dead were all right, but Dave was a little too freshly buried.

"Where's this billet of yours?" I asked as we came onto the Square with a few late buses still standing at the bus depot. Bournemouth had double-decker buses, which, like the pubs, quit operating at ten o'clock sharp.

"Straight ahead along High Street for two blocks, and we're practically there. It's a beautiful old place, a sort of private hotel before the war. Some of the girls are lucky enough to be two in a room. I'm in a larger one on the ground floor with ten beds in it."

"Are they very strict about this ten-thirty business?"

"Very. There's a duty-sergeant makes a bed check at eleven."

"That's a spoil-sport trick. Sounds a little like some of the air training schools I've been on."

"I suppose it's a good thing, really. Some of the girls would stay out half the night if they could."

"No doubt. This way I suppose it at least cuts down a little on the number of medical discharges."

"It doesn't seem to help that much, I'm afraid. There seems to be a couple of pregnancies every month. Most girls are plain stupid. Some of them don't even have the slightest idea who the father is."

"I guess it doesn't make that much difference, does it?"

"I suppose you're right. But it does seem to me it's a little too close to the alley cat."

"These are crazy times," I told her, "people are doing crazy things. I don't think it's the best excuse in the world for doing them, but perhaps it's reason enough. Look at me. Two hours ago I didn't know you even existed, now I'm talking to you as if I've known you for years. Things move fast because they have to. Next Tuesday I'll be back in Yorkshire, a few days later I could be over Germany again. Who knows after that?"

We'd walked along High Street now for several blocks, past all the deserted shop fronts, their windows full of dark emptiness. There was hardly any traffic in the streets, everything was very quiet, as if holding its breath. I had my right arm around Midge's waist, hardly in the best military tradition, but a very practical way of strolling with a girl. I think we'd both have been content to wander on all the way to Boscombe like that, walking very slowly, closely together, talking about anything that came into our heads, some of it silly, some of it serious. But there wasn't time tonight.

"We've still got five whole days," I reminded her. "Let's both of us think about the best way of spending them."

"I know how I'd like to spend some of the time."

"How?"

Midge squeezed my hand in answer and pulled me into a darkened shop entrance. I didn't know whether she was standing on her toes or not, but I didn't have to bend my head down as far as I thought I would to meet her lips.

"That's how," she laughed softly as we took a breather a good minute later.

"Where'd you learn to kiss like that?"

"You inspire me, that's all," she said. "Now I've got to run. I don't want to have any privileges withdrawn this week of all weeks."

"That would be a calamity. Where's this billet of yours?"

"Around the next corner. When will I see you again?"

"How much time do you get for lunch?"

"An hour and a half. The Grand Hotel where I work is right next door. You can't miss it. We go at twelve."

"I'll see you out front then. Let's hope it's a nice day."

"It'll be a nice day," Midge said. Her hand tightened in mine again. I still hadn't gotten over how small it was. And very warm, very soft.

"Now walk me the rest of the way," she said.

"Aren't you afraid some of the girls might see you? I know how catty you females can be."

"I want them to see you. I want to show you off."

"You could always say I'm your older brother."

"You think they'd believe that for a minute?"

"Who knows how girls think? I've never been able to figure that part of them out."

"You won't have any trouble with me, Bill."

"If I do I'm simply going to put you over my knee and spank you."

"Don't try it," Midge said, "you might be surprised how much I liked it."

24

"Didn't I tell you we'd leave all the good weather behind us?"
I asked Midge as our train rolled along at a good clip trying
to make up a little time as we entered the outskirts of London.

"I'd hoped for better myself, but I promise I'll make you
forget all about the weather."

"I'll hold you to that."

"I'm quite sure you will, you nasty lad," Midge half-whis-
pered in my ear. The other occupants of the carriage, a
middle-aged minister and his older and severe-looking wife,
glanced across at us in polite disapproval. No doubt they
thought I was robbing the cradle. If they only knew, I
thought, if they only knew.

It was now almost eleven o'clock. We'd boarded the train
at Bournemouth West Station at eight-thirty. It had seemed a
long, slow trip getting up to London.

Today was Saturday. Midge was on a forty-eight hour
pass. That gave us both today and tomorrow together. Sunday night she'd have to return to Bournemouth; Monday afternoon I'd have to leave London and go north. Our time
together was slowly but surely growing shorter. I think we
both felt this and were determined to make every minute of
our weekend count.

Frankly I hadn't been keen at all on coming up to London.
I'd have much sooner stayed under warmer, bluer skies in
Bournemouth. But Midge had planned on going home this
weekend for a whole month and had talked me into making
the trip.

"You'll get a kick out of my mother, she's a wonderful
cook, and you'll have a lovely room all to yourself. Besides,
we can go anywhere and do anything we want to."

I didn't know what I was getting into, but if that's what

162

Midge wanted I suppose I wanted it too. In the few short days I'd known her in Bournemouth she had come to mean a great deal to me. I'd met her at a time when my whole life had been turned upside down, when I'd begun to wonder whether I could go on living in a world which killed so many of the good people in war and seemed to spare so many of the true bastards, the cream of the scum, to reap the dividends in peacetime. And I'd wondered if I'd ever find a woman who would return my love as eagerly as I gave it. More and more, with each new day of my leave in Bournemouth, I began to believe that Midge, tiny, adorable, good-natured Midge, might be the answer.

Life had suddenly become joyous and worthwhile again. I had begun to enjoy the little things I'd simply taken for granted before, or worse still, hadn't even been vaguely aware of. A fine day, a walk in the park, a run across the sands, the moon shining on the Channel, the tree-shaded streets of Bournemouth, a fox trot on the radio, cream buns from a certain bakery in the High Street washed down with strong cocoa, sitting high up in the back row of the Odeon Cinema—all these things had become cherished and memorable because Midge was there to share them with me. And then most cherished, most memorable of all, our spending the previous night together in my hotel room. The nervous way the two of us had worried whether anyone had noticed us coming up the back stairs, the shy way in which we'd undressed, Midge in the bathroom and I outside, our first long, never-ending kiss together on the small bed. Then still almost like two small children, our slow, curious examination of each other's physical parts between the cold sheets. The not-unexpected surprise of Midge's well-shaped, sturdy little body suddenly unbearably close, instantly demanding, waking me to tenderness, ecstasies never before thought possible. . . .

The last ten minutes on the train seemed easily an hour. Then we were stepping down onto the platform and walking into the huge overwhelming echo-vault of Waterloo Station, thick with soldiers in full pack and rifles, school-children, holidayers, all hurrying to meet friends, to catch trains, to find taxis.

We were lucky ourselves to get a taxi almost right away. Midge gave the address I was to remember so well, 15 Harwood Street, Shepherd's Bush. We were suddenly swept up into the swirl of London's wartime traffic.

Midge snuggled up to me in the back seat.

"You know, I can hardly believe I'm here with you right now. Any moment somebody is going to pinch me and I'm going to wake up and find it's only a beautiful dream."

I put my arm around her waist.

"Funny, I've felt a little like that, too. But it's no dream, and it's even more beautiful."

"I know we're going to have a fine weekend. It's all the time we'll have together for ages and ages."

"At least until I can get some more leave. Maybe the war will end before we know it."

"It can't end one day soon enough to suit me."

"One thing, little one. You're sure you're doing the right thing bringing me home with you?"

"I told you I've written Mom to expect us both. It's going to work out fine. I have a very understanding mother. Don't worry your head any more about it."

We arrived almost before we knew it at Harwood Street. Number fifteen had a large old-fashioned front to it, complete with solid oak door and knocker, very similar to others on the street. Midge had told me it was built in the early 1900's, had twelve rooms on three floors, and had come through the Blitz and the later bombings without a scratch. Some houses not too far down the street hadn't been so lucky, being completely destroyed in a raid early in the war.

Midge let us in with a key and led me through the hall into a large kitchen in which a middle-aged woman was at work. Midge gave her a kiss and introduced her as Mrs. Thomas.

"Your mother got fed up with things this morning and sailed out early on a shopping spree. She said she'd be home later in the afternoon and for both of you to make yourselves comfortable."

"Don't worry, Margaret, we will. What can we have for lunch? We're both quite peckish."

"There's some ham and eggs. And I made some blueberry tarts only yesterday."

"Wait till you taste her blueberry tarts, they're super," Midge enthused, then led the way upstairs with me following close behind carrying her small suitcase and my haversack.

The second floor was quite spacious, and must have had at least five bedrooms. Midge, however, continued up a second flight of stairs, these being much narrower; they ended at a very generous attic with high ceilings in both of the adjoining bedrooms. There was also a four piece bathroom for good measure.

"My brother and I have used these two rooms ever since we were children," Midge explained. "You're to have this one, which belonged to him. That's a picture of him over on the dresser, in case you're interested."

It was a very pleasant room, with a view out the window of at least a hundred other roof tops, each with their innumerable small chimneys jutting up. The bed was large, double-bed size. And there were a couple of very comfortable-looking chairs.

"It's very cosy," I said. "Your brother must have liked it very much."

"I only hope he's back in it soon," Midge said. "He's with the B.L.A. right now up at the Rhine. We've been hoping he'd get some leave but his regiment has been right in the thick of it apparently."

"I'll bet he misses this house. I know I would. Now let's see your room. I'm very curious about it."

"It's actually not much different from this one, except it's smaller, because of the bathroom squeezed on the other half."

It was a nice room as well, looking out onto the street and the houses opposite. It held only a single bed, which looked, however, ample enough for Midge. There was a picture of her with a schoolgirl's uniform on complete with broad-brimmed hat. It was a very feminine room, somehow, and I could see Midge's personality clearly showing in it.

"Now as soon as I change into something more comfortable I'll make you some lunch," Midge said. "Perhaps you want to clean up a little. If so go right ahead and use the bathroom."

"Good idea. Tell me one thing, can I risk sampling your cooking?"

"I can't do very much to ham and eggs, can I? Besides which I'm a very good cook. Mrs. Thomas and my mother have both been coaching me every chance they've had these last couple of years. My mother still claims good cooking is the best way to a man's heart."

"You were cooking on both burners last night, let me tell you."

"Very funny. I always seem to get the comedians. Now run along and let me change."

By the time I'd washed and put on a clean shirt, then found my way down to the kitchen again, Midge had a frying-pan going over a hot stove. Before I knew it I was sitting down to three fried eggs and several slices of ham. I was told to cut myself some bread, and by that time Midge was seated opposite me at the big kitchen table.

"Are the eggs the way you like them?" she wanted to know.

"Just right. You know, you're a good cook."

"I'm glad. You've got to keep your strength up, you know." And she smiled a very knowing smile at me which made her look so damn cute that I wanted to lean right across the table and kiss her.

"So I'm finding out. You women are such demanding creatures."

"You wouldn't have it any other way, would you?"

After we'd washed down some of Mrs. Thomas' blueberry tarts with strong hot tea we climbed the stairs to the big roomy attic as if by common agreement. Midge had exchanged her uniform for a black sweater and grey skirt and looked almost smaller, more delicately-shaped than ever to me. Without her high WAAF cap she looked considerably shorter than I remembered her. Her red hair contrasted beautifully with the dark sweater.

"You know," she said as we went into my room, "we shouldn't be doing this right now. My Mom could come back at any time. What would she think?"

"Let's ask her, shall we? I'm sure she'd approve."

"You're awful, Bill, really awful. I'll wager you've been the ruin of many a nice girl."

"As one of my old buddies used to say, all girls are nice. Some are only nicer."

"Come on, then, let's not waste time talking, shall we?"

This time our love-making did seem forced, as if we both really did have the idea of being interrupted right in the middle of things.

We must have dozed off a short time later in each other's arms. When I opened my eyes the watch on my wrist said ten minutes to three. Midge was sleeping softly beside me, her face turned toward me relaxed and so childish-looking in the slight mould of the pillow.

I heard the slightest of noises behind me. I turned slightly and froze in the bed. A middle-aged woman was standing there beside the half-opened door looking in at us. Her rather handsome face was expressionless, unless the eyes that looked at mine sparkled ever so gently.

Then the door was closed very softly. She was gone. Midge and I were alone again in the room. It had all happened so quickly that I hadn't had the time to react at all. Now I could feel the sweat trickling down under my armpits. It was one of those times which you experience perhaps two or three times in your whole life. They're among the most uncomfortable moments you'll ever know. This was certainly one of them.

The woman in the doorway could only be Midge's mother. My worst fears had been realized. We'd been caught cold. She might as well have walked in during our most passionate love-making.

Thank God she hadn't wakened Midge. I had to give her credit for that. I could easily imagine someone else causing an instant, disagreeable scene. And our whole weekend together ruined, and with it perhaps everything between us.

Well, the worst has happened. I told myself. So there's no use worrying any more about it. You'll just have to be a big boy and take your medicine. And hope it all works out somehow.

I waited another ten minutes and then gently kissed Midge awake. She seemed to open her eyes almost at once, eager to return my kisses.

"Come on, sleepy-head," I told her, summoning up a light-heartedness that I certainly didn't feel at that moment, "we're letting the best part of the day slip by on us. Let's get dressed and get some of that sunshine outside before it's all gone."

"Wouldn't you sooner stay in bed?" she teased, her small warm fingers at work under the sheet.

This was madness, I told myself, what if her mother should come back again? But Midge was close against me now and my argument was losing more weight every second.

And in another minute had lost completely.

25

It was Sunday evening. In another ten minutes the train for Bournemouth would pull out. Midge and I sat in a corner of one of the waiting rooms at Waterloo Station, both trying a little too hard to be cheerful. It wasn't working very well. In five minutes she'd have to board the train and we wouldn't see each other again for God knows how long. Something inside my head kept thinking maybe never, but my heart refused to believe it. We'd talked about spending my next leave together. If the war lasted it could be another ten weeks. If by some miracle it ended before that there'd probably be a three-day stand-down at least. No matter how you looked at it the time we'd be apart was too damn long.

"Promise me you won't listen too hard to my mother," Midge said. "She'll probably get you alone before you leave tomorrow and give you an endless list of my faults. But don't believe her. I don't have any."

"I'll just let her talk on and on. Do you think she knows we slept together at the house?"

"I have a small confession to make, darling. I felt so guilty yesterday afternoon doing it behind her back that I told her all about us before we turned in last night. She didn't seem half as shocked as I thought she'd be. 'You're a big enough girl now to look after yourself,' she said finally. 'I only hope you know what you're doing.' That's all she said."

"I wondered why you were so wonderfully relaxed," I said. "I don't think I was." I didn't tell her that having her mother look in on us in bed together Saturday afternoon hadn't helped matters any. There wasn't any point in bringing that up now.

"You were fine, dear," Midge said. "That was a wonderful night. And we're going to have many many more like it, only even more wonderful, aren't we?"

"If I have anything to do with it we are," I said. "Say, I just had a crazy idea. Why don't I get a ticket and come down on the train with you? I can sleep at the transient officer's quarters and get a train back in the morning."

"That's a nice thought, but it's a lot of extra trouble for you and we'd only have to say goodbye tonight anyway. It might be a lot harder then than it's going to be now."

"I suppose you're right," I said. "Anyway, you have my address at West Moor, haven't you? I expect plenty of letters from you. I'll do my darndest to answer them. If they're slow in coming you'll know I'm too busy flying. Now I think you'd better get on that train if you're even going to find standing room."

"I suppose you're right." We both got up reluctantly with me carrying Midge's small suitcase. We moved slowly across to the station entrance and out into the seething hive of noise and humanity that was Waterloo Station at this hour.

"There's my train, darling," Midge said. "Put down my suitcase for a moment."

I took her in my arms and we kissed very long and very deeply, oblivious of everything around us. When we'd finished I saw she had tears in her eyes. I think there were one or two in mine as well.

"Goodbye, darling," Midge said. "Take care. Keep alive for me, won't you?"

"Just for you. It's all the reason I need, believe me. Take care of yourself now."

We walked over to the train. It was packed. Midge would have to stand to Southampton. I should have insisted on her taking an earlier train. But she'd been stubborn about staying that extra couple of hours and I hadn't argued too much with her.

She stepped up and I handed her the small suitcase. She'd be lucky to get standing-room in one of the corridors.

She turned and blew me a kiss with her free hand. She was trying very hard to smile. Then she disappeared inside the train.

I didn't wait for it to pull out. For some reason I wanted to get out of Waterloo Station as quickly as possible. There was something vaguely evil about it now, something sinister, foreboding. It was as if it had suddenly swallowed up the one thing in this world I really cared about at the moment. And for all I knew it could be for good. This world I was living in now held out no guarantees on anything. Not for love, not for life. But still demanded that I somehow kept going, blindly, groping my way through the darkness.

I had had some vague notion of wandering up by the River past the Houses of Parliament. Now I didn't feel like walking anywhere. I found the Tube entrance to Bakerloo and went down the deep endless escalator. Why I didn't know either. Going back to Midge's place would only remind me of her all the more. I had a feeling the attic room and especially the bed in it would be unbearable without her. Yet I didn't have any better ideas.

Almost before I knew it the Tube had carried me back to Harwood Street. I let myself in with the spare key Midge had given me. The downstairs lights were mostly off, so I went right up to my room. I lay down on the bed and tried to unwind a little. Before I knew it I'd dozed off to sleep.

It was almost eleven by the luminous dial of my watch when I woke up. I felt wide-awake and slightly more cheerful. I wondered whether Mrs. Wilkins might be downstairs now; if so, perhaps I could coax a cup of tea out of her. I was really more in the mood for a beer or something stronger, but I'd settle for a hot cup of tea or coffee.

The downstairs lights were still off as they had been when I'd come in. I was about to give it up as a lost cause and start up the stairs again when I heard the front door opening. It was Mrs. Wilkins and behind her an R.C.A.F. P/O with pilot's wings up.

"Don't go upstairs, Bill," Mrs. Wilkins called out to me, "I've someone here I want you to meet."

"Does that mean an invitation to a cup of tea?" I asked.

"Certainly. This is Pilot Officer St. Pierre, Bill. Jacques, this is Bill Sutcliffe. I believe you're a Flying Officer, aren't you?"

"I'm afraid so. Pleased to meet you, Jacques. I'm an air bomber with the Algonquins."

"Hello, Bill. As you see, I'm a pilot, or was. I'm afraid my flying days are over." He spoke excellent English with an interesting French-Canadian accent. He was good-looking, and Mrs. Wilkins told me the next day that he was twenty-two, the same age as me. "Mrs. Wilkins tells me you're on sick leave yourself."

"I'm finishing up a week tomorrow. Then it's back to Yorkshire and the old rat-race, I suppose."

"You seem in fine shape right now. You look like you've made a good recovery."

"All I had was a bump on the head and some bruises. But I lost all my crew and I think the M.O. thought I was close to going around the bend. So he gave me seven days to get over it. I suppose I'm as right again as I'll ever be. Who were you with, by the way?"

"I was at Croft with 434, Bluenose Squadron," Jacques said, "so I wasn't that far away from you."

"Look, boys," Mrs. Wilkins interrupted us, "why don't the two of you go in the living-room and get comfortable while I make us a pot of tea? Then you can talk all night if you want to."

"Sorry," I said, "I got carried away like I usually do."

"That sounds like a wonderful idea," Jacques told her. "If I don't sit down soon I'm going to fall down."

We drew the curtains in the living-room, put on some lights, then sat down in a couple of comfortable chairs. Jacques had taken Mrs. Wilkins out to the nearby cinema and they'd walked both ways. That apparently had been a little too much for him.

"I'm as weak as a kitten," he told me. He'd had the latest of three stomach operations only two weeks ago and his recovery was slow-going.

"I was lucky as hell to find this place," he went on. "A nurse phoned the Beaver Club and they got me a room here. I've lived here now for three months off and on. Mrs. Wilkins is like a mother to me. She tells me you're going with her daughter Midge."

"I met her in Bournemouth on my leave," I said, "and I came up with her for the weekend. She's a wonderful girl. I've known her less than a week but it seems like months."

"Well, if she's anything like her mother you're lucky to be going with her."

"I guess she's a chip off the old block. She's a tremendous girl, Jacques."

"What I can't figure out is why Mrs. Wilkins hasn't ever married again. She'd make someone a fine wife. And she's not that old. Mr. Wilkins must have been quite a man himself."

"Midge has never talked very much about him. Apparently he was a gentleman's bookie, whatever that is."

Our conversation was interrupted at this point by the arrival of Mrs. Wilkins with the tea. After she'd poured she led us into a lively conversation about the differences of living in Canada and England. I found it interesting to get Jacques' point of view about things. He was from Quebec City so he could be said to be a typical French-Canadian. By the time Mrs. Wilkins excused herself saying it was way past her bedtime I'd learned a few things about Quebec that I hadn't known before. And not surprisingly found that Jacques was no ordinary French-Canadian or any average member of the R.C.A.F.

After Mrs. Wilkins had gone it wasn't long before our talk turned back to the Air Force and the war. Jacques had flown Halifax B.III's since they'd gone into service with Bluenose Squadron in mid 1944 and he'd been shot down over Hamburg in late June. All of the crew had jumped clear of the aircraft as she went down in flames, but he'd never seen any of them again. He himself had been grabbed right away and roughly handled as they took him into the city. The whole area was still burning from the raid. The soldiers turned him loose in the centre of a large angry crowd on one of the big streets, and everyone, men, women and children went at him.

"I was pushed down and it felt as though a hundred pairs of boots were kicking me all at once. After three or four kicks in the groin and stomach I passed out, probably luckily for me. When I came to I was covered with blood, but an old veteran of the First War in Volkstürm uniform had managed to drag me away from the mob. He saved my life right there. I was three weeks in military hospital getting over that beating, including an operation to close a rupture in my stomach wall."

"The day I was discharged the bastards took me out to a Hitler Youth Camp and let the kids work me over again. They didn't beat me up as badly this time, but they didn't need to. My stomach wall ruptured again and I thought I'd die with the pain. But another six weeks in the hospital and another operation and I was hobbling around again. I'll say one thing—the Jerries have only the best doctors."

"After that the Gestapo took over and put me on a train for Brussels. There at Headquarters they tried to get me to talk. They figured I was French-Canadian, not English-Canadian, so naturally I hated the English. But what the hell did I know anyway? I played dumb and they gave me the full treatment. One little trick took place down in a huge cellar they had under this great old house. They tied a group of us up and stood us facing a wall about six inches back from the rough stone. Then a goon in soft shoes walked around behind us with a long rubber truncheon. You couldn't hear the bastard coming and suddenly he'd whack you without any warning, driving your face right into the wall. I had six sessions like that lasting one hour each. I broke my nose and one eye was cut and my face was covered with bruises. See my nose?—it's still a little crooked. Then they suggested I talk. I told them to stuff it this time. They got mad and worked me over with clubs. My damn stomach ruptured again. I was still in hospital in pretty poor shape when the Americans liberated Brussels early in September."

"How's your stomach now?"

"I hope the next operation will make a big difference. I also hope it'll be the last. But they tell me it's never going to be completely normal."

"Christ, I don't think I could stand a quarter of all that pounding you took," I said.

"I didn't think I could either, to tell you the honest truth. But it's surprising how much you can take when the chips are down."

I dreamt about Jacques that night. The dream wasn't very pleasant. God, that kid had courage. And now with his health perhaps ruined forever he could still be cheerful as hell. All my troubles seemed so small by comparison it wasn't even funny.

I saw Jacques at late breakfast the next morning and we talked some more. Then, shortly before lunch, Mrs. Wilkins and I had a nice little chat for a few minutes over the inevitable cup of tea.

"Bill, promise me one thing," she said, somewhere along in the conversation, "if you find you want to break things off with Midge, don't beat about the bush, tell her straight out. I think she loves you a lot and you'd hit her very hard if you play along when you aren't really serious."

"Don't worry," I told her, "I'll never let that happen. As a matter of fact, I'd have liked to become engaged right now, but I don't think I should until I quit flying." And I went on to tell her a little bit about Fred and his little Scots lass up in Edinburgh.

"You do whatever you think is right, Bill. I'm sure you'll find my Midge will never let you down."

That afternoon I boarded my train at Charing Cross and spent the three hours to York with a hundred thoughts running through my head. It was so different to the last time I'd come off leave. I'd had the crew to keep me from being too down in the mouth. Whatever lay ahead of us back at West Moor we'd been facing together. But not this time. I was strictly on my own.

So that when I got off the train at York and walked through the station, it was like moving through a gloomy mausoleum. I took a taxi out to the base with none of the high spirits of that last time with the crew, when we'd all piled into my Standard Nine and driven to Betty's Bar for a pint to get the travelling dust out of our throats. No Betty's Bar, no beer this afternoon. But I found myself humming under my breath for some unknown reason the same old familiar song which would float around somewhere at the back of my head as long as I lived—humming the words as a few tears came slowly in spite of everything:

"There was flak, flak, bags of bloody flak,
   In the Ruhr, in the Ruhr,
There was flak, flak, bags of bloody flak,
   In the Valley of the Ruhr."

"Come on, you bastards, sing," Walt seemed to be shouting out in the silence of that taxi:

"My eyes are dim, I cannot see,
   The searchlights they are blinding me,
   The searchlights they are blinding me."

26

When the M.O. told me to take off my shirt and tie right away I had an idea what he might be up to. Otherwise I wouldn't have been prepared for him giving my shoulder a good slap, and probably would have jumped at least an inch off the floor. As it was I sucked in the pain and gave a low grunt.

"Still pretty tender, eh?" he asked.

"Hardly feel it at all."

"How about that thigh? You had a whopping big bruise there."

He pinched right in the centre of the bruise and it hurt worse than the shoulder. But again I was ready.

"That doesn't bother me either," I volunteered.

"You either heal a lot quicker than average or you're a hell of a liar, Bill," the squadron-leader said. "But I've got to give you the benefit of the doubt, don't I?"

"I suppose you do."

"Well, let's test your eyes a bit. You took a real bash on the head, you know. Now read the bottom line on that chart over there."

I didn't have a worry about my eyes. It didn't take long to convince him either.

"I'm sending you back to active duty effective immediately," he told me after he'd finished writing up some papers. "I think that's what you want, isn't it?"

"It can't be soon enough to suit me," I said.

"Have any recurring nightmares from the crash?"

"Almost every night," I said, then wished I'd kept my big mouth shut.

"If you told me you didn't have any I'd be really worried. You're reacting very normally, and that's good. How was the leave, by the way?"

175

"Bournemouth was beautiful. Only rained once all week. If we could only bring some of that weather up here."

"That would make it too easy," the M.O. said. "Now I suppose you'll see Ralph Bowman. Tell him to give me a call when he's finished with you. Lots of luck, Bill."

I did up my tie and put on my tunic. Then I shook hands with the M.O. and left. He was one of the best I'd met in the Service. They didn't come any better. I'd have to watch out for him in the mess and stand him a drink. I owed him a couple and he was just the guy who would drink them.

I walked out of the hospital and headed down to the dispersal hut. I was hitting it lucky so far today. Ralph Bowman was in his office, hunched up behind a small mound of paperwork. For a moment I thought he looked annoyed as he glanced up after my knock, then his face seemed to brighten and I got the impression he was glad to have an excuse to take a break for a few minutes.

"Looks like you're putting your day off to good use," I ventured, settling into the chair opposite him.

"Very funny. But we can use it. They gave us a real good clobbering yesterday. I suppose you picked up on all the gen outside."

"A little. Too bad that last Lanc gaggle was late hitting the target. Otherwise they'd have had plenty of fighter cover."

"You can bet someone is having his ass chewed off over that. Well, we're in good shape, anyway, and Muskrats only lost one."

"I was just over paying the M.O. a visit. He says I'm O.K. to fly any time. I was hoping you could fix me up with something, Ralph. I hope to hell I won't have to sit around some Pool at a holding unit waiting for a raw crew."

"Matter of fact, old bean, we can use you right away. Know Tommy Thompson?"

"The wild man of Johnny Allen's crew?"

"The same. Well, to make a long story short he came in off leave last night from London with a beautiful dose. Some young virginal-looking thing has loaded him up with the bug. So he'll be two weeks and more out of circulation. Too bad that guy thought rubbers were only something you wear on your feet if it rains."

"Poor old Tommy. He deserved a better fate. Does Johnny know I'm available?"

"Yes, as a matter of fact. He and the rest of the crew are damned glad to have you instead of some greenhorn from the Pool."

"How many ops have they chalked up?"

"Twelve. They're a bloody fine crew. I'm going to expect big things of you from here in."

"Thanks a million, Ralph. You can count on me."

"Don't thank me. Just put those bombs on the aiming-point. That's all the thanks I need."

"I'll do my damndest," I told him.

"I know you will. So why not slide down to Stores and draw a new kit? I'll try to get you an H2S run or two before you do an op but it may not be possible. They're really pulling them out of the hat these days."

"Don't worry, Ralph, I'm not that rusty."

"We'll see," he said. And went back to his paperwork.

I left the dispersal hut hardly believing my good luck. Back in a seasoned crew with no sweat at all! I guess I had Tommy Thompson to thank. Or more correctly some cute little dosed-up London doll.

27

I found an empty locker in the flight hut, hung up my stuff and walked back to the dispersal hut. Whoever had used the locker before me had left his key in the lock. Everything seemed to be working for me today.

I looked around for Johnny Allen and found him watching a poker-game in lively progress at the far end of the room. He was an older pilot than most, perhaps twenty-five, a wavy, blond-haired guy who always acted very friendly but still gave you the distinct impression you'd never get very close to him. I knew he and Tommy Thompson had chummed around a lot, which probably wouldn't make him any more approachable at the moment.

"Hi, Bill," he said by way of greeting, "just watching a couple of my dumb friends lose their next week's pay. Say, let's sit down somewhere."

We moved across the room and sat down on a couple of folding chairs.

"How was your leave?"

"Wonderful," I said. "I understand you were on a week too."

"Yeah. We tried to take London apart and drink it dry at the same time."

"That was rough about Tommy."

"Rough for me, tough for him. We were over at the Hammersmith last Saturday night. I picked up this kid, a real looker. Honestly, Bill, she'd have taken your breath away. Reminded you of the girl back home and all that garbage. Then Tommy cut in and practically stole her away from me. When he saw I was a little cheesed off about it he offered to toss to see who took her home. I lost the toss. End of story."

"Some story," I said.

"Which leaves me without a bombardier. Did Doc pass you out?"

"No trouble. I'm still a little sore, that's all."

"I'll bet you are. So how about it. Bill? Want to give us a go?"

"Suits me fine, John. I thought you'd never ask."

"Great, Bill, really great. Suppose I fix us up with an H2S run? That'll get your eyes used to the set again. How about 0200 hours if we can manage it? I'm supposed to get back to Ralph on this."

"The sooner the better," I said, but I was only kidding myself. I was starting to tighten up a little already. God knows what I'd be like by take-off time.

I walked back to my room. One thing that hadn't changed since I'd gone on leave was the hut's unique smell, a mixture of coal dust, coal gas, unwashed clothing and hot-plate cooking.

Dave's old bed had been empty when I'd turned in the night before, but now it was made up differently, with a strange new complement of litter around it.

I still had that small packet in my locker Fred had made me promise to send on to his beloved in Edinburgh if anything happened to him. Until I put it in the mail I'd have it on my mind. I almost forced myself to bring it out, put it into a slightly larger envelope I happened to have, then addressed and sealed it after slipping in a short awkward-sounding note to his girl. The packet no doubt contained all the letters she'd written him. Whether or not she'd appreciate getting these now was hard to say, but a promise was a promise. After I'd licked stamps onto the envelope and it was done with I felt somehow much better. I'd mail it right after lunch.

I'd barely finished that chore when my new roommate put in an appearance.

"Sorry to make all that noise last night. I was too loaded to even notice you there in the bed, believe it or not. I'm Russ Gordon, but everybody calls me Flash, so why should you be the exception?"

"I must have been really pooped, Flash. I didn't hear a thing. I'm Bill Sutcliffe, by the way."

"That makes me feel a lot better, Bill," he said. "Say, I heard about your crew. That was a tough one."

"They're all tough," I said. I didn't want to talk about it. Flash had hair almost as red as Midge's and didn't look more than nineteen. That was pretty young to be a P/O. But then they were turning them out on the youthful side these days.

I managed to eat a fair lunch at the mess. Afterwards I ran into Harry Sanders, a fellow bombadier in our squadron. He offered to buy me a beer but I said no thanks, I was flying in an hour.

"What's new?" I asked him. "Were you on the Hamburg milk run yesterday?"

"Milk run, hell. We came so damn close to cashing it in that it wasn't even funny."

"What's left to bomb there anyway?"

"They told us we were going after the Bohm and Voss shipyards. Of course our crate has to have trouble in two engines, and by the time our engineer gets them back in shape we're ten minutes back of our gaggle. So our pilot gets the brilliant idea to form up on a bunch of our Lancs going in to the target. The cloud cover's solid so we're bombing on skymarkers. All of a sudden 262's start zooming out of the cloud banks by the dozen. We've lost our fighter umbrella so we're on our own. A couple of Lancs go down flaming almost at once. Our pilot told me to drop my bloody bombs and down they went, miles from nowhere. Then we got out of there fast. Our rear-gunner saw a couple more Lancs get hit behind us, but we seemed to have a charmed life. It was plain murder, Bill. And here we thought Jerry was cooked. Hell, those 262's go by at five hundred per and you feel like you're standing still."

"Which our Hallys damn well are by comparison. Anyway, you're still in one piece, Harry, with a drink in your hand. Now I've got to blow. I'm going to sweat out an H2S run. And I mean sweat."

"Who's the lucky crew?"

"Johnny Allen's."

"They're a good bunch. Lots of luck, Bill."

"Thanks. I'll need it."

I still had half an hour until I was due at the flight hut. I decided to go back to the billet and write a letter home. I hadn't written the folks since I was in hospital except for a card or two scribbled at Bournemouth.

The letter took a little longer to write than I'd bargained

for, and it was twenty-five to two when I arrived at Flights. Johnny was already suited up; when I'd dressed he introduced me to the rest of my new crew. There was Pat Crawford, the navigator, from Edmonton, Guy Lalonde, wireless operator, from Sherbrooke, mid-upper gunner Sam Yarnowsky from Winnipeg, tail-gunner Soup Campbell from Trenton, and Don Wilson, the engineer, from Orillia, Ontario. Like my old gang they were a real cross-section of Canada. With twelve ops under their belts they had a quiet confidence about them that gave me a good feeling right away. Only Johnny, myself and Pat Crawford held commissions, all the rest were flight-sergeants. When Johnny told them I had sixteen trips in I could tell they didn't mind having me on board too much. This in spite of the fact that I was filling Tommy Thompson's shoes, apparently the most popular member of the crew.

Shortly before the lorry taking us to dispersal pulled up I allowed myself the luxury of a last nervous pee. Then I zippered up the heavy, awkward flying suit and was as ready as I'd ever be. I could feel the weight of the suit a little on my tender shoulder but I'd probably forget all about it once we got under way.

It was a brighter than usual afternoon, sun out strongly, clouds white and swift-scudding in a solid blue sky, Perfect bombing weather. But in spite of this Tannoy had announced a stand-down until 0800 a half hour ago. So for nearly all crews it was a lazy day.

At dispersal I saw we were flying my old girl "N" for "Nan". The thought struck me as we looked her over whether or not it would have helped our luck any that day of the crash if we'd been in "Nan" instead of "Charlie", but I had to admit now it was pretty wild dreaming. The last time I'd seen "Nan" was inspecting her after we'd diverted to Croft on Black Sunday following the Munster pasting. She'd been full of holes that afternoon, twelve good-sized jagged ones. Today she looked slightly patched-up, but it wasn't that obvious. The airframe boys had done a lovely paint job on her and she showed hardly a scar now. Good old Nan!

A few minutes later Johnny had finished running up all four engines and we were ready for take-off. I was sitting awkwardly on the fuselage floor midway back in the aircraft. All of my new crew but Johnny and Don were hunched over around me in a group. The sweat was starting to pour now. I could feel it under the suit even down to my legs. I didn't feel too bad yet, though. Up front Johnny had the engines shrieking, every fibre of the aircraft shaking, fighting the brakes holding her. Then he released them and old Nan started to roll, slowly at first, then faster, faster, faster as she surged down the runway. I could feel myself shaking all over now. My whole body ached. Now the faces around me no longer seemed strangers. Dave was sitting there next to me, Joe and Pete and Fred on either side. We were being pushed by the wind like a feather. Now we were off the runway, and still she wouldn't lift up. And over there was the hatch, the only way out. . . .

A sudden gentle swaying underneath told me we were off the deck, airborne and slowly rising. We'd made it. The faces around me somehow blurred, then focused again. The still strange but smiling, friendly faces of my new crew.

"Up off your butt," the one they called Soup Campbell told the mid-upper gunner, "and how about giving me a little shooting competition for a change?"

Sam, the gunner in question, looked at me and shook his head as he pointed to the rear-gunner.

"Listen to him flapping his gums. Last time up he almost shot down the crate towing the bloody drogue."

It was now 0205 of a Sunday afternoon. I was back at my airman's trade and there was still a war to win. I moved along behind Pat Crawford, following him up to the navigator's compartment. Now it was all coming back very fast. Everything was almost as it had been before. The aircraft was the same, the bombs the same, the enemy the same. Only I had changed. That and the faces that I'd fight with, perhaps even die with, now.

28

The fifteenth of April was a very ordinary day but somehow the date stuck in my mind. Perhaps it was because the fog had lifted enough to allow us to fly back in the morning from Long Marston. Perhaps because the extra day we'd been forced to spend there had seemed to me like a small eternity.

Since joining Johnny Allen's crew I'd sweated out three more ops, Harburg, Hamburg and Leipzig. At Harburg, a suburb of Hamburg, we'd tried to complete the damage done to the Rhenania oil refinery on previous attacks. It had been a lively night with some trouble from searchlights. Apparently there'd been fighters up after us but we hadn't seen any. That was on the fourth. On the ninth they'd given us another night shot at Hamburg. I'd always remember that session in the briefing room. When the target had been announced a low murmur of incredulity had seemed to sweep across the crowded rows of aircrew. Several very distinct voices had gasped out "Not again!" in complete disbelief. It showed how these last few attacks on what seemed to us veterans as very secondary targets were bothering more than a few of the new crews. Perhaps the way the Me 262 was being talked about at every bull-session as some fantastic adversary had something to do with it. To me the jet fighter was preferable to that sea of death-black flak over Munster. And Hamburg wasn't defended now like it used to be, far from it.

Luckily the worst fears of the gloom-merchants had gone unrealized that night. Over Hamburg a thick cloud cover had built up. By the time we'd approached the target the Master Bomber had come over the R/T with his crisp precise tone: "You will now bomb on sky markers." Which we did. It was only on the first leg of our return heading that Don Wilson had reported the number four engine pressure dropping. It was the first engine failure I'd been involved in since O.T.U.

183

and old Slim. But Johnny had simply feathered the engine and we'd gone home with no sweat on three Hercules XVI's.

Coming back from clobbering the Mochau marshalling yards outside Leipzig on the tenth, we'd watched three Mustangs chasing a bat-winged Me 363. The 363 had looped and twisted, trying to escape. It was a little like watching an unequal World War One dogfight in the movies. With its fuel running out the pocket jet had lost height rapidly. Finally two of the Mustangs had closed in and smoke had begun to pour from the doomed fighter. He'd nosed straight down, more smoke trailing. Kaput.

We'd had several wonderful days off after that. I'd found a first long letter from Midge in my mail slot at the mess, and it had been a very welcome tonic to my slightly sagging spirits. I'd sat down right after lunch and written a reply almost as long, which was very unusual for me. Bournemouth was dead without me there with her, she'd written. She was keeping very busy at work and was counting the days until she'd see me again.

The afternoon of the Kiel attack I'd been playing softball most of the afternoon with a dozen or so guys, including two or three of the crew. It had been a warm sunny day. I'd found I wasn't as rusty at throwing and hitting a ball as I thought I'd be after such a long lay-off. It felt good using a few muscles I'd almost forgotten I owned. I'd showered and lain down for a short nap around four only to be awakened at a little before five by Tannoy announcing a stand by.

There'd been more grumbling than usual that night as we'd taken off shortly after eight o'clock on a night attack against the Deutsche Werke Shipyards at Kiel.

"I don't know how you guys feel about it, but this war is starting to get on my bleeding nerves," Pat Crawford had told us as we'd waited for Johnny to gun "O" for "Oboe". He and Johnny had been in Ye Olde Starre with their first pint in front of them when the S.P.'s had come into the saloon bar and told all West Moor personnel to return to base.

"Pretty grim when they start cutting in on a man's beer time," I'd agreed. "Looks to me like the brass were caught with their pants down on this one. I wonder how many crews they weren't able to round up?"

A good question. But we hadn't been one of the lucky ones. And we'd had problems right from the time the west coast of the Danish Narrows showed up on my H2S. First Pat and I couldn't agree if we'd strayed off our flight plan or not. Then, after we'd straightened that out and were approaching on target, I'd seen two distinct sets of ground target markers ahead. We'd been warned about dummy markers. Finally I'd picked out the ones straight ahead as closer to the colour our Pathfinders used and got away what I thought was a good release.

We'd had one extra problem on the Kiel op. The base had closed in on us and we'd had to touch down at Long Marston. That evening we'd bummed a ride to the nearest village. The local pub had been crowded, the beer wet. They'd poured us out of the bar at ten, and we'd walked back to camp arm-in-arm, singing at the top of our voices, feeling no pain at all. It had been a damn fine evening and I'd spent it with a damn fine crew. That night for the first time in several weeks I had the feeling that I'd outlive the war. That I wasn't going to die. That I was going to live for a long long time and experience life to the full. Of course in the morning, if my nightmares were bad, I might not believe it as strongly, or even at all. But it was a wonderful feeling while it lasted, even if only for a few hours. For that I suppose I had to be thankful.

29

At five-thirty on the morning of the eighteenth they dragged us out of bed for a daylight to Heligoland, or more specifically the airfield on the island of Dune. Over one hundred Hallys of the Group were to make up part of a force of almost a thousand heavies from Bomber Command.

"They're really scraping the barrel now," I grumbled to Pat Crawford over powdered eggs and bangers in the mess, "next time it'll be the Channel Islands."

"Let's not knock it, sport. Quite a pleasant change from Hamburg and Leipzig."

"N" for "Nan" was waiting for us again at dispersal, to my great secret joy. Looking better than ever, with not a patch showing. I actually patted her awkward flanks a couple of times during our last-minute inspection to show the old girl how glad I was to see her and fly in her again. I was sure now that she wouldn't let us down. My best insurance on these last few trips. Like today, my twenty-first.

When we left the English coast behind us Johnny wasted no time telling us over the intercom how he felt about the whole outing.

"You can see now how we're boxed in on every side. It's a real bugger from up here. So let's have everyone on their toes. Keep a sharp look-out from your own spot, and I do mean sharp. Sing out loud and clear if you don't like the looks of anything at all. Better be safe than sorry. That's all, folks."

Only a few minutes after Johnny's pep-talk it happened. Two Hallys collided up ahead. I yelled the news from my bombardier's compartment, where I watched with a strange fascination as the two aircraft clung together for a moment, then separated. A wing fell off one, the other lost his twin fins and turret. It had all happened in a flash. The one without a

186

tail nose-dived toward the sea. It was only mid-April; you didn't need much imagination to guess how icy-cold the waters of the North Sea would be. Now parachutes blossomed out from the other Hally spiralling downward. One, two, three, four. That was all. These poor bastards would be even worse off than the ones dead or dying in the plummetting aircraft. They'd last ten, fifteen minutes at the most after hitting the water. There was no way they'd get any help from Air-Sea Rescue. No one could get to them in time, they were too far off the coast. They'd float with their Mae Wests until they died from the cold. When the wreckage and the bobbing survivors had faded from view I left my compartment and slumped down beside Pat at his navigator's table. He was busy entering something in his log book, probably the details of the crash as Johnny had given them to him. He was a lot like Dave in this respect; personally I couldn't be so cool after a thing like that. But I'd seen it happen and he hadn't. Tonight I'd be the one with the picture of it all in my mind when I tried to sleep; he'd have probably forgotten all about it by then.

More by an effort of will than anything else I'd managed to snap out of it to some extent by the time we approached Dune from the north and swung south on our bombing run. There wasn't much time for sentiment in a war. It wasn't a pastime for bleeding hearts. As we drew closer the island was revealed in the brilliant sunshine like a picture target shown at briefings, all runways clearly visible. Already sticks of bombs from the flight ahead of us were bursting on the centre of the "X" formed by the runways. Then as we made our run the centre of the island began to turn into one great cloud of smoke billowing upward.

That was our shortest op of the war: 4.40 I penned the time into my log book. We were through at de-briefing by four in the afternoon. I still felt too shaken by that mid-air collision to even want to try to sleep. I knew it would simply mix together my usual nightmare and I wasn't ready to face that at the moment.

I drove a car load of the boys into York with me. Then, promising to join them for a few beers later on I strolled around town. Ever since I'd broken off with Prue I'd kept pretty close to Betty's Bar and a couple of other pubs in York. The chance of running into her on the street was still a thousand-to-one shot, but I hadn't been in the mood before to gamble even that much. Today I simply didn't care. Somehow it didn't seem to matter any more.

Coming up past the Art Gallery I noticed a fairly large crowd gathered. About twenty slightly bored policemen were scattered at a respectable distance from the edge of the crowd. Evidently someone thought trouble might develop. I moved in closer to get a better look.

A man about thirty years old dressed in a leather windbreaker and sporting a striking full red beard was standing on an elevated metal stand. He was speaking quite forcefully to perhaps three hundred people, most of them factory workers by the look of their clothes. Apparently he was almost through his speech. "To conclude," he said, "after six years of fighting for freedom we're worse off now than we were before we started. Freedom to do what?" he wanted to know. "To give you a thick ear," someone in the crowd yelled. "You can't even do that," he countered, "you'd have one of these coppers on your neck in no time flat. What we have to do, my friends," he went on, "is to stop this war right now. Each day longer it's allowed to go on the more senseless it becomes. Soldiers must refuse to fight, workers must lay down their tools and stop the machines. If we all do this together the present government of capitalist stooges will collapse immediately under its own dead weight. Then a new government of the workers, elected by you and working for you, can take its place. Yes, I'm called an Anarchist, and I'm proud to be one. But don't get the idea we still go around throwing bombs and murdering kings. That's far in the past. This is the year 1945. Besides, we don't have to resort to terror tactics any more. We depend simply on the good common sense of you, the worker, the real backbone of this country of ours."

He was finished and stepped down. There was scattered applause. Then the chairman of the meeting, an older, serious-looking man standing beside him, invited questions. Any not put through him, the chairman, wouldn't be answered, he cautioned. The questions came, slow at first and then one after another. They were mostly banal, I thought, and the red-bearded man fielded them easily. The crowd was quiet and well-behaved, it was a waste of time for the police to be there. But perhaps they'd been sent to intimidate the meeting in the first place. If so they hadn't succeeded. I listened until the questions became very silly and the speaker in turn slightly irritated. Then I walked on.

From what little I'd seen in England it seemed fairly obvious that these working men who had eaten crow for centuries weren't about to change their diet overnight. Maybe they'd still eat it for another fifty years. They were stubborn enough, however, to prefer to grub along under a Parliament than under a dictatorship. Several hundred thousand of them had died in this war so that people like this leather-jacketed revolutionary could speak his mind in a public place with the police in attendance to protect him if he began to suffer at the hands of the crowd. Today in Germany he wouldn't last thirty seconds; it was inconceivable that anyone there would even think of taking such a radical step as speaking out against the government in public or elsewhere. That Anarchist was right, however, in many ways. Our fathers had bungled this war and it looked as though the same old gang would run things after it was over. We might get rid of Hitler but that was all. So it was up to us, the ones who had fought this war, to do something about it. But I was afraid that we were very tired and very disillusioned. We could very easily let things slip back into the same old rut again. Perhaps the labels would be changed but the old hatreds, the familiar injustices would still be the same in the end. That made our dead the biggest losers of all. They'd been sold a bill of goods and marched to their graves without a complaint. And we who fought on after them could do no more than drink to their memory the same day they died and then try to erase their faces from our minds before we had to risk death the next time ourselves.

Maybe I should have told the red-bearded Anarchist that I'd just come back from being over the North Sea and watched fourteen Canadians die trying to finish off the war he wanted over so badly. But he'd have an answer for me, no doubt, a smart logical answer for which I could only return anger and frustration in reply. The ones who had to do the fighting, the real dirty work, were always the poorest ones with words.

I'm sure the rest of the crew must have thought I was bloody poor company when I joined them a little later at the Starre. It took at least two mild and bitter to mellow my mood. I hoped I could down at least three more, I knew that sooner or later I'd have to lie on my bed and try to sleep. I was afraid what was coming. Those two Hallys plunging like dead birds. The bodies trapped in the turrets, the cockpits. The reek of smoke, the flames of death. The last trapped, terrified human cries. And far below the bodies, the faces floating in the water.

30

Four days later after lunch Tannoy sounded a stand-by. Up until that moment you could have got pretty good odds from any number of guys that our flying days were behind us. The operational ones, anyway. Now I was glad I hadn't made any bets.

This raid looked like another last-minute job, an attack on Bremen, which was supposed to be surrounded by British forces. The Jerries must have been putting up a fairly stiff resistance to cause the brass to lay on an op like this one which called for pin-point bombing, something we weren't exactly noted for.

I was in a fairly good mood until I reached dispersal. There we found a strange aircraft, "X" for "X-Ray", waiting for us. I didn't know how the other boys felt but I had that sudden sinking feeling in my stomach. This was op twenty-two for me. The strain was beginning to tell a little.

All the way across the North Sea I had the repeated picture of those four chutes opening below the two falling Hallys on the Dune raid. It had been much the same kind of afternoon, too.

As we approached the Dutch coast our number two engine packed up. So "X-Ray" had been a jinx after all. If we'd had "Nan" there wouldn't have been any trouble, I told myself.

We began to lose height rapidly. Johnny announced almost immediately: "We're going to have to turn back, gang." Then he said to me: "Let's get rid of the bomb load pronto, Bill."

Our first abort. I hunted up the nearest designated spot to jettison bombs in a case like this. Luckily it wasn't that far away. All the same it seemed like a long time before we reached the area. With one squeeze of the "tit" the whole load went down, making quite a splash. That sent "X-Ray" bouncing up again, and we regained our old height without too much trouble.

A short time later we heard the Master Bomber order the attack abandoned. That made us feel a little better for the moment. With us aborting and so not getting credit for an op, it softened the blow a little to know that everybody else had taken a screwing as well. It wasn't until de-briefing that we found out the brass had decided that the other crews had carried the attack far enough to be given credit for an op. Maybe it was a gift, a morale-booster, but an op behind you was one op closer to a tour, no matter how you looked at it. That generosity of Group really topped it off. Soup Campbell said it for all of us: "Something told me this morning I should have stood in bed, fellows."

A little before eight-thirty I stopped by the mess with Johnny to get ourselves a well-earned late supper of bacon and eggs. I picked up the mail in my box. There was a letter from Midge and one from my mother. There were also two scribbled slips of paper telling me a Miss Warwick had called at five and again at eight. A phone number was given in each case.

I suddenly had that strange uneasy feeling I'd had earlier in the day before taking off for Bremen. What could Prue possibly want? We hadn't spoken a word or seen each other since that last night a month ago. It was very seldom that I thought about her any more. And now in a moment the whole thing was alive again.

I recognized the number. It was the pharmacy in York. I'd memorized it long ago. If Prue had called me now, and twice at that, it must be important. I went out to the lobby. Luckily both telephones were not in use.

An older man's voice answered. Mr. Warwick? I couldn't tell at first.

"Is Miss Warwick there, please?"

"No, she's gone to Harrogate. Who's speaking, please?"

It wasn't Mr. Warwick. I was fairly sure of that.

"It's Flying Officer Sutcliffe. Prue and I are old friends. Can you tell me when she left?"

"About half an hour ago. She's catching the 9.20. Is there any message you want to leave?"

"No thanks," I said and hung up.

It was a quarter to nine now, which gave me plenty of

time to drive into York and to locate her at the station if I left right away. If it wasn't important there wouldn't be much harm done. I didn't feel nervous now about meeting her. Enough water had already gone under the bridge, I suppose.

I was parked and heading in the entrance to the station shortly after nine. There was a good chance Prue hadn't arrived yet but I couldn't take the chance and wait outside. I decided to give the station platform a good look, then hang around the ticket office.

I'd barely finished checking out the platforms and walked back into the main waiting room when I saw Prue walking in through the entrance carrying a suitcase. My heart began to beat faster at the first sight of her. She still had a lot of that old magic; I hadn't got her entirely out of my system yet.

When I saw her heading straight for a ticket window I decided I'd better move in. I caught up to her as she was setting down her suitcase.

"Where do you think you're going, young lady?"

For a moment she looked startled, then she seemed to relax into her usual assured manner.

"Oh, hello Bill. I'm very glad you caught up with me. Did you have any trouble with Henry at the shop?"

"No. Was that who I was talking to?"

"Yes. He used to work with father, then retired when I came on the scene. He's going to fill in while I'm away."

"Which I understand is to Harrogate."

"That's right. Would you mind waiting a moment while I buy my ticket? Then we can talk until the train comes in."

"Why bother?" I asked. "I can easily drive you over. Now that I'm here it seems silly not to make use of me."

"It's too much trouble to put you to, really. I'll just get my ticket. It'll be far easier all round."

"I insist," I said, "so no more arguments. I'll take your bag and we'll walk out of here to the car. Then you can tell me what this is all about on the way over. And I'm not going to take no for an answer. So there."

"All right," Prue said. "I'm too tired to argue."

And some of that tiredness did show in her face. But it still couldn't do much damage to those sparkling eyes of hers, that fine skin, her assured, graceful bearing. She was a thoroughbred, no doubt about it. As I walked slowly beside her out of the infernal noise of the station I couldn't help wonder why I hadn't fought harder to keep her.

I opened the car door, put her suitcase in the back seat, then closed the door behind her after she settled in the seat. I had the car parked on Station Road, but it wasn't busy at this time of night.

I offered her a cigarette, which she accepted. After we'd lit up and both exhaled, with our breathing the only sound breaking the deathly silence in the car, Prue said rather awkwardly, "I'd given up on you tonight, you know. The chap who answered the phone was very nice but he simply wouldn't say anything at all about you."

"It's the security. He's not allowed to say anything. You could be a beautiful spy trying to learn our deepest secrets, you know."

"That occurred to me later. But it still was frustrating. Especially when I debated quite a long time before deciding to get in touch with you. Even now I'm not sure I've done the right thing."

"Why don't you let me be the judge of that? But first you're going to have to tell me what it's all about."

"I'm coming to it. This may be something of a shock to you. The fact is I'm pregnant."

She was right. I wasn't prepared for that at all, and the expression that came over my face must have shown it very clearly.

"See, I knew you'd be upset. That's why I didn't want to call you. I couldn't see what good it would do, really. But the plain simple fact is that I had to tell somebody. And as the father you seemed to be the logical person."

"No doubt at all about that," I agreed. "When exactly did you find all this out?"

"Last week."

"And there's no possibility of an error?"

"None whatever. The doctor was quite positive. He even got carried away a little and said I'd make a lovely mother."

"No argument there. Of course you would."

"But which I can't be. Right? The doctor's our family physician and brought me into the world, as a matter of fact. So I felt I could talk very honestly with him. He was a little shocked at first, but finally agreed that under the circumstances an abortion would be the best solution."

"Under what circumstances, Prue?"

"The fact that I don't want to be a mother and have no intention of being one, even if I have to kill myself first."

Her voice had risen to a slightly hysterical pitch. I'd better watch what I said. It certainly wasn't the time for any flip phrases.

"What did he suggest, if anything?"

"He's actually done more than that, Bill, he's made arrangements with a fellow colleague in Harrogate to do a clinical abortion on me. Tomorrow morning at eight as a matter of fact."

"How did you explain this little jaunt to your parents?"

It was the wrong thing to say but it apparently didn't bother her.

"I'm simply taking a short holiday and visiting a girl friend. I'll stay in a hotel a couple of days and go back. Then it'll be all over and done with. Nobody will be hurt and nobody will have to suffer for our little mistake."

"You've planned it all very carefully," I said.

"I hope I have."

"And you're sure you want to go through with it?"

"There's just no other way, Bill."

"I could marry you. Does that sound so impossible?"

"It really does. It simply wouldn't work. You'll have to find yourself a girl who wants to be a mother and have children. This girl doesn't. Make no mistake about that."

"You seem to have made up your mind pretty completely."

"I certainly have."

"But will you promise me one thing in spite of what you're saying now?"

"What's that?"

"If you feel like changing your mind at any time between now and tomorrow morning you won't hold back on me."

"All right. But I know right now I won't, Bill. Now, are you still sure you want to drive me over? You don't have to, you know. I can still very easily catch the train."

"Hell, you're carrying my child, aren't you?" I said. "I think I have one or two privileges."

"If you say anything more like that I'll get right out of this car," Prue retorted, her voice shaking slightly.

"I'm sorry, I shouldn't have said that. Of course I want to drive you. Please sit back and take it easy."

We drove over to Harrogate without saying more than a few words to each other. Prue apparently had made reservations at one of the smaller hotels. The operation was at eight in the morning; she'd spend the balance of the day resting at the clinic. She refused to tell me how much the operation was costing. "Enough" was all she'd say. "Don't worry," she added, "I can afford it." I didn't say anything more. I had exactly ten pounds in my drawing account at the moment.

I'd never had the chance to visit Harrogate before. It was supposed to be one of the most beautiful spots in England. Perhaps I'd have a little time to look around it in the morning. On the drive over I'd decided to stay the night here. It seemed the least I could do.

Prue directed me through unfamiliar streets to the hotel, a quaint, interesting-looking building in an older part of the town.

I got her bag out of the car. I'd decided I wouldn't tell her I planned to stay over. It might only cause another row. Prue seemed more her old self as we made what she thought were our goodbyes.

"Thanks very much for driving me over," she said. "I must say it was reassuring having you with me. Now you run along and don't worry about a thing. These operations are nothing with a good doctor and I've got the very best. And you take care of yourself. Remember, you've got the best part of your life still ahead of you."

"You're sure there isn't something more I can do for you?" I asked her.

"Absolutely nothing. Cheers, Bill. And thanks again."

"Don't thank me. And goodbye, Prue."

I watched her disappear through the hotel entrance, carrying her bag and moving with that splendid way of hers, head high. Only I knew that at this very moment she must be very far from being sure of everything. Very possibly she was going through the biggest ordeal of her young life.

I drove back through the town and stopped at the first hotel I came to. It was slightly larger than the one Prue was staying at. I signed the register, paying for one night in advance. Then I got on the telephone to the Officer's Mess at the base. I asked for the bar steward, Andy MacFarlane. Luckily he was still on duty. I told him where I was, gave him my hotel number, and he agreed to call me the moment

Tannoy sounded. There'll be a quid in it for you when I get back tomorrow, I told him.

Then I went through to the bar, had a very quick ale and took the lift up to my room. I was feeling very tired now. Bremen had been harder on my nerves than I'd realized at the time. And then this operation business on top of everything.

I still had one phone call to make. I asked the switchboard to get me Prue's hotel. She should be settled down in her room by now.

She answered after three or four rings.

"It's me again," I told her. "There's been a slight change in plan. I'm staying overnight at the Belvedere. I want you to do me one very big favour. When you feel up to it after the operation ring me here. I just want to know you're all right. Then I'll go. Is that possible?"

"You're going to a lot of trouble for nothing," Prue said, "but if it'll make you feel any better I'll try to ring you. I can't promise when it'll be, though."

"I know. That's fine. Good night then. I hope you get some sleep. And all the best for tomorrow."

"Thanks, again, Bill. Goodnight. And for God's sake don't worry about me."

I felt better after that. I'd done all I could for now. The only other thing that remained was to wait for her phone call. It looked as though she was definitely going through with it. The more I thought about it now it did seem the only logical way out for us. We hadn't wanted this to happen but Nature had thrown us a big curve. Had she ever.

The hotel was comfortable but I couldn't get used to it for a long long time. It must have been after one before I finally fell asleep. And then it must have been a fairly restless sleep, if what I remembered of my crazy dreams in the morning were any indication.

I woke before eight. It was a beautiful morning outside. I felt in the mood to take a nice long walk, followed by a leisurely breakfast. But I couldn't leave the room on account of the telephone call from Prue. I simply had to be there when it came.

At least I could take a shave while I was waiting. So I spent most of the next half hour washing up, then carefully removing the stubble. I always felt better after using my trusty safety razor and shaving lotion. I seemed to go through a bottle of after-shave in no time. Dave at one point had accused me of drinking the stuff on the sly.

I'd barely finished drying my face when the telephone rang. Even though I was expecting it and shouldn't have been too surprised when the noise jangled through the room, I still must have jumped half a foot. It showed how good my nerves were at the moment.

Then as I went to pick up the receiver the thought went racing through my head: with my luck it's got to be the bloody base.

Instead it was Prue's voice, fairly flat, tired-sounding, but still slightly cheerful, perhaps just for my benefit.

"It's over, Bill. Everything's fine. I'm going to take something now to give me a nice sleep. I'm afraid I didn't get too much last night."

"Me either," I said. "Are you sure you'll be all right? There's nothing you need? Just say the word."

"Quite sure. I'll be as good as new by tomorrow. And I do have a friend I can visit here. So don't worry any more. You've been a dear. I won't forget it."

"I wish it could have been a lot more, Prue. It's too bad we didn't hit it off better."

"I know. But that's life. Now goodbye and all the luck."

"Goodbye," I said. Even my own voice had a final sound to it. I put down the telephone. So it was over. Just like that. Yesterday we were linked together somehow, now it was finished. And the sooner I forgot about it the better.

I decided to take my walk, then have some of that breakfast I'd promised myself. Then I'd better get back to West Moor. Something told me the war couldn't wait for me much longer than that.

31

At 1510 hours two days later Johnny coaxed old "Nan" up into the air and we began to form up for a mid-afternoon attack on Wangerooge Island at the eastern end of the Frisian chain. This was one of the last Jerry strongholds in Holland, shielding two troublesome coastal batteries we had orders to wipe out.

It proved to be another textbook precision bombing raid, almost a carbon-copy of the Dune attack. Except that about the time I released my bombs well in the centre of the smoke and dust rising almost to our bombing height, both light and heavy flak began to break around us in rapidly multiplying bursts. Johnny moved us out of there sharply. While we hadn't spotted any mishaps on the ride over or seen any aircraft around us shot down, we heard later at de-briefing that no less than seven kites had bought it that afternoon from accurate ack-ack fire on neighbouring islands. Two of the aircraft were from Six Group. But both coastal batteries had been totally obliterated.

I hung around the de-briefing room after interrogation, sipping rum and coffee. It was only eight-thirty, but even so I felt dead-tired. My log book flying time read only four hours, forty minutes, and we'd had a fairly easy time of it. That was number twenty-two for me, but three ops more to go at this stage of the game felt more like thirteen. The same old question that had nagged thousands of aircrew before me now loomed larger and larger in front of me: will I make it or will I crap out? One thing was fairly certain, I'd had almost all the flying I could take, milk runs or no milk runs. Each time up now was simply too much strain, too much blood-sweat.

Tonight for some reason I didn't feel particularly hungry, but went along anyway with the rest of the gang for the usual bacon and eggs. Perhaps the rum had got to me and my whole thinking process was a trifle fuzzy, but I had the strangest feeling sitting there in the dining hall that this would be the last time we'd be there together having a meal after a raid. Whether or not that was supposed to mean that this new crew of mine along with myself were down on the books to go for the chop on our next outing I had no way of telling, but I felt it as strong as death. Knock it off, you nit-wit, I told myself. Maybe it only means that there's simply no more targets to hit, that we're going to hang up our skates for good. What you need to do is log some sack time. You've had these mixed-up thoughts before after a raid and they all came to nothing. You're letting it get too close to you. Maybe it's only a prelude to your usual night's torture program. Will it be that old crash on take-off nightmare back again? The one that ends with Pete Yarish's face falling apart like tissue paper when you reach out to touch it through the turret door?

All at once I wanted to stand up there at the table and tell each member of this crew I'd sweated out these last six ops with that they were a great bloody bunch. That I was proud as hell to be one of them and fly with them. That I'd remember them always, no matter what else happened.

But something told me very very firmly, no, you can't do that, you stupid bastard. They'll only laugh at you, tell you to sober up and stop shooting the crap. And you'll probably embarrass them as well.

So I ended up very sensibly buggering off to bed, dragging my two feet like two lead weights all the way to the hut. A world traveller at twenty-two, Canada's typical fighting airman, scared almost to tears to fly any more, fed up with the grinding monotony of Service life, wanting only to be out of it. No more cities to scan on the H2S, no more targets to bomb, no more senseless killing. With only one thing left to fill up the blinding darkness of his life, the love of a tiny, red-headed WAAF. Paste that up on your recruiting posters.

Only they weren't recruiting any more. Only they'd almost run out of targets. And soon, very soon they'd settle with me. Give me a handshake and say, thanks very much. We had you marked down as expendable, but you somehow escaped out of our clutches. Oh well, perhaps we'll get you next time around.

Faced with this final comforting thought I said to myself, to hell with it, let it all come down, made the last restless turn in my bed and surrendered to sleep, to the nightmares waiting. To the oblivion offered afterwards, that total satisfying dark.

32

"Almost everyone here has his own special rumour, his own guaranteed official gen," I wrote Midge early the following week. "The most imaginative ones have the squadron disbanding within the next couple of weeks. The other chief school of opinion has us flying food in to Holland and Germany and bringing out prisoners-of-war and then the long-service troops. It'll probably be one of these but I don't know which to put my money on myself. I'd like to back the disbanding theory, because that would mean I'd be sure not to fly again. But we'll simply have to wait and see what the brass decides. One thing seems fairly certain: we'll get at least a three-day stand-down when V-E Day comes, and I'm going to try to wangle an extra day or two on the end of it. Then I'll be heading for Bournemouth by the fastest possible means."

Following Wangerooge there'd been no more flying, not even practice flights. After longing for a break in the deadening routine of operational flying, I wasn't able to adjust very easily when it finally came, to relax and enjoy it. I wandered around the base or rode into town without any special feeling of release. I couldn't concentrate on reading books or magazines; I was drinking too much beer and sitting around the dispersal hut torturing myself with each new fantastic rumour. In a way it would have been a relief to fly again, to have to do something ordered and meaningful.

The British newspapers were packed with more dramatic news day after day. Hitler had committed suicide in his Chancellory bunker. The Russians had reached the Reichstag building. What was talked of as perhaps the last R.A.F. raid of the war had been made by Mosquitoes on Kiel. Montgomery was meeting with German envoys. The war couldn't last much longer than a few days any way you looked at it.

Even now all the ops I'd flown since February seemed like

202

events I'd sweated through many months or even years ago. Already an undertone of nostalgia was beginning to colour many of them. Seemingly unimportant moments like looking out of an aircraft window soon after becoming airborne on a daylight raid and having the eye take in a perfect picture of Yorkshire countryside caught only for a moment before it swung away far behind. The way our aircraft would suddenly lift through a dense patch of fog at night, and there, brilliantly glowing, the moon in a perfectly clear upper sky. Or belting along with the nose down and flak coming up much too close, too loud and too concentrated around the target area, your heart still in your mouth as you got up from the bomb-sight, your work done and the clothing under your flying suit bathed in sweat, hoping, praying no lucky burst would wing you. Then a little later old Max's good-humoured voice over the intercom: "Only enough petrol left to make the coast, you guys. So where do you want to touch down— Hamburg, Amsterdam or Kiel?" And the stock answer coming back in a chorus: "Make it Brussels, Max", because we all knew Brussels was a real, wide-open town. And Walt cutting in right after: "Enough of that b.s., gang. Everybody back on the ball." Or Dave the day of the bad Munster show crapping his pants in his fear and telling me about it a little sheepishly that night in the shower at the flight hut. And the feeling so many nights of being in a completely different world locked up there in upper darkness, only intruded on by ominous clusters of searchlights around the flak belts or mysterious flashes of gun-fire from the ground action far below. And a thing to really grate on already over-taut nerves—the loudly-cursed red enemy fighter markers hanging too brightly in the air to indicate our homeward route—spelling out the certain fact that we might be jumped on from all sides by enemy fighter packs eager to draw Allied blood. But even more straining on the nerves what seemed like the simple business of turning into the Station circuit after a long tiring op. Good old Yorkshire was somewhere below, but not too much of it visible, the runway lights showing very faint and flickering. And knowing there was still five, ten, or even fifteen minutes still left to hang up there while we waited our turn to land, moving ponderously around and around in the same endless circuit. That's when a lot of the real sweating started. And it was so much in the mind that you totally forgot frozen hands

and feet under the gloves and the boots as you crouched in
the fuselage, still dreaming of that hot coffee and rum waiting
at de-briefing. With all the time Walt checking Max every
couple of minutes to see how much gas we had left, then finally getting the nod from the tower and starting his approach that slid us lower and lower through the half-haze
until the small miracle of wheels touching down, of brakes
squealing not too protestingly, occurred. And home free once
more. . . .

Wednesday Johnny informed me and the rest of the crew
that he'd had a talk with one of the top brass and had this almost officially: no more flying. And that there was a good
chance the squadron itself would be disbanded by mid-May.
Then at the mess that night there was a sign up announcing a
big party Saturday night. Ladies were invited with escorts;
music for dancing by the Station orchestra. The theme of the
evening was announced as "The Last Round-Up", which
sounded pretty final to most of us.

So it looked like I'd made it after all. Though why I
couldn't understand. If it was by the grace of God it was a
God I didn't really know. All I knew for certain was that I
was very glad to be alive. But whether I was better off than
the ones I'd flown with who had died I certainly couldn't tell
at the moment. I might never find that out. I'd come very
close several times to discovering all about death. Perhaps in
the years ahead I might be lucky enough to find out something about life.

33

By noon that Saturday I could feel even in our hut and certainly up at the mess the beginning of that delicious abandonment which would build into the big blow-out that night. Later in the afternoon I drove Johnny and Pat Crawford into York. We drank beer at Ye Olde Starre until eight-thirty, with only a brief pause for some bread and cheese, after which the two of them went off to corral the four girls they were bringing out to the base by taxi to help liven up the proceedings. For some reason known only to them they didn't want me along and had refused my offer of transportation. I shrugged my shoulders and drove back to camp. I had the feeling it was going to be quite a night before it was all over.

I parked my car in the usual place by Number One hangar and walked back down the road to the mess. They must have had the windows open in the lounge because even from a distance I could hear first the brass section, then the softer saxes of the station dance-band swinging out loudly. As I got closer to the brilliantly-lit, huge double Nissen hut, I had to concede that they were producing a very fair imitation of the Squadronaires, the Air Force's top-flight dance-band from A.F.H.Q., London. But after a few drinks nobody would care very much about the music, as long as it was sentimental and wildly swinging in turn. Tonight, in the mood I was in, the band sounded very good indeed.

The first thing that hit you as you went inside the mess was a huge sign above the door that read: *The Last Round-Up*. Below the bright lettering was hung a large pair of genuine steer-horns. They seemed wildly out of place, but still a real symbol of the Western Canadian theme of the evening. Other signs were in evidence. Where a cloak-room had been set up the letters read *Check Your Hardware Here*. Over the bar area another read *The Last Chance Saloon*. When I got as far as the lounge I made out a line of beer barrels right up one side of the room with a fancy cover over them. The old pool-table had been covered over as well to serve as a huge informal table.

There were a lot of civilian girls in bright party dresses already dancing, as well as a sprinkling of WAAFs. I noted with quiet satisfaction that I didn't see anyone half as cute as Midge among those in uniform. I wondered if she'd been available whether or not I'd have brought her here tonight. I decided that I wouldn't have risked it. These parties usually started out innocent as hell but had a way of quickly degenerating into brawls. Simply because the party was being held in the officer's mess was no guarantee those present wouldn't forget they were ladies and gentlemen at some stage of the proceedings. Far from it. Well, all I had to do was hang in for another week or so and I might find myself dancing with Midge at the Pavilion in Bournemouth. With a prospect ahead of me like that I could afford to play it cool tonight. Not that I didn't mean to enjoy myself. No fear of that.

I pushed my way up to the bar and came away with a large glass of Scotch and water. The Scotch was Haig and Haig. We were travelling first class. It looked as though they meant to make a real dent in the Mess Account tonight. And why not? I made a mental note to drink steadily and keep close to the bar. That Scotch wouldn't last too long once the word got around.

I joined a group of Muskrat boys nursing drinks near the band stand. They were all in various stages of intoxication, having made an early start on the evening. One by one they put down their drinks to dance with the girls who seemed to be arriving every minute at the party. Somebody asked me where Johnny and Soup had got to. I said I hoped they hadn't stopped along the way to sample the merchandise. Don't put it past them, either, someone added. But Soup's sudden arrival with four bright-looking things in tow made an instant liar out of me. My group scrambled to get to them. I went back to the bar, had another Scotch, and with that much comfort inside of me, decided to try my luck on the dance-floor. I had a succession of partners, all very charming. One graceful-looking blonde I swung around the floor danced very close, her belly rubbing up against me ever so softly, ever so insinuating, and all the time her face held the most expressionless look. It was all I could do to keep from laughing out loud. And of course it made you wonder what you'd have to do to change that look on her face. I wisely decided to leave it to someone else to find a possible answer. My life had had enough complications lately. I wanted the pure simple life for a while. At any rate simple.

About eleven-thirty the first of half a dozen fights, major and minor, erupted without warning. A Flying Officer desk jockey from our squadron, generally regarded as none too bright, was threatening a Squadron Leader on the Headquarters staff. At least one foot shorter and thirty pounds lighter, the Squadron Leader quickly peeled off his dress jacket. "Forget about rank, let's finish this right now," he told the other man. They started in trading pretty good punches for the shape the two of them were in. The Squadron Leader, however, had learned to box somewhere, and began to make a monkey out of the bigger man. Finally, with the Flying Officer's nose bleeding quite freely, they'd both had enough. They shook hands and dancing continued as though this had only been a short intermission feature.

At two in the morning a couple of us still more or less on our feet went outside for a little air. I almost tripped over a Flight Lieutenant pilot lying on the grass in the half darkness not too far from the door. We lifted him up. He was very drunk and still out cold. He had blood all over his face, both lips were cut and swollen, both eyes blackened. He wasn't an Algonquin pilot and I couldn't place him as a Muskrat either. It looked very much as though someone had finally settled an old score. We managed to lift him up and dump him on an empty bed in the nearest officers' hut. On the way back to the mess we found a second unconscious body, this time a Flying Officer without any wings up, lying at the entrance to an air-raid shelter. He was also very drunk and even more seriously worked-over than the first victim. We were all in from hauling the first one, but still we felt we couldn't leave him lying out there all night, even though he had all the anti-freeze he needed inside him to see him through sub-zero weather. We half-carried, half-dragged him to the nearest bed. You had to hand it to whoever had settled this double grudge that night. He'd simply waited until his victims were well oiled and had gone outside in turn to relieve themselves. Then he'd followed them out and beaten the crap out of them one at a time. No fuss, no muss, and no chance for either of them to get a good look at their attacker. And best of all, no witnesses, so they'd never make a charge stick anyway.

By the time we returned to the mess even in that short interval the dance had slowed to a crawl. The band had packed it in shortly before. Nearly all the civilian girls were gone and their escorts with them, many no doubt all set to shack up for the night. All the people left seemed to be formed into aimless, melancholy little groups. The party was taking on all the signs of a minor wake.

A pilot I knew in the Muskrats came along and suggested a little runway racing to break the monotony. He had an Austin in even worse shape than my Standard. I packed half a dozen guys into my car, each accompanied with at least one bottle of beer. We belted up and down the runways in the pitch darkness, headlights flashing dimly ahead, trying to race three or four other fools who'd joined us in their beat-up hacks. I had the pedal solidly down to the floor with the needle on the speedometer quivering around the seventy mark. We were close to being airborne.

After about twenty minutes of this a station lorry headed down the runway toward us. A figure standing on the running-board waved me down to a halt. It was the Duty Control Officer. He told us very nicely but firmly to be off the runways in three minutes or else. We weren't going to kill ourselves on his tour of duty if he could help it. Then he drove off after the other cars.

I turned my old bus around and headed back up the runway. Two of the boys jammed in the front seat with me had started up a half-hearted chorus, keeping time with their now-empty beer bottles:

"There was flak, flak, bags of bloody flak,
    In the Ruhr, in the Ruhr,
  There was flak, flak, bags of bloody flak,
    In the Valley of the Ruhr."

I hadn't sung that song for what seemed like a short eternity now. It sounded almost like a dirge, a bitter-sweet memory from a fading past, a past that was still almost yesterday. Now the three boys in the back seat took up the words, this time with considerably more gusto. It sounded much better, more like I remembered it from before.

Right at that moment we drove past a dispersal area, and I could swear I spotted "N" for "Nan" silhouetted against what little moonlight there was. I hadn't seen her since our last op, the milk-run to Wangerooge Island in late April. It seemed now almost ingratitude on my part, not having walked at least once down the runway to take a look at her hunched there like some abandoned and completely forgotten thing. Not much of a reward after the brave and faithful way she'd carried us safely out and back again, both day and night, to those places on the map of Europe, those testing hours of our young, impatient manhood. But I suppose I'd wanted to forget all about that time back there, at least for the present. To pretend that it had all been one continuous bad dream that had no basis in reality.

All at once a swift succession of crazy, mixed together memories began flooding through my slightly spinning head. . . .

"Sing, Bill, goddamn you, sing," someone was suddenly shouting in my ear.

"Goodnight, old girl, sleep tight," I whispered under my breath. Then half-shouting along with the others took up the closing verse:

"My eyes are dim, I cannot see,
The searchlights they are blinding me,
The searchlights they are blinding me."

I seem to be driving up that West Moor runway one moment, and the next something is persistently tapping my right shoulder. That's when I open my eyes and see Midge bending over the side of my chair. She has that amused smile on her face that instantly makes me feel good all over.

"Come on, dream boy, you're not going to snooze all the afternoon away, are you?

I'm suddenly wide awake. The section of newspaper with the Six Group story is on the floor at my feet. I look at my watch. I can't believe it, but I've somehow relived a tour of ops in a little under an hour and a half. Then I remember the record on the turntable. Good old Buck and Ruby. That's the first time I've ever gone to sleep listening to jazz played by either of them. I must be getting very old indeed!

"Some dream," I tell her. "Especially the nightmare parts. There was this cute little WAAF who looked so nice and innocent . . ."

I half-pretend to duck the blows her small hands rain on me. Then suddenly I reach over, grab her by the arms, and drag her onto my lap. I'm still amazed by how light her whole body feels.

"Now it's my turn," I tell her, and start to tickle her in the ribs. But before I can really begin to bother her she throws her arms about my neck and her lips move onto mine. I find I'm suddenly not interested in doing any more tickling. . . .

Half an hour later I start out for a walk with Sam, the next-door neighbour's big Afghan hound, for company. We cut down through Langmuir Wood and come out at the Humber River. It's late March and the water flowing by me is brownish-coloured, more turbulent than usual because of the early spring run-off. With Sam pulling at the leash every step of the way we move south, following the bend of the river right down to the Old Mill bridge.

The light-hearted mood I'd left the house in has suddenly vanished. Perhaps because of my dream of old nostalgia I've got Vic Harrison on my mind again. But that's not quite true either. Vic has been weaving in and out of my thoughts constantly since he died without warning only a month ago. And not, I realize now, merely because he was an old acquaintance and a lovely person to boot.

I suppose without really knowing it I've always considered him the typical Canadian airman of World War Two. Typical, yes, but certainly not average. For one thing I know very little about his Air Force career, beyond the fact that he was a navigator and had won the D.F.C. He'd joined the R.C.A.F. in 1940, a handsome eighteen-year-old kid with a big build that had been put to good use during his three years on the line for the Oakwood Collegiate football team. He made aircrew, washed out as a pilot, then graduated as an observer and was shipped overseas. One of the stories he told me concerned his posting to an R.A.F. training unit in northern England with a group of other Canadians. They'd arrived in mid-winter at a base close by the sea to find their barracks freezing cold and heat almost nonexistent. Their request for more coal for the laughable barrack stoves was turned down cold. So they systematically began to break up and burn the barrack furniture, such as it was. When that was exhausted they refused to go on parade and stayed in bed with their greatcoats on. They were all put on charge but still wouldn't leave their huts. The C.O. then threatened to charge them all with mutiny. They still held together and didn't budge. Finally an Air Commodore from R.C.A.F. Headquarters arrived and listened to their story. It didn't take very long before more coal was provided and the barracks became almost livable. Vic never did tell me if they were provided with a new set of barrack furniture. . . .

When I reach the Old Mill bridge I turn back with Sam and, at a leisurely pace, retrace my footsteps up the path beside the river. Come to think of it, I used to cross a bridge over the Ouse in downtown York that looked a lot like the Humber River here; that is, if you added a host of old buildings on either side of the river bank to the English scene.

Vic told me he'd flown in the first thousand-plane raid to Cologne in May, 1942. He was then at O.T.U. It was a strictly volunteer mission, with instructors and students forming makeshift crews to somehow fly their old training Wellingtons to the target and back. Soon after that he joined 61 Squadron, R.A.F., and flew the first raids to Turin and Milan among the thirty trips of that first tour. He got the D.F.C. and "bloody well earned it." Then, after a short leave in Canada, he'd chosen to return to England to do a second tour in Six Group rather than accept a safe instructor's job at home. He never said a word about his second tour with the R.C.A.F. and Goose Squadron, but I gathered it hadn't been too great.

I've said before that Vic was a typical aircrew type, but that isn't completely true. He felt closer to the air force than most. How else do you explain his involvement with a reserve squadron after the war, giving up a lot of his weekends to work at a ground job for little or no financial return? He simply liked being involved with aircraft and those who enjoyed the air force as much as himself. It was a part of his life and he held on to it always. Even when all that was left of it were the two poker games a month at the officer's mess on Avenue Road. So while it was horribly tragic, it was at the same time very appropriate that he'd dropped dead in the early hours of

*a Saturday morning a month ago near the end of a game.
He'd laid his hand down, gone out to the head, and when he
failed to return after a considerable time they went to look
for him and found him stretched out in the washroom. He
never regained consciousness. His son told me his father
wouldn't have wanted it any other way and I believed him.*

*In conversation Vic hardly ever mentioned his flying, even
though I was a Six Grouper myself with over twenty trips
under my belt. Perhaps he thought my tour in the last couple
of months of the war didn't really count for much, that I'd
flown a bunch of milk runs. In a way our failure to commu-
nicate with each other was a pity. It explains, perhaps, why
so much of what hundreds of Vic Harrisons had experienced
has died with them.*

*No doubt those who shared Vic's views considered it "bad
form" to talk about their wartime exploits, especially to those
who hadn't served in the air force, and therefore couldn't
really have any idea what it was all about. Talking about the
old times with one's wartime buddies was a different matter.
That was something to be jealously guarded from the uniniti-
ated.*

*These are a few of my thoughts as I continue my stroll,
away from the river now, up again through Langmuir Wood
on the homeward leg of my walk. Sam keeps pulling me
along, evidently thinking the middle-aged man holding his
leash needs a little help. Well, perhaps he does at that.*

*Suddenly I know what I have to do. In some way, though
I'm not exactly sure how I'll go about it, I have to get down
on paper what I know and have seen of the war, even for the
little that it's worth. I'll try to tell it as simply and as directly
as possible. But it won't be only my story that I'll be telling.
It'll be Vic's and a thousand others like him. A whole generation of Canadians, who though raised to reject war, still
took up the challenge of the dictators and went out to meet
them head on. The last group of citizen warriors to fight a
war they hated but could still believe in.*

*It probably won't end up being too much of a book. But
it'll be a little better than the present conspiracy of silence, a
small chink of light shining through the door. You can't bury
a whole generation and not even leave a few grave-markers.*

*I climb the many wooden steps leading up from Langmuir
Wood, then finally come out on the street. I'm puffing hard,*

my heart pounding from the exertion. My boy, I tell myself, you're older than you care to believe. You'd better not waste too much time putting to paper what you have to get down. . . .

And I hurry home along the street, the first words already forming in my head.

About the Author

John Holmes is the pseudonym of a Canadian writer better known for his verse than his prose. During World War Two he served with the Royal Canadian Air Force in Eastern Canada and in England, ending the war as a member of Eagle Force. Author of an earlier novel, *The Winter Of Time*, he also collaborated with Douglas Alcorn in the latter's air force memoir *From Hell To Breakfast*.